THE ESSENCE OF MALICE

By Ashley Weaver

Murder at the Brightwell
Death Wears a Mask
A Most Novel Revenge
The Essence of Malice

a&b

THE ESSENCE OF MALICE

ASHLEY WEAVER

Allison & Busby Limited
12 Fitzroy Mews
London W1T 6DW
allisonandbusby.com

First published in Great Britain by Allison & Busby in 2017.
Published by arrangement with St Martin's Press.

A CIP catalogue record for this book is available from
the British Library.

First Edition

ISBN 978-0-7490-2225-9

Typeset in 11/16 pt Sabon by
Allison & Busby Ltd.

The paper used for this Allison & Busby publication
has been produced from trees that have been legally sourced
from well-managed and credibly certified forests.

Printed and bound by
CPI Group (UK) Ltd, Croydon, CR0 4YY

For my beautiful niece, Larson Rose Lea.
Auntie loves you, Lolly!

CHAPTER ONE

Lake Como, Italy
April 1933

If my husband didn't die attempting this foolishness, I was going to kill him myself.

It was a glorious spring afternoon on the banks of Lake Como, but my mind was on neither the weather nor the stunning views of the lake with its backdrop of hazy blue mountains that lay before me. Instead, I stood on the balcony of the villa, a hand shading my eyes against the sun, and watched as a seaplane dipped and glided high above the glittering surface of the water. My husband, Milo, was at the controls, and to say I was displeased would be putting it mildly.

The morning had started out with no hint that such dangerous activities were impending. Milo had slept late, and I had gone for a walk along the shore after breakfast. I had arrived back at the villa an hour later to find a hastily scrawled note from Milo informing me that he was going out to fly a seaplane. I had had to read it twice to make sure I had not misunderstood. Considering he had never, to my knowledge, flown a seaplane – or any other type of plane, for that matter – in his life, the prospect was somewhat alarming.

I could not, however, say it was entirely surprising. Milo had been lamenting only yesterday that it was still too cold for waterskiing, and so it seemed that he had seized upon another, more drastic way to risk bodily harm.

What was more, I knew perfectly well who was responsible for introducing him to this newest type of peril. It was André Duveau, our neighbour here at the lake. He had the villa nearest ours, and he and my husband shared an affinity for racing, gambling, and, apparently, endangering their lives. It was no wonder they had become fast friends.

The plane swooped low towards the water, and my heart leapt to my throat. Unconsciously, I reached out to grip the rim of the stone flowerpot that sat on a pedestal near the railing. Just when it seemed that the plane was going to plunge into the water, its nose rose and it swooped upward once again. I suddenly had the distinct impression that Milo knew I was on the balcony and was frightening me on purpose.

I watched the plane climb higher until, unable to stand there any longer, I turned around and went back into the villa. If Milo was determined to kill himself, I was not going to watch him do it.

Not an hour later, I heard footsteps approaching the sitting room where I had been examining a French fashion magazine and hoping I would not be required to wear mourning in the summer.

My husband came into the room, followed by André Duveau. They were both dressed casually in shirtsleeves and trousers tucked into boots, the requisite flying costume, I supposed.

Milo had become tanned during our weeks in the Mediterranean sun, and his darkened complexion set off his black hair and made his blue eyes appear even brighter. I was not, however, in the mood to be swayed by how handsome he looked this morning, his hair tousled by the wind. I made sure to give no indication of my relief that he had arrived home safely.

'So you made it back alive, did you?' I asked, setting the magazine aside.

'Got my note, I see,' Milo said, smiling. He came to where I sat and leant down to brush a kiss across my cheek before dropping into the chair across from me, apparently not fooled by my show of indifference. 'You needn't have worried, darling. You know no one brings me back to earth as well as you do.'

I refrained from a retort and turned to our guest, dropping the pretence of acceptance. 'I should be very cross with you, Mr Duveau.'

He smiled. 'Allow me to beg your pardon, Mrs Ames. I should be devastated to find myself in your bad graces.'

Despite his very French name, he had almost no trace of an accent, having spent the majority of his childhood, he had told us, in England. He currently made his home in Paris, among other places, but Como was his favourite retreat. He owned an expansive villa and kept several aeroplanes that he flew frequently.

'I cannot lay the blame entirely at your feet, in any event,' I said to Mr Duveau as he took a seat. 'Milo always does just as he pleases.' Considering how Milo loved to live recklessly, I supposed I was lucky that he had not taken to the skies before this.

Fortunately, we would not be in Como for much longer. We had only let our villa for a fortnight and would be returning to London within the week. Having spent the past month on holiday in Capri, we had been about to start the journey home when Milo had suddenly decided that a stop at Lake Como was in order. I had been perfectly willing to extend our stay in Italy, and our time here had been lovely and further improved by Mr Duveau's acquaintance.

'Then I am forgiven?' Mr Duveau pressed, his eyes twinkling with amusement.

'Yes,' I allowed. 'I suppose.'

He flashed another smile, and I thought it would be difficult for anyone to be cross with Mr Duveau for long. Like my husband, he possessed the irresistible combination of startling good looks and a great deal of charm. His fair hair always looked a bit windswept, whether or not he had been out flying, and, in the short time I had known him, I had seen many women flush under the dual appeal of his warm dark eyes and roguish grin.

'It is I who shall have to work to earn forgiveness,' Milo told him. 'My wife doesn't approve of aeroplanes.'

'I fully appreciate the benefits of aeroplanes,' I said. 'It is the idea of my husband careening about a thousand feet above the ground that doesn't appeal to me.'

'You may rest assured, Mrs Ames, that your husband has the makings of a fine pilot. A few more outings and perhaps we might be qualified to vie for the Schneider Trophy.'

I was not at all assured at the thought that Milo might

make a habit of flying, let alone take up participating in seaplane races. If that was the case, I certainly had a few things to say about the matter, but now was not the time to discuss it.

'Will you stay for lunch, Mr Duveau?' I asked.

'It is a tempting offer, but I'm afraid I haven't time. I'm returning to Paris in the morning, and I have a great many things to attend to before I leave.'

'Oh, I didn't realise that you were leaving so soon,' I said.

'I hadn't intended to, but there are . . . certain matters that require my attention.'

A woman, I thought at once. The careful way he avoided mentioning just what urgent matter called him back made me suspect that there was an affair of the heart involved. I assumed that the lady in question would appreciate his flying to her side. It was rather a romantic gesture.

'It's a shame you must leave,' I told him. 'But I wish you safe travels.'

'Thank you. It's been lovely making your acquaintance. I feel as though I shall be leaving old friends behind. In fact, I've brought a parting gift for you.' I hadn't taken much notice of the small box in his hand until he held it out to me.

I took it and opened it to find a small glass bottle nestled in a bed of velvet. It was a bottle of perfume. I removed it from the box and examined it. The glass was cut in facets that gleamed in the light shining through the big windows behind me. 'How lovely,' I said. I removed the stopper and the rich floral aroma drifted upward.

'It's a brand-new scent,' he told me. 'You'll be one of the first women to wear it.'

'That's very kind of you,' I said, taking the stopper from the bottle and dabbing it against my wrist. It smelt wonderful, soothingly familiar somehow and yet exotic.

'I noticed that you wear gardenia,' he said. 'I thought you might like this. It's called Shazadi. It's floral, but there is a warm, sensual undertone to it that suits you.'

'Thank you,' I said. 'I shall enjoy wearing it.'

He smiled. 'I hope so. Now I must bid you adieu. It's been a pleasure meeting you both. Perhaps I shall see you in London sometime?'

'We should like that,' I said.

'And perhaps next time a fighter plane, eh, Ames?' he said. Then he winked at me and made his exit.

When I was quite sure that he was gone, I turned to my husband. 'I know it's useless of me to ask you not to do such reckless things, but you might at least wish me farewell in person before you make me a widow.'

Milo, as I knew he would, dismissed my concern. 'You worry too much, my lovely. Seaplanes are perfectly safe. Not much different than driving an automobile.'

I was not going to argue the point with him. I had learnt over the years to pick my battles. I could only hope that, with André Duveau gone, Milo would be left without access to this particular vice.

'Seaplanes aside, it's too bad Mr Duveau had to leave,' I said. 'He's very charming.'

I waved my wrist before my face and breathed in the perfume once again. There was something rather intoxicating about the scent.

'As far as that goes,' Milo said, rising from his seat, 'when a fellow starts noticing what scent one's wife wears and gifting her with perfume with "sensual undertones", it may be time to dispense with his friendship.'

I laughed. 'Is it so strange for him to remember that I wear gardenia? I thought it was very kind of him to give me the perfume.'

'It wasn't as kind as you think. He's got some sort of financial involvement in a perfumery. They've probably given him crates of the stuff to foist off on people.'

'How charming you are this morning,' I said wryly.

He came to me and took my wrist in his hand, bringing it up to his nose. 'It does smell lovely on your skin.'

'Do you think the sensual undertones suit me?' I asked softly.

'Oh, immensely.' He pulled me to him and lowered his mouth to mine, and I felt again that unaccustomed sensation of perfect contentment that had encompassed me as of late. I was rested, relaxed, and very happy. Only a year ago I had been convinced that my marriage was coming to an end. Now I felt that things had never been better.

Then suddenly Milo stilled, pulling back ever so slightly. 'When did the post arrive?'

I looked up at him and saw that his gaze was directed over my shoulder. Apparently this non sequitur had come to pass as he looked down at the little table behind me where the morning post was stacked. 'A little while ago,' I said. 'Winnelda brought it in. I haven't looked at it yet.'

Milo released me and reached to pick up a letter. He was always terribly difficult to read, but I could sense a change in his mood as he examined the envelope.

'What is it?' I asked.

He hesitated ever so slightly and, though his expression

didn't change, I felt suddenly apprehensive. 'There's something I haven't mentioned to you,' he said.

A variety of scenarios sprang immediately to mind. Given my husband's somewhat colourful past, I imagined it could be any number of unpleasant things. I waited.

'I had an ulterior motive for stopping in Como,' he continued, doing nothing to set my mind at ease.

'Oh?' I enquired carefully.

'It has to do with Madame Nanette.'

I tried not to show my immense relief. Madame Nanette was Milo's former nanny, the woman who had, for all intents and purposes, raised him. Whatever Milo's secret was, it could not be as bad as I had feared.

'What about her?' I asked.

'I had a letter from her, forwarded by Ludlow, while we were in Capri. She's taken a post in Paris and will be travelling with the family to Como. She had seen in the society columns we were in Italy and wondered if we would stop to visit her.'

Milo had received several letters forwarded by our solicitor while we had been abroad, so it would not have attracted my notice. I did wonder why he had chosen not to share this with me before we left Capri. It was not as though the news was something unpleasant. Quite the contrary, in fact.

'How nice,' I said. 'I shall be glad to see her.'

He walked to the desk in the corner and picked up the letter opener, slitting open the envelope and pulling the letter from inside. His eyes scanned the words, his features impassive.

At last he looked up. 'She's going to remain in Paris. She asks that we come there.'

'Is she unwell?' I asked, suddenly worried. It was unlike Madame Nanette to request a visit. While she and Milo held each other in the highest regard, they did not remain in close contact. I had only met her twice, once at our wedding and once when we had passed through Paris at Christmas.

'She doesn't say. The letter is very brief.'

'May I read it?'

He held it out to me without comment. I looked down at the piece of paper in my hand. It was thick, high-quality stationery embossed with a coat of arms, the crest of the house in which she now worked, I supposed.

Her penmanship was exceptional, beautiful script flowing in perfectly straight lines across the page.

My dear Milo,
I am unable to leave Paris after all. If you and your lovely wife could find the time to stop and see me, I would be most pleased.
Fondly,
Madame Nanette

In the postscript she had given her telephone number and asked him to ring her upon our arrival.

'There isn't much to it,' I said.

'No, there isn't.'

There was something unsettling about the brevity of the letter, though I didn't know what exactly.

'Would you mind going to Paris?' he asked.

'Of course not. I think we should go as soon as possible. We'd better begin packing at once,' I told him, mentally

15

beginning to make the necessary preparations. 'We can take the train tomorrow.'

He smiled suddenly, and it was one of those smiles that made me instinctively uneasy. 'Darling, how would you like to fly to Paris?'

CHAPTER TWO

We took the night train from Milan.

'We might have been in Paris by now,' Milo mumbled as we prepared for bed in our private cabin after dinner, the dark landscape rushing by outside the window.

'But trains are so much more romantic,' I replied.

'Perhaps if there was a bed we could both fit into,' he retorted, glancing through the door of our small lounge at the narrow bunks in the adjoining sleeping cabin.

I ignored his complaints as I took a seat on the banquette sofa. Flying was, perhaps, the quicker route, but I preferred to journey with my feet firmly planted on the ground.

Besides, I liked to travel by train. The glossy wood panelling glowing warmly in the soft yellow light of the lamp; the gentle sway of the car; the soothing, rhythmic clatter of the wheels on the track. It all combined to create a comforting effect that left me feeling sleepy and peaceful.

I looked up at Milo, who appeared neither sleepy nor peaceful. There was a restless energy about him tonight, and I knew that being confined to our small compartment wasn't likely to appeal to him. Yet he had brushed aside my suggestion that he take a drink in the train's lounge and had retired with me as soon as we had finished our after-dinner coffee.

'Come and sit,' I said, patting the sofa beside me. He finished tying the belt of his dressing gown and did as bidden. Taking his silver cigarette case and lighter from his pocket, he lit a cigarette and leant back against the seat with a sigh.

I studied the smooth lines of his profile for a moment before asking, 'You don't really mind that we didn't fly to Paris?'

He turned his head to look at me. 'No, darling,' he said, reaching out to squeeze my hand on the seat between us. 'Duveau was likely flying his Avions Fairey Fox fighter anyway, and it only has two seats.'

'You might have flown without me.'

'I'm not so fond of Duveau's company that I would choose it over yours.'

'But you would have liked to make the trip in an aeroplane.'

'I'd rather a cramped train compartment with you than all the aeroplanes in the world,' he said, bringing my hand up to his lips to kiss it.

I smiled, but I felt a growing wariness. As a general rule, Milo always said just the right things. But when he was this sweet, it was cause for suspicion. I had had the feeling since reading Madame Nanette's letter. There was more to this trip to Paris than met the eye.

I shifted on the seat to face him. 'Milo, there's something I've been meaning to ask you.'

'Oh?' he asked, picking up a French newspaper and unfolding it, his eyes scanning the headlines. 'What is that?'

'Why didn't you tell me in Capri that Madame Nanette had written to you?'

He shrugged. 'No reason in particular.'

'But you might have mentioned it was your reason for stopping in Como,' I persisted.

He hesitated for a fraction of a moment, and I had the distinct impression that he was debating whether or not to lie to me.

'It slipped my mind, I suppose,' he said in a careless tone, his gaze not leaving the paper.

Now I was certain that he was lying. Milo was many things, but forgetful was not one of them.

There had been a time in our marriage when I would have allowed this dismissal, but things had changed in recent months. I was not in the mood to be thwarted. I looked at him, my eyes narrowed. 'What aren't you telling me, Milo?'

'You've a suspicious mind, my sweet,' he said dryly, folding the paper.

'Whose fault do you suppose that is?' I replied, only half in jest.

'Entirely mine.' He smiled, tossed the newspaper aside, and leant towards me. 'I'm very wicked indeed, tainting your innocent heart with constant mistrust.' There was a look in his eyes that made it clear that he was going to do his best to distract me from the conversation.

This was confirmed as he pressed his mouth to mine and slid his arms around me, and for a moment I almost forgot that I was growing cross with him. Almost.

I pulled back from his kiss and firmly pushed him away. 'Answer me, Milo.'

The corner of his mouth tipped up, an expression that was a mixture of amusement and exasperation, and he sat back with a sigh. 'I didn't mention it because I was afraid you would do what you are doing now: baying at the scent of trouble like an overwrought bloodhound.'

My brows rose. 'I will overlook, for the time being, that highly insulting description of my interest and ask only that you explain yourself. What trouble?'

He leant across me to grind out his cigarette in the brass ashtray on the little table near the window. 'I'm not entirely sure. There was something wrong about Madame Nanette's first letter.'

'What do you mean?'

'For one thing, she wrote of a private matter she wished to discuss with me. The vagueness of it was what caught my attention. She has never had trouble expressing herself, so the careful wording was unusual. Something about the tone of the letter was off.'

Vagueness was not, in itself, cause for alarm, but I trusted Milo's instincts. He was unnervingly astute when he wanted to be.

'She didn't come out and say it,' he went on, 'but I had the impression there was some difficulty with the family for whom she's working.'

'They were supposed to holiday in Como,' I said.

'Yes. I didn't mention it because I didn't know if there was anything in it. I thought I could go and speak with her without causing you alarm.'

I didn't entirely buy this excuse, especially given his

unflattering reference to my proclivity for sniffing out trouble.

'But then you received the second letter this morning,' I said, 'saying that she had been detained in Paris.'

He nodded. 'That seems to confirm that something is amiss. She would not have asked me to come otherwise.'

Even from the meagre details at our disposal, I could not disagree with his assessment that something seemed wrong. I wished that he had seen fit to confide in me before this.

'You might have told me, you know,' I said.

His expression was unrepentant. 'You've been in enough danger as of late. I have determined to keep you out of trouble, and I won't apologise for it.'

I frowned. It was true that we had found our way into several less-than-desirable situations over the past year, but wasn't that all the more reason for us to do what we could to solve Madame Nanette's problem? We were becoming experts at such things.

'Surely it's not a question of danger,' I said. 'And if Madame Nanette is experiencing some kind of difficulty, we should do whatever we can to help her.'

'I shall do whatever is necessary,' he said with an air of finality that irritated me.

'Well, you won't be doing it without me,' I said.

He studied my face for a moment and then shook his head.

'Why are you looking at me like that?' I asked.

'That expression of yours. I know what it means.'

'And what is that?'

He sighed. 'Trouble.'

We arrived in Paris on a warm morning full of sunshine and the scent of heliotrope.

Despite my concern about Madame Nanette and my irritation at Milo's initial secrecy, I had been lulled into a deep sleep by the motion of the train and had awoken feeling refreshed and hopeful. Perhaps there was nothing so very wrong after all. Perhaps Madame Nanette merely wanted to visit with us. It had been a long time since we had seen her, after all.

We had lunch at a cafe and then went to our hotel, a lovely stone building with blue shutters and window boxes full of bright flowers. It was not where we usually stayed when in Paris, but it was in close proximity to the address on Madame Nanette's letter, and we thought it would be best to be near her.

Milo had wired her about our arrival and he stopped to enquire at the desk as to whether there were any messages.

'There is a message, monsieur,' the desk clerk said, handing Milo a slip of paper.

Milo took it and glanced at it. 'She says she will call tonight after dinner, if she can get away.'

I nodded, my optimism suddenly beginning to fade. I sincerely hoped there wasn't something seriously amiss, that she wasn't ill. Though Milo was not one to confide his feelings, I knew that he cared very greatly for Madame Nanette. His mother had died shortly after giving birth to him, and Madame Nanette was the closest thing to a mother that he had ever known.

He seemed to have sensed my concern, for he smiled reassuringly and gently squeezed my arm as we exited the lift and followed the bellboy towards our room.

I stepped into our suite and looked around as the bellboy deposited our hand luggage inside the doorway.

Our trunks had come ahead with my maid and Milo's valet from the station.

'Everything in order?' Milo asked, as he tipped the young man and then closed the door behind him.

'Yes, it's lovely,' I said.

The door from the hallway had opened into the sitting room, which was tastefully decorated in pastels and muted florals. A satin sofa and armchair sat before the marble fireplace, and there were a number of pleasant art pieces on the walls. Floor-to-ceiling windows lined one wall, and I walked across the plush carpets to them and pulled back the drapes. Below us, the Seine sparkled in the afternoon sunlight.

'It's nice to be back in Paris,' I said. 'It seems as though it's been ages.'

Though the words were sincere, I heard the lack of enthusiasm in my own voice. I couldn't seem to shake my growing unease. Milo must have noticed it, for he followed me to the window and stood close behind me.

'There's no need to fret, darling,' he murmured, sliding his arms around me and brushing a kiss on my neck. 'I'm quite sure everything will be fine.'

'Yes,' I said, his confidence making me want to believe it, too. 'I'm sure you're right.'

There was a polite shuffling of feet behind us, and I knew that Milo's valet, Parks, was making his presence known. Parks was extremely uncomfortable with any displays of affection between Milo and myself, and he took great pains to make sure he never stumbled onto one unknowingly.

'Yes, Parks?' Milo asked, releasing me and turning to face him.

'Your things are all arranged, sir, and I've set out your evening clothes. Is there anything more?'

'I don't think so,' Milo said. 'Why don't you take the evening off, Parks. I daresay even you could find something to amuse yourself with in Paris.'

'Undoubtedly, sir,' Parks said, with an absolute lack of enthusiasm. 'Thank you.'

'Is Winnelda somewhere about?' I asked.

'I believe she went to a nearby shop, madam, to collect some, ah, reading materials.' The words were rife with disapproval.

I knew very well what type of reading materials Winnelda would be collecting. Gossip rags. She loved nothing more than juicy scandals, and I was certain Paris would have plenty of them for her. I was doubtful, however, that she would find much written in English.

'Thank you, Parks,' I said.

He nodded and then noiselessly exited the suite.

'Poor fellow can barely contain his excitement at the prospect of an evening off in Paris,' Milo remarked dryly.

I smiled. 'I do wonder sometimes what Parks is like when he's alone. Do you think he's always so respectable?'

'Eminently. I half expect he sleeps in his suit.'

'I know working in proximity with Winnelda has been trying for him.' Winnelda was as flighty as Parks was dependable, and I suspected that she vexed him greatly.

'He may not have to worry. You're likely to lose that girl in Paris,' Milo commented. 'Either she'll be swept off her feet by some mustachioed scoundrel or she'll wind up kicking her heels in a chorus line.'

'No, not that,' I said. 'She hasn't balance enough.'

It was just then that the door to the suite opened, and Winnelda came inside, a stack of magazines in her arms. She stopped when she saw us and bobbed an awkward little curtsey. 'Oh, madam, Mr Ames, I didn't realise that you had arrived. I just went down the street to purchase a few things. That is . . . I . . . well, I have your trunks almost unpacked, madam. Shall I unpack the little valise you had with you?'

With one last look at the picturesque view outside, I turned from the window and pulled off my gloves.

'Yes, Winnelda, thank you. And will you lay out something for me to wear this evening?'

'I thought you'd be buying new gowns,' she said, her tone expressing shock that I should wear something I already owned when all the shops in Paris were at my disposal.

'I may do some shopping,' I said with a smile, 'but not before dinner.'

She looked a bit disappointed, so I resorted to a topic I knew would cheer her.

'Anything of interest in the society columns?' I asked. Winnelda took great pleasure in the bad behaviours of the rich and famous. Now that Milo had managed to keep himself out of the gossip columns for the last several months, I was much less averse to them than I had been when his name was bandied about with those of beautiful socialites and cinema stars.

'I had to go through a lot of magazines to find anything interesting,' Winnelda said glumly. 'Most of them were in French and had an old man on the cover.'

'An old man?' I repeated.

'Yes, his photograph was on the cover of many of

them. He was quite old and not very handsome at all.'

'That's too bad,' I said, fighting back a smile.

'I bought the ones I could find in English and a few of the French ones, too. I thought, perhaps, you might tell me what some of them say later.'

'Certainly.'

If I had known the direction our Paris visit was about to take, I might have paid a bit more attention to the gossip columns from the beginning.

CHAPTER THREE

We had an early dinner and returned to the hotel to await Madame Nanette's arrival. Milo ordered coffee to be sent to our room in preparation for her visit, and there was nothing to do but wait. I turned on the wireless and Milo sat smoking, giving every appearance of perfect ease.

I couldn't help but feel relieved that both Parks and Winnelda had been given the evening off so that we might have some privacy. Parks was the soul of discretion, but Winnelda was an inveterate eavesdropper. She meant no harm by it, but it would be easier to focus on our visit with Madame Nanette without wondering where Winnelda might be lurking.

Shortly before ten o'clock a light knock sounded on our door. Milo moved to open it, and Madame Nanette stood before him. They exchanged greetings in French, and there was a transparent fondness in Milo's tone that I seldom heard there.

She caught both his hands in hers, looking up into his face. 'You look very well,' she pronounced at last. 'Too much sun is bad for the skin, of course, but you have never minded about that.'

He laughed, leaning to kiss her forehead. 'I might have known you would notice.'

She smiled and reached up to pat his cheek before coming into the room.

My gaze swept over her face, searching for any sign of illness. I felt relieved to see that she looked radiantly healthy. She had a sweet countenance and sharp, dark eyes. She was of average height and slim build and wore a dark grey dress, a bit old-fashioned in style but of excellent quality. Her once-black hair was now streaked with silver, but her skin was almost unlined, and she might easily have passed for a much younger woman.

She came then to me and gently grasped my arms and brushed kisses across both cheeks. Then she stepped back, her hands still on my arms, to examine me. 'You look wonderful, Mrs Ames. Very happy.'

'Oh, call me Amory, please.' I had told her the same thing each time we met, but she had yet to become comfortable with the informality.

She squeezed my arms and then she turned to Milo. 'Your wife glows with happiness. It must be because you've been behaving yourself. I've scarcely seen a word of you in the gossip columns for several months.'

Milo smiled, passing off what might have been a gentle rebuke as a compliment. 'Yes, I've been extraordinarily well behaved as of late. It's almost a pity, really. I haven't had a good scolding in many a year.'

'I'm sure you have a few that are long overdue,' she replied, the twinkle in her eyes belying the sternness of her tone. 'You are still much too handsome for your own good, but I suppose that can't be helped. Now, Amory, come sit beside me and tell me about your trip to Italy.'

We moved to the cluster of furniture near the fire. Madame Nanette and I sat on the sofa, and Milo took a chair near us. I poured coffee from the silver pot into the hotel's fine white porcelain cups. Madame Nanette took her coffee with two sugars, no milk, just as Milo did.

I was, of course, anxious to hear why she had really come, but she seemed in no hurry to divulge the reason for her visit. Instead, I told her about our time in Italy as Milo sat, smoking a cigarette and contributing an occasional comment. I could almost believe that we had imagined the undertone of trouble in her letters, except for the slight hint of some private worry that flickered occasionally in her eyes before she pushed it away.

Finally, it seemed that Milo had had enough of the niceties. He set down his cup and saucer and ground out his cigarette in the crystal ashtray on the table. Then he set his gaze on Madame Nanette. 'There was more to your request that we visit than wanting to hear what Italy was like. Why have you really asked us to come to Paris?'

A smile touched the corner of her lips. 'Always intuitive and always impatient.'

'Yes, well, I think I've been remarkably patient thus far.'

She clicked her tongue disapprovingly at his tone, but it seemed to have prodded her forward and, after a moment's hesitation, she began. 'There is something wrong,' she said. 'I suspected as much when I wrote to you. Now I'm sure of it.'

'Why don't you tell us about it?' I encouraged.

'It is about my employer,' she said.

Milo nodded. I knew he had thought it likely that the matter concerned her employer.

'For whom are you working?' I asked.

'You have heard of Helios Belanger?'

I was surprised. I certainly had heard of him. Helios Belanger was one of France's premier parfumiers. He was the creator of more than a dozen popular perfumes. 'Worthy of queens,' the Parfumes Belanger slogan proclaimed. No respectable society woman was without a Belanger scent. I had several bottles of them on my dressing table at home.

I glanced at Milo. He did not look at all surprised, and I had that strange inkling that he knew more than he admitted.

'I don't know if you heard,' Madame Nanette went on, 'but he took a very young wife four years ago.'

'Yes,' Milo said. 'I believe I did hear something about that.'

'They had a child the year after their marriage, a girl, Seraphine. It is she who is my charge.'

Milo nodded.

'And there is something about working in Helios Belanger's home that has caused your concern?' I asked.

Again, she hesitated. Then she folded her hands in her lap. 'Perhaps I should start at the beginning,' she said. 'You know about Helios Belanger, but perhaps you do not know all that is necessary for my story to make sense.'

Milo sat back in his chair. 'By all means, tell us.'

I poured more coffee into her cup, and Madame Nanette began her story in her warm, musical voice. Her accent had been considerably softened by twenty-odd years in English service, but there was still the melodic fluidity of the French language in her speech.

'Helios Belanger has a long and illustrious history of wealth. He is a man who has met with success at every turn, thanks to both a relentless nature and a Midas touch. His beginnings were not so illustrious, though few know much about that part of the story.

'He was born in Marseilles, the son of a Frenchman and his Greek wife. Neither of them survived past Helios's youth. He had no family and made his way here, to Paris, where he spent many years on the streets. But those years were not wasted. He learnt how to use his wits and how to be an excellent judge of character. Not only that, he always claimed that his keen sense of smell was developed from nights spent in the open air in the Jardin des Plantes and amid the follies of Parc Monceau.'

I could picture him in my mind, the young boy, ambling along the pathways of the park at dusk, finding a spot to lie down amidst the lush foliage, and looking up at the stars.

'He was quick and smart, and he got a job at an apothecary. His employer was a former soldier who told Helios of his travels around the world and instilled in him a desire to experience foreign lands,' Madame went on. 'When Helios wasn't working behind the counter, he spent time mixing herbs and flowers, making amateur perfumes that his employer eventually let him sell. That was how I first met him.'

I looked up, a bit surprised. I had not expected this development, that Madame Nanette had known him in the past. My eyes flickered to Milo, but he wasn't looking my way.

'As a very young woman, I spent a summer working in a flower shop,' she went on, 'and Helios would often come to buy flowers. He could talk for hours about the fragrances, the subtle differences between them. He would sometimes walk me home and could tell, before we turned a corner, what types of flowers were in the window boxes on the next street. He was exciting, charming, and I began to be very fond of him.'

There was a faraway look in her eyes as she related this part of the story, and I thought that some of the years had melted away from her face. For a moment, I saw what she must have looked like as a young woman.

'You were in love with him,' Milo said suddenly, his sharp gaze on her face.

She smiled, a bit sadly, I thought. 'That is difficult to say. I certainly thought that I was, as a girl of eighteen. But what do the young really know of love?'

This time Milo did glance briefly at me. I think we were both surprised at the turn this story had taken and were wondering where it would lead.

'For a time I entertained hopes that we might be married, but it was not meant to be,' she said. 'We parted ways.'

It was an abrupt way to end a tale of romance. I was certain that there was more to that story than she was willing to tell at the moment, and I wondered what it was that had come between them.

'Helios went off to see the world and shortly thereafter I got a position as a nanny. I went to England to begin my life there with you.' She smiled at Milo, and I could feel the warmth and affection in it.

'And you didn't hear from him again?' Milo asked.

'Not until last year,' she said. 'I was living in Lyon, having just left a post, when I received a letter from him. He told me that his first wife, Elena, had died. He had remarried and was wondering if I would be interested in a position as the nanny for his young child with his second wife.'

'How insulting,' Milo said.

She smiled gently. 'It was no such thing. One cannot expect him to have held a *tendresse* for me after all these years. I thought it was kind of him to have remembered me at all and to have wanted to entrust me with the care of his child.'

Milo didn't look convinced, and I was somewhat in agreement with him. It seemed to me that Helios Belanger must have had some motivation for seeking out a woman he had not seen in thirty years to be the nanny of his child with a young wife.

'And so I went to work at his house,' she continued. 'He was very much changed, but at first I still saw some hints of the boy I had known in the man he had become. He was very kind to me when I arrived.'

'Was he indeed?' Milo asked, reaching for another cigarette from the box on the table.

'You mustn't frown so, *mon cher*,' she said. 'There was nothing between us that was romantic, no lingering hint of love. I barely saw Helios after my arrival. What is more, I had not been in the house long before I began to sense that something was amiss.'

'How so?' Milo asked.

'It is difficult for me to say exactly. The child, Seraphine, is perfectly lovely. The young wife, too, is very pleasant. Yet there has been something wrong. It is difficult for me to put into words what I mean. It was just that there was a great uneasiness in the house. The atmosphere was strained. Despite all appearances, it was not a happy home. At first, I thought little of it. I have worked in many unhappy homes, after all.'

I glanced at Milo, wondering if this included his, but his expression was unreadable. He had never spoken much about his childhood. His father had died when Milo was at university, but I had never had the impression that Milo had mourned him much.

'But then things began to get worse,' she said softly.

'In what way?' I asked.

'As I said, the Helios Belanger that I began to work for, the one whose name was in all the advertisements, was much changed from the boy I had known. Though our paths rarely crossed, it was plain enough to me what he was. This man had become a tyrant. He was unpredictable, often irrational, and ruled over his business – and his family – with a will of iron.'

'That has been known to cause unhappiness,' Milo commented. 'Who else is in the house?'

'All his children live with him. I had the impression he wanted always to keep them near him. There are two sons and an older daughter, in addition to the child. Anton is the eldest. He's very serious, very reserved. He has always been his father's right hand, but I do not think his heart is in it. To Anton, the scent of money surpasses all else.

'The same cannot be said for the eldest daughter, Cecile. She shares her father's love, his passion, for perfumery. She spends hours in the greenhouse and the laboratory that Helios built for her, creating and perfecting scents. Also like her father, she has a very strong will, and is often in conflict with her brothers.'

She paused almost unnoticeably before adding, 'And then there is Michel, the younger son. He has a very bad reputation.'

'Yes,' Milo said. 'Michel Belanger and I are acquainted.'

Somehow I was not surprised to hear that the black sheep of the Belanger family should be acquainted with my husband. Milo had spent a good deal of time in Paris, and the wanton younger son of an illustrious household seemed like the sort of company he would keep.

Madame Nanette nodded, as though she, too, was not surprised. 'He is handsome, spends far too much time drinking and carousing, and there have been a number of scandals with women. He has an unruly temper, as well, and there was an incident with a woman's husband that Monsieur Belanger paid a good deal to keep quiet.'

'What kind of incident?'

'I do not know the details, but I believe the husband was badly injured.'

This Michel Belanger sounded like an unsavoury character indeed.

'What about the young wife?' Milo asked. 'What's she like?'

'She is English and very pretty,' Madame Nanette said. 'Her name was Beryl Norris before she married. She came from a good family in Portsmouth. From what I understand, Helios met her when he was on holiday and had married her by the time he returned home, which was a great shock to his children. I cannot say much about her, but I think she is a good mother. I don't know if she loved Helios when she married him, but she loves her child.'

'And so they all live together in the big house in the Faubourg Saint-Germain, this unhappy little family,' Milo said. 'When was it that it dawned on you that they might be more than just unhappy?'

Madame Nanette seemed to consider the question. 'I

think it first began to seem evident around six months ago. Monsieur Belanger and Monsieur Michel quarrelled loudly one night. That was not unusual. They often quarrelled. I thought very little of it at the time.'

'But you thought of it later,' I said.

She nodded. 'The following morning Helios left early, went to Grasse.'

'Where his factory is located,' Milo supplied. Grasse was home to many perfume factories, the climate making it particularly suitable for growing jasmine, lavender, and other flowers widely used in perfumery.

'Yes. He came back a few days later and was sullen, grim. It seemed from then on that he became erratic in his moods, pleasant one moment and surly the next. Every so often, I would see him staring into the distance, as though something weighed heavily on his mind.

'And then everyone began to seem very much ill at ease in his presence. Mademoiselle Cecile often tensed when he spoke. What had been an unhappy household became something worse. Something had changed. There was something heavier in the air. Fear. Perhaps even malice.'

'This is all very interesting,' Milo said.

'Yes,' I agreed. 'Perhaps we should find a way to introduce ourselves to Monsieur Belanger.'

She looked up, her dark eyes troubled. 'That's just it. That is how my suspicions were confirmed. Helios Belanger is dead.'

CHAPTER FOUR

'Dead?' I repeated, shocked. This was not at all how I had expected her story to end. 'How? When did this happen? Surely we would have heard something about it.' Then I thought of Winnelda's dismay at the 'old man' on the cover of all the Paris gossip magazines. I wondered if that man had been Helios Belanger.

'It happened only three days ago,' Madame Nanette said. 'Rather suddenly.'

There was something in her tone that gave me pause, and the familiar sensation of unease began to creep along my spine.

Milo did not seem to be suffering from the same shock, for his tone was completely unmoved as he asked, 'Sudden, was it?'

She looked at him, and it seemed to me that there was some sort of unspoken communication that passed between them. They understood each other. I fought down a bit of envy, for it was almost always impossible for me to tell what Milo was thinking.

'Yes,' she said. 'It has been blamed on an aeroplane crash.'

I couldn't help but shoot a significant glance at Milo. I knew that flying was unsafe, and this was proof of just what I had been worrying about.

'He went to visit his factory in Grasse two nights before his death. He was finalising the plans for his newest perfume with the manager of his factory. When he arrived back in Paris, he had some difficulty with the landing. The plane landed roughly, veered badly, and ended up smashing its nose into the ground.'

'And he was hurt?'

'They said he did not appear to be. He got out under his own power, and waved away the men who had rushed to help him.'

'He was alone?'

'Yes. He had taken up flying over the past year. He found it a more convenient way to get to Grasse. He could get to his factories much more often.'

'Was it a problem with the plane?' Milo asked.

'The plane was badly damaged, of course, but I have not heard that they found there to be any trouble with it.' She hesitated. 'It . . . it was assumed that there was something wrong with Monsieur Belanger.'

'Intoxicated?' Milo asked. I glanced at him. He was leaning forward slightly, his gaze particularly intent. I seldom saw him take such an interest in anything, but it appeared he was intrigued.

'I do not know. I think that is what they assumed. They said he appeared a bit dazed, was unsteady on his feet.'

'I see,' Milo said.

'Then again, it may have been that the crash upset him,'

Madame Nanette added. 'Such a thing is enough to try anyone's nerves.'

'Yes, of course,' Milo replied.

She smiled. 'You needn't humour me, *cherie*. I know you think that my feelings may cloud the issue, but I can assure you that is not the case. I do not think he was drunk because he was not a man to drink to excess. He liked always to retain control of his senses, even as a young man. He told me once that his mind was his most powerful weapon and he didn't like to dull it.'

Milo seemed to accept this. 'Was his driver there to pick him up?'

She shook her head. 'No. He had left his automobile there, and they said that he insisted on driving himself home.'

It seemed a rather reckless action for them to have let him drive home alone, considering he had just crashed an aeroplane. Then again, I suspected Helios Belanger was not the type of man against whom one would easily win an argument when he had made up his mind to do something.

'He made it home all right?' I asked.

'Oh, yes. The butler let him in, and did not notice anything particularly amiss. He said Monsieur Belanger seemed a bit tired, said he leant a bit heavily on the bannister, but he did not think much of it. The next day he seemed much better, and the matter was all but forgotten. But two days later he was gone. He had had a pleasant meal with his family that final night and the next morning the maid . . . found him.'

'The maid?' Milo asked. 'His wife was not in bed with him?'

It was something of a personal question, but Madame Nanette did not seem taken aback by it.

'No,' she said. 'They keep separate rooms.' It was not an unusual practice, but it did lead me to wonder what the relationship between Helios Belanger and his young wife was like.

'What did the official report say?' Milo asked, voicing my own question.

'Heart failure.'

'Brought on, perhaps, by shock from the crash,' Milo said.

'Yes.' One look at Madame Nanette's face, however, was enough to convince me that she did not believe the simplest explanation to be the true one.

'But?' Milo prodded her.

'But Helios has always been possessed of excellent health. I don't believe for a moment that there was anything wrong with his heart. His own doctor seemed very much surprised.'

I didn't argue, but I did not think it was entirely unlikely that heart failure might have been the cause of his death. A man of volatile personality with family troubles and an empire worth millions to run might certainly have been under a great deal of strain. Such things were hard on the heart.

'If it wasn't his heart, what was it?' Milo asked.

She met his gaze, her expression grim. 'I believe he was murdered.'

I had suspected, somehow, that she was coming to this, but it was still something of a surprise to hear the words uttered aloud.

It seemed that Milo had been anticipating a similar revelation, for he did not look at all taken aback by her announcement.

'You think the aeroplane crash might have been the first attempt on his life?' Milo asked.

'It is possible,' she said. 'He might have been drugged or poisoned, the killer hoping that he would die in the crash. When that did not work, the second attempt proved successful.'

'Who was there the night before he died?' Milo asked.

'The entire family plus Herr Jens Muller, the German sculptor. Everyone ate the same things at dinner, but anyone might have introduced something into his after-dinner drink. He usually took a glass of brandy as a digestif.'

'And is there a suspect you have in mind?' I asked, unable to keep silent any longer.

She glanced at me, a rueful smile flickering across her mouth. 'That's just the thing, Amory. There are too many. As much as it pains me to say it, I fear that any of them might be capable of it.'

'And what is it that you would like me to do?' Milo asked.

I disliked that he had said 'me' instead of 'us', but I decided to let it pass for the moment. We could argue about my involvement after Madame Nanette had gone.

'I can't, of course, go to the police,' she said. 'I have no proof. They would laugh at me. Even if I did have evidence, it would be unlikely that they would take the word of a nanny over one of the most influential families in Paris.'

'And so you would like us to look into the matter?' I said.

She nodded. 'I know that you have been instrumental in solving other crimes of this nature, and I thought that you might be able to find out something that I cannot. You will be able to interact with the family and those they know. It would cause suspicion for me to ask questions, but they will talk to you. There may be something that you can do.'

'Then again, there may be nothing,' Milo said. It was put a bit bluntly, but he was right. I didn't see what there was that we could do. How could we find evidence of a murder, especially one that had been officially declared a natural death?

'That is true,' she said, 'but if we have done all we can, then that will have to suffice.'

Milo smiled. '"Your best will suffice." I remember you told me that often.'

She returned his smile. 'It is still true.'

'Then we will do our best,' Milo said.

'That is all I ask.' She rose from her seat. 'Now I suppose I must be getting back. This is not really my evening off, but Madame Belanger has been sitting with Seraphine at night since her husband's death, and I knew that it would be all right for me to come to see you.'

'You don't have to work, you know,' Milo said, his tone edged with the faintest tinge of impatience. 'I do wish you'd cash the cheques I've sent you.'

'I don't need your money.' Her tone was stern, but her dark eyes were smiling. 'Working with children keeps me young.'

I believed her. There was something very youthful and alive in her expression. I could see why Milo had adored her as a child.

She smiled then, mischievously. 'Perhaps someday when I am old, I will accept it.'

Milo sighed, but his amusement was plain on his face. 'Very well. Let me know when that day comes.'

'It will not be soon, I can assure you.'

'You'll likely outlive us all,' he said.

This seemed to please her, and she let the matter of money drop. 'Thank you for having me. I'm so glad that I was able to talk to you. You will let me know if you have made progress?'

'Certainly,' Milo said, 'though I feel it is probably best that we don't make our connection known.'

She nodded. 'Yes, I thought the same.'

'When is your next day off?'

'Tuesday.' That was five days away. I wondered if we would have anything to report by then.

'Come have tea with us then,' Milo said. 'If something arises beforehand, send a message and I will arrange to meet you.'

'Very well.' She hesitated. 'You will be careful?'

'Of course.'

Her gaze narrowed, and for a moment I could imagine it must have been the look she had given Milo when he was a naughty child challenging her nursery rule. 'I mean it. I do not want you putting yourself in danger as you have done in the past. I have read of your exploits.'

'Amory's exploits, you mean,' Milo said. 'She's the one who insists on taking risks.'

'You needn't worry,' I hurried to assure her. 'We will be very careful.'

She studied me for a moment as though to make sure I meant it. Then she nodded. 'I thank you for what you are doing.' She kissed us both and then Milo walked her to the door and she was gone.

I stared for a moment at the closed door, trying to take in all that had just happened. In all my worries about

43

Madame Nanette's problem, I had not thought it would be something like this. Perhaps, given my recent history, I should not have been quite so astonished.

'And so we find ourselves at the scene of another murder,' Milo said, coming back to the sitting area. He didn't seem much troubled by the fact, for he lit another cigarette and settled back into his chair. I couldn't help but think that he looked particularly content.

'What do you make of it?' I asked. 'Do you think it's likely that Helios Belanger was killed?'

'Madame Nanette is not one to make accusations lightly. If she thinks that something sinister is at work here, I'd place odds on her being correct.'

I didn't know her at all well, but I had had the same impression. There was something calm and steady about her. She did not seem a woman who would jump to conclusions or make hasty assumptions. She had not given us the names of her suspects, but the sweeping accusation that it might be anyone in the family was troubling. A family as prominent as the Belangers would be difficult to infiltrate, let alone accuse of murder. We had our work cut out for us.

'This won't be easy,' I said, voicing my thoughts.

'No,' Milo agreed. Then the corner of his mouth tipped up. 'But that's what makes it interesting, isn't it?'

It occurred to me that he was taking a singularly sanguine attitude about all of this. He had taken it completely in stride when she told him that her very famous employer might have been murdered, and I wanted to know why.

'You didn't seem much surprised by anything she had to say,' I remarked.

'I was expecting trouble. It wasn't particularly surprising.'

'Murder is not particularly surprising?' I demanded.

'Not any more,' he replied.

Despite the nonchalance of his tone, suspicion was beginning to build. 'But Helios Belanger is a well-known name. You didn't bat an eye when she mentioned him.'

'Murder is murder, darling. No matter to whom it happens.'

The realisation hit me suddenly. 'You knew Madame Nanette was working for the family of Helios Belanger.'

He blew out a stream of smoke. 'You don't suppose I would receive a troubled message from her without making a few enquiries?'

Milo could be incredibly resourceful when he set his mind to it. Naturally he would have wanted to know the details of Madame Nanette's situation.

'Then you already knew that Helios Belanger was dead?'

'Yes. It was in all the papers.'

I could not exactly fault him for my ignorance on that score. I hadn't had much interest in news on holiday. I suppose I ought to have tried harder to stay au courant. What I could fault him for was his silence on the subject.

'You heard Madame Nanette's employer had died suddenly, and you didn't think to mention it to me?'

He sighed. 'Darling, as I told you last night, I didn't want to trouble you with every little detail. I was attempting to gather information before I alarmed you.'

Though this was a very poor excuse, I decided to move on, for the time being at least.

'You said you know the younger Belanger son?'

'Michel, yes. He and I know each other fairly well, though I haven't seen him in a year or two. We were in a few scrapes together in our younger days.'

I could only imagine what Milo's definition of 'a few scrapes' was. He had once described the time he and the drunken heir to a dukedom had nearly been arrested for driving a car, the back seat full of scantily clad women, into an Italian fountain as 'a minor mishap'.

That particular event had occurred before we met, but there had been a handsome array of reported transgressions since then, and I wondered what Michel Belanger must be like if Milo disapproved of him.

He replied in that uncanny way he had of seeming to read my thoughts. 'The problem with Michel is that he has never grown up. While I have become rather staid in my old age, he hasn't changed much since our carousing days.'

My brows rose. 'Staid, are you?'

He smiled. 'Why, darling, haven't you noticed? I'm developing into a perfect paragon of virtue.'

This did not deserve a response. 'So this Michel isn't a very nice sort of fellow, then?' I enquired, directing the conversation back to reality.

'To give you some idea, his father finally sent him away from home when he was nineteen or twenty after the maids kept turning up pregnant,' Milo said.

'Oh,' I replied.

'You see? I may not enjoy a spotless reputation, but at least I don't have half a dozen illegitimate children scattered across Europe.'

'How very staid of you,' I replied wryly.

'Well,' he said, rising from his chair, 'I don't suppose

there's anything more to be done tonight. Shall we go out?'

'Now?'

'Certainly. We're in Paris, after all, and the evening is young.'

There was a certain logic in that argument that I couldn't deny. 'Why not?' I replied, rising from the sofa.

An hour or two of music and dancing might be just the thing to clear my head before we began our enquiries.

Besides, Milo had just spent the past several minutes revelling in the memories of his glory days. It was probably best that I kept an eye on him.

CHAPTER FIVE

My first steps towards solving the mystery of Helios Belanger's death were taken the next morning at breakfast. I sat at the table enjoying some of the excellent pastries and strong coffee provided by the hotel and glancing through the newspaper. I was certain that the sudden death of so noted a person would have made for several juicy articles, but the majority of those had apparently been written in the days immediately following Helios Belanger's death. In this morning's newspaper, there was only a small piece describing reported funeral preparations. It seemed the funeral was to take place that day.

I set the paper aside as Winnelda moved to the windows and flung two of them open, a gust of cool spring morning air billowing into the room and swirling the curtains.

'It's such a beautiful morning,' she said dreamily. 'Paris is just as wonderful as I ever thought it would be.'

'I'm glad you're enjoying yourself,' I said, pouring myself a second cup of coffee from the silver pot as I pulled my pale blue silk robe more closely around me to ward off the chill.

'Isn't it glorious, madam? So beautiful and romantic.'

'Yes,' I replied, as I lifted my cup to my lips. 'It's lovely.'

She wasn't the only one succumbing to the charms of the city. After our visit to a nightclub, Milo had seen me back to our room and had gone off to one of his favourite gambling clubs. He had come in shortly before dawn smelling of the traditional scent of such places: cigarette smoke, liquor, and traces of inferior perfume. Whatever women had frequented that particular gambling establishment had clearly not been wearing Belanger scents.

I didn't expect he would be rousing himself anytime soon, but I had arisen determined to make myself useful this morning. I had always worked best at these little puzzles by speaking to the people at the heart of the matter, but it seemed unlikely that I would be able to meet any of the members of the Belanger family anytime soon. After all, it would be unseemly to approach them at such a time. What I could do, however, was learn as much about the family as possible.

I could think of an excellent way to start.

'Would you like to look over your gossip magazines this morning, Winnelda?' I asked.

She turned from the window, her excitement clear on her face. 'Oh, yes, madam. I would like that ever so much. You and Mr Ames are so clever, speaking French just like real French people. I spent a long time last night looking at the photographs, but they're not as good without the words. Shall I fetch them now?'

'If you like.' I stirred a bit more milk into my coffee as she went to collect her magazines.

While she was gone, I tried to figure out how I might be

able to form some sort of connection with the Belangers. Madame Nanette being a nanny, it was unlikely that she would be able to introduce me to the family. What was more, they were all in mourning and would no doubt retreat from society. It was going to be difficult, but I would do my best to find a way.

Winnelda returned, her magazines in hand, with remarkable speed.

I moved to the sofa and patted the seat beside me. She came to sit, and I took the magazine at the top of the stack and examined the cover. I knew that Winnelda was more interested in the vagaries of young socialites and the love affairs of cinema stars than she was in the 'old man' she had seen on the cover of the other magazines, but I hoped that we would both find something worthwhile in our reading.

Choosing what I thought would most appeal to her sense of the dramatic, I read to her the tragic, if dubious, account of a penniless Russian princess who had wed a commoner against her family's wishes only to succumb to pneumonia shortly thereafter.

'It's romantic, isn't it, madam?' she said, clasping her hands together. 'Romantic and so very sad.' I was fairly certain she was about to come to tears.

'Yes,' I said. 'Very sad indeed.'

'To die so young, and so very much in love.' She sighed, removing a handkerchief from her pocket and dabbing at the corners of her eyes. 'Life is very unfair sometimes.'

'You're quite right,' I agreed as I sifted through the magazines and found one for which I had been searching. Helios Belanger's picture was not on the cover, which was why it had escaped Winnelda's rather discriminating tastes, but his name was in the corner along with the sensational headline: 'The Crash That Led to Death: Helios Belanger Dead After Devastating Aeroplane Accident'. Despite the somewhat misleading headline, I hoped the article might prove useful.

'This is rather a sad story as well,' I said.

She looked over at me. 'What is it?'

'It has to do with the elderly gentleman you saw on some of the society magazines.'

'Oh? Who is he? Someone important?'

'Have you ever heard of a gentleman called Belanger?'

'The name sounds familiar to me,' she said, 'but I can't place it.'

'He is a well-known parfumier.'

'Oh, yes, madam!' she exclaimed. 'I remember now! My friend Edith is saving her salary to buy a bottle of one of his perfumes called Tigress because she thinks it will make her boyfriend wild for her.'

'I wish Edith every success,' I said.

Winnelda shook her head, her expression unhopeful. 'Edith's boyfriend has a wandering eye. I don't suppose the perfume will be much good.'

I couldn't disagree with her on that score.

'I'd like to see if we can find any information about the Belanger family,' I said, attempting to bring the subject back around to the task at hand. 'I'm very interested in what will happen to the company now that Monsieur Belanger has passed.'

'Very well, madam. I'm sure there must be something here.'

And so we set to flipping through the magazines with gusto. I found one article discussing Monsieur Belanger's sudden death and speculating on who would ascend to the Parfumes Belanger throne. As Madame Nanette had told us, it was commonly assumed Anton Belanger would take the reins, but there was mention of Cecile Belanger's influence in the perfumes her father had released to great acclaim over the past several years. The article even hinted at a bit of an internal struggle between the siblings.

There was also talk of a new perfume Madame Nanette had said was forthcoming. It was called L'Ange de Mémoire, and there was a great deal of anticipation surrounding its release. In addition to the sensation of the scent itself, which was rumoured to be comprised of rare, luxurious, and highly secret ingredients, the bottle had been designed by Jens Muller, a rather famous sculptor. The Belangers had been planning a grand party to reveal the bottle's design ahead of the perfume's release.

I wondered what sort of impact Helios Belanger's death would have on the sales of the perfume. It would be the last scent to be created under his governance, and I couldn't help but think the demand for it would be very high indeed.

We continued flipping through the pages until Winnelda stopped, examining the caption on a photograph.

'Here's a picture of the youngest son, Mitchell,' she said.

That would be Michel. I took the magazine from her and looked at the photograph. The quality was not very high, likely owing to the fact that it had clearly been taken when he was moving towards the photographer at an accelerated speed. It seemed Michel Belanger had not wanted his picture taken. The caption of the photo – 'Michel Belanger leaves the home of Pierre and Georgette Rochart in the pre-dawn hours while Monsieur Rochart is away on state business in

Brussels' – gave a good hint as to why he had been trying to avoid being photographed.

The common assumption was that the French were a bit more lenient when it came to romantic relationships, but Michel Belanger leaving the home of a government official's wife in the early hours of the morning, while the official was away, seemed a bit beyond the pale.

'He seems to be very handsome,' Winnelda said, leaning towards me to peer at the photograph again.

'Yes, I suppose he is,' I said. Though, from what I had heard from Milo and Madame Nanette, his personality was not at all attractive. I wonder if he had assaulted the photographer, another example of his temper.

We had been reading over the magazines for the better part of an hour when my vision began to blur from staring at the tiny print. There had been surprisingly little information about the Belanger family in them. I could only assume all the relevant stories had been in the magazines that Winnelda had avoided because the photographs of Helios Belanger had not appealed to her.

'Let's stop for the time being, shall we?' I asked at last. 'Perhaps we can acquire more magazines later.'

'Yes, madam. There were ever so many more, and several of them had Monsieur Belanger on them. I would have chosen some of them had I known.'

She gathered up the magazines just as Milo made his appearance in his dressing gown.

'Good morning,' he said, walking towards the sitting area.

'Good morning,' I replied. He looked well rested, despite the fact that he had slept only for a few hours.

'I'll just lay out your clothes for the day, shall I,

53

madam?' Winnelda asked. 'The blue suit, perhaps?'

'Yes, that will do nicely. Thank you.'

'What fresh mischief have you schemed up this morning?' Milo asked as Winnelda disappeared into the bedroom, magazines in tow.

'Nothing as dramatic as all that. We were looking for clues in her gossip rags,' I said, 'though we found surprisingly little. The problem, as I see it, is that we have no way to introduce ourselves to the family. Even if we were inclined to inject ourselves into their lives, it can't be done while they're mourning. If only we had some sort of connection.'

He made a non-committal noise and turned in the direction of the coffee pot that still rested on the table behind the sitting area.

'I want so much to help Madame Nanette, but I just can't see at this point how we are going to do it.'

'Don't give up hope just yet, darling,' he said. 'Something will turn up.'

Something in the way he said it made me look sharply at him over my shoulder, but he was pouring coffee and didn't appear to notice my inquisitive look.

Another thought occurred to me. 'Why are you up so early?' I asked. 'I rather thought you'd be abed until noon, considering your late night.'

'Too much fresh air in this room,' he replied, glancing at the open windows. 'It was seeping into the bedroom. I couldn't sleep.'

'I suppose it is rather bracing when compared to the thick, airless atmosphere of your gambling club.'

'You'll be glad to know my evening there was a success,' he said, stirring sugar into his coffee.

'You won, did you?' I asked, settling back on the sofa, my back to him.

'A thousand pounds, give or take a few francs,' he said, 'but that's not what I mean.'

'Oh?' I asked, only marginally interested in his gambling exploits.

'You said we need a connection to the Belangers, and we have one,' he said.

I turned again to look at him, suddenly very interested in what he had to say. 'What do you mean?'

'Just what I said. We have a connection to the Belanger family.' He lifted his cup to his lips and took a drink, clearly enjoying leaving me in suspense.

'Who?' I demanded.

'André Duveau.'

I frowned. 'He knows the Belangers?'

He slathered butter on a croissant. 'Darling, he told you he was in the perfume industry.'

Of course. How silly of me not to think of it before now. He had given me the bottle of perfume, and I had never stopped to think there might be a connection. What a dismal display of deductive powers.

'You don't mean to tell me that he's associated with Parfumes Belanger?' I demanded.

'That is exactly what I mean to tell you.'

'Why on earth didn't you say something before this?'

He brought his cup and saucer to the sofa and sat beside me. 'In the course of my enquiries about Madame Nanette's position, I learnt that Helios Belanger once did business with André Duveau. In fact, they often holidayed together in Como. I thought it might be a good means of forming a link to her employer's family.'

My lips parted in surprise as the implications of what he had just told me sank in. 'You cultivated Mr Duveau's friendship deliberately.'

He shrugged. 'We share many common interests. It wasn't difficult.'

Sometimes it still surprised me how very devious Milo could be.

'Turns out it was a lucky thing I did, given recent events,' he went on. 'He mentioned in Como that he enjoyed gaming at a particular club. I telephoned him last night to see if he would introduce me there. So you see? I was gathering information.' He smiled. 'You don't think I spent the night out gambling purely for my own amusement?'

I declined to answer that question. 'And so when he had to leave Como so urgently it was because Helios Belanger had died.'

'Yes. He received word that morning, I believe.'

I thought of the urgent matter Mr Duveau had spoken of when he was prepared to depart for Paris. I had assumed it was a woman, but it had been a more urgent matter than that. I wondered what the relationship between him and Helios Belanger had been. He certainly hadn't seemed overly upset at the news.

Another thought occurred to me. 'André Duveau is very fond of flying, and Helios Belanger died following an aeroplane crash.'

'Yes,' Milo said. 'I had thought of that. I mentioned it to Duveau, in fact. He admits that it was probably his enthusiasm for flying that drew Helios to the hobby. He lamented it, or seemed to.'

I wondered. Was it possible that André Duveau had something to do with the crash that had killed Helios Belanger? But, no. He had been in Como with us at the time. It didn't seem likely that he might have been able to participate in a murder plot in Paris, especially if Helios Belanger had been poisoned the night he died.

'He also mentioned that Monsieur Belanger had taken to drink in recent months. Perhaps that might account for the plane crash.' That contradicted what Madame Nanette had told us about Helios Belanger not liking to dull his mind. Which one of them was mistaken?

I didn't know whether to be impressed with Milo's investigative skills or severely put out that he had gone sleuthing without me. My curiosity got the best of me. 'Did you learn anything more?'

'Not much, I'm afraid. I tried to bring up his dealings with Belanger during a casual conversation at a baccarat table, but he was losing badly and his focus was on the game.'

That was a pity, but a connection with the family was still an excellent development. André Duveau was the answer to all our difficulties. He would be close enough to the Belangers to provide valuable information, but, as an outside connection to the family, we would not be intruding upon his grief. I began to wish that we had made plans to dine with him in Paris. Perhaps he would be too occupied to see us. What then?

'I can see the wheels turning,' Milo said. 'But for pity's sake, darling, let me finish my coffee before you begin concocting schemes.'

'I might remind you that it was you who brought this mystery to us,' I said.

'Yes, I suppose you're right,' he said. 'Which is why I am going to deal with it. I don't want you getting too deeply involved.'

'Milo . . .' I began to protest.

He held up a hand. 'All right, all right, darling. Before you start formulating some outlandish plan for meeting with him, I've taken care of that, too. We're having dinner with him tonight.'

'Tonight?'

He smiled. 'You are not the only one capable of underhanded behaviour.'

'Yes,' I said, sweetly returning his smile. 'I realised that a long time ago.'

CHAPTER SIX

Winnelda had been very distressed that I did not intend to purchase a new gown for my evening out in Paris, but I felt suitably turned out in my gown of pale mauve satin crepe. It had a high neckline and flutter sleeves with a low-cut back that ended in a chiffon bow. It was the perfect colour for spring, and I had been in the mood for something less severe than my wide array of dark gowns.

André Duveau had suggested a nightclub called Arabique for dinner, and Milo had agreed to it. I had never visited it before, nor even heard of it, and was not sure what to expect. I found it was a very elegant establishment. Leaving the cloakroom, we went down a short flight of marble steps into an interior courtyard of sorts, created by marble pillars that met high above our heads to form keyhole arches. Coloured fabric draped down from the ceiling and large potted palm trees added to the exotic effect.

'We are meeting Monsieur Duveau,' Milo told the head waiter.

'Of course. Right this way, monsieur.' I had noticed that

there were tables outside the courtyard, set into little alcoves with vaulted ceilings. Others were situated near carved wooden screens that provided some measure of privacy. The waiter, however, led us to a table near the dance floor. André Duveau rose when we reached the table. The waiter pulled out the chair nearest Mr Duveau for me, and Milo was just about to take a seat when a lovely blonde woman in a chartreuse evening gown appeared at his side, speaking excitedly in French.

'Milo, it *is* you! I was sure it was. There can't be two men in the world who look like you.' Then she flung herself into his arms and kissed him squarely on the mouth. I watched this exchange with great interest.

'Hello, Nadine,' he said, gently prying her off him. 'How are you?'

'Very well. It's been *ages* since I've seen you.'

'Yes. Allow me to introduce my wife, Amory. Darling, this is Nadine Germaine.'

'How do you do?' I said politely, examining her gown and only slightly jealous that her colouring should be so complemented by a shade that would look absolutely hideous on me.

I took it as a good sign that she was not at all flustered to learn that I was Milo's wife. 'I am pleased to meet you, Mrs Ames. I adore your husband.'

'Don't we all,' I replied.

'And this is Mr Duveau,' Milo went on smoothly.

'How do you do?' she said before grasping Milo's arm. 'Come and meet my friends, will you? I've told them all about you. They'll be thrilled to meet you.'

He looked down at me. 'Do you mind?'

'Not at all,' I replied. I had learnt to be gracious in the face of Milo's many admirers, though one had never been quite so admiring in my presence before.

'I won't keep him long,' she promised, leading him away.

I smiled at Mr Duveau, who appeared to be doing his best not to appear too curious. For my part, I was actually glad that Milo had been called away. It would give me the opportunity to talk to Mr Duveau alone. Perhaps he would be more receptive to my questions than he had been to Milo's.

'This is a beautiful nightclub,' I said. 'Milo and I have been to Paris many times, but I've never been here.'

'I thought you would appreciate the ambiance,' he said. 'I must admit, many of the places I prefer are not quite so . . . savoury.' He smiled that rakish smile of his. 'I hope you are not scandalised by that admission.'

I smiled dryly. 'Mr Duveau, as you've just witnessed, years of marriage to Milo have made me practically immune to scandal.'

He grinned, and his eyes flickered in the direction Milo had gone with his young friend. 'I expect he appreciates that you take his reputation in stride.'

'Not in stride, perhaps,' I replied, 'but I have come to understand that not everything is as it seems.'

'An excellent philosophy. One that is true of life in general, I suppose.'

'Yes, I suppose.'

He took a drink of his wine, and I took the opportunity to change the subject.

'I've greatly enjoyed the perfume you gave me, Mr Duveau.'

He smiled. 'I'm glad. I thought it would suit you.'

'What was it that made you decide to go into the perfume industry?'

'My father died a few years ago and left me a rather sizeable inheritance, but my mother had hoped that I would do more with my life than simply risk it flying aeroplanes after the war. I had a . . . friend, a woman, who was terribly fond of perfume. Her enthusiasm was contagious, and I began to develop something of an interest in it myself. I thought I might as well invest in something worthwhile.' He flashed a smile. 'It's business, but a bit frivolous by some standards, so it suits me.'

'I did not know that you were connected with Helios Belanger.'

I said it abruptly to gauge his reaction, and it seemed to me that his smile faltered ever so slightly. Whether it was the pain of loss or something else, I wasn't sure.

He took another drink of his wine and when he spoke again his expression had returned to normal. 'I worked with him, yes. When I realised that I wanted to work with perfumes – seriously, as something more than a hobby – he was the first person I sought out. He is one of the top names in France, in all of the perfume industry, and I have always wanted to have the best.'

'How did you manage to meet him, to convince him to work with you?' It was forward of me to ask, but I did wonder how it was that someone who had no experience had gained the ear of the top man in the profession.

Mr Duveau hesitated for a moment, and then smiled somewhat ruefully. 'Well, to be honest, it was his daughter, Cecile, who was my friend. She introduced me and, I am sure, influenced her father to take an interest in me.'

'I see.' So Mr Duveau and Cecile Belanger had had a romance. This was becoming quite interesting.

'Monsieur Belanger and I worked together closely for nearly a year, in fact, but there were . . . difficulties.'

It was very apparent he did not intend to elaborate upon the difficulties. I could well imagine, however, that they had something to do with his relationship with Cecile Belanger. Romance and business were seldom a successful combination.

I thought sympathy might elicit further confidences. 'He sounds as though he might have been a difficult partner,' I said.

'Oh, we were not partners,' he said with a laugh. 'Helios would not have accepted me as an equal. We worked well enough together, however. We disagreed on many things, but he was a man with an excellent head for business and unwavering determination. We parted on fairly good terms, and of that I was glad.'

'Then you no longer work with the Belangers?'

'No, I decided to venture out on my own sometime last year.'

'So you're now a competitor?'

'Hardly that. I can never hope to equal his success, but I enjoy dabbling in perfumery and am hoping to find a niche for myself. Shazadi is my first scent.'

'I'm sure it will be a great success.'

'Thank you.'

I ventured back once more to the subject of Helios Belanger. 'Monsieur Belanger's death was such a tragedy. I'm sure it's a very great loss for the industry.'

'Yes, I'm afraid so,' he said in a tone that revealed nothing of his feelings. 'He was a genius, in his way.'

I leant forward slightly. 'It's fascinating to meet someone who worked with him. What was he like?'

He took a cigarette from his pocket and took his time about lighting it. I wondered if he was trying to decide what to tell me. 'It is hard to say what he was really like,' he said at last. 'He was a dragon of a man, always looking around a room as though trying to determine who he could breathe fire onto next. Everyone was in awe of him, and a bit afraid. I suppose I was the same, but I admired him greatly.'

'I'm rather interested in perfume,' I said, lest he think I was prying too deeply into his personal affairs. This statement of interest was not a falsehood. I was becoming more intrigued by the moment. 'The science of it fascinates me. I feel the process is rather like magic.'

He smiled, much more at ease now. 'Yes, well, I wasn't much familiar with the process itself, though I've started a small laboratory of my own. If you want to know how such things work, I can introduce you to Cecile. She has a mind for all of those kinds of details.'

So he and Cecile Belanger were still on speaking terms.

It seemed he had followed my train of thought, for the corner of his mouth tipped up. 'It was not a bitter parting. Cecile and I both find that there is no need to hate each other just because love has faded. She would be happy to show off her gardens and laboratory to you.'

'I'm sure the family will be concerned with mourning at a time like this.'

A hint of amusement crossed his features. 'Do you

think so? I'm afraid you don't know the Belangers.'

I didn't have time to find out what he meant before Milo returned to the table.

'I'm sorry about that,' he said, taking his seat. 'Nadine is the younger sister of an old friend of mine. She's a model now and lives here in Paris. Have I missed anything?'

I leant to remove Milo's handkerchief from his pocket and handed it to him. 'Just that little spot of lipstick on your chin.'

He smiled and wiped it away as I continued. 'We were just discussing the death of poor Helios Belanger,' I said. I wanted Milo to know that I had been working while he had been enjoying being fawned over by a pretty young woman and her friends.

'Ah, yes,' Milo said, with the perfect imitation of barely concealed boredom. 'Amory's developed rather an obsession with him. She's gone mad about perfume as of late.'

'It's not an obsession,' I protested, a bit irritated, despite the fact that this description of my interest fit perfectly with what I had been telling Mr Duveau. I turned my gaze back to him. 'But I am terribly interested.'

'You see?' Milo said. 'You mustn't indulge her or she'll never stop pestering you.'

I kicked him under the table, but I recognised the warning in his words. I was, perhaps, pressing too hard. My interest was already extremely apparent. I didn't want to overdo it.

'There we disagree, Ames,' Mr Duveau said with a smile. 'I'm always happy to indulge a beautiful woman.'

I glanced with poorly veiled triumph at Milo before turning my attention back to Mr Duveau.

'You mentioned Cecile Belanger worked closely with her father. What about the others in the family? Are they involved in the business as well? It's not nice to be so interested in gossip, I suppose,' I said lightly. 'But when my friends find out that I was in Paris after Helios Belanger died and met one of his business associates, they'll want to know all about it, all the inside information on what the family is like.'

'Then I won't disappoint you.' He flicked the ashes from his cigarette into the crystal ashtray on the table. 'The older son, Anton Belanger, is a cool customer, not much like his father. He has always been a very serious, ambitious man, but intimidated by his father. For years, he has been fighting his father's rule as much as he dared and waiting for the moment when he might be able to implement his plans for the business. Perhaps he will make a success of it. He is intelligent, sharp.'

'Married?' I asked.

'Widowed. His wife died shortly after Helios's first wife, Elena, did. It was a difficult time for Anton, I'm sure.'

'I see. And there is a younger son, I believe?' I asked to prod him on.

'Yes. Michel.' Though he tried to answer the question casually, there was no mistaking his dislike for the younger Belanger brother. I wondered what had caused it.

'I know Michel Belanger,' Milo said. 'If there was ever a single thought of business in his head he didn't let it interfere with his drinking or his women.'

Duveau smiled. 'That is an accurate assessment.'

I felt suddenly that we had pushed the conversation far enough for the time being. I had been so inquisitive that I was afraid he would soon grow suspicious, if he wasn't already.

The waiter came to take our orders then, and after he left I let the subject drop. Milo followed my lead and shifted the conversation to gambling clubs. While they talked, I pondered Mr Duveau's description of the Belanger family. It was much as I had heard from Madame Nanette and the gossip magazines. I felt somewhat discouraged. I didn't really see how second-hand accounts of the personalities of the Belanger family members might be useful in determining if one of them had killed their patriarch.

Our dinner came, and we ate, the topics of conversation ranging from gambling to horses and then to aeroplanes. More than once I fought the urge to yawn.

At last Mr Duveau pushed his plate away. 'But enough of this dull talk, Ames. I'm afraid we're boring your wife.' He rose from his seat and held out his hand. 'Will you dance with me?'

'I'd love to.' I took his hand and he pulled back my chair with the other hand as I rose.

'You don't mind me sweeping your wife away, do you, Ames?' he asked, when I was practically already in his arms.

'By all means,' Milo said.

André Duveau moved around the dance floor as the band struck up 'Fascination', and a mellow-voiced gentleman began to sing. Mr Duveau was an excellent dancer, and for a moment I took simple pleasure in our movement around the floor.

'I'm sorry if I appeared too inquisitive about Monsieur Belanger,' I said at last. 'Milo always says I'm much too interested in other people's business.'

'Not at all,' he said. 'I find your interest charming. In fact, I have an invitation that I think will appeal to you.'

'Oh?' I asked. He had mentioned introducing me to Cecile Belanger. Perhaps he had meant it. I hoped that was the case.

'Helios Belanger was poised to release his newest fragrance soon. It's been something of a closely guarded secret. There is a grand party scheduled for tomorrow at the Belanger residence to reveal the design of the bottle.'

This was the event I had read about in Winnelda's gossip magazine. The timing of Monsieur Belanger's death was unfortunate, to say the least.

'I imagine it will be costly to cancel such a thing,' I mused aloud. 'But perhaps they can reschedule it for some future date.'

He gave a dry laugh. 'They're not going to cancel it.'

This truly surprised me. I had not even considered the possibility that the party might go on. 'But in the wake of Monsieur Belanger's death . . .'

'The family is more desperate than ever to make sure that Parfumes Belanger goes on being the success it has been for the last twenty years. They want to prove that they can carry on without him.'

'But what will people say?' I asked.

'People will whisper behind closed doors that the party is in poor taste and then come out in droves to attend it.' He shrugged. 'I don't think Helios would have wanted it any other way. He was very proud of his creations.'

'I'm sure it will be an eventful party,' I said.

'Would you like to come?' he asked.

The invitation was more than I could have hoped for. In

addition to being the ideal opportunity to meet the members of the family and evaluate Madame Nanette's suspicions, I would, on a more superficial level, enjoy attending such a highly anticipated event.

Still, I hesitated. I didn't want to appear too eager.

'I know you want to come and are too polite to say so,' Mr Duveau said with a smile. 'So I shall spare you the dilemma of deciding. I insist that you come. It's going to be the talk of all Europe, and I know you'd regret missing it.'

'I am a bit curious,' I admitted.

'Then that settles it,' he said.

I let it go at that. After all, I had no intention of declining such an invitation. Murder or not, I imagined this would be a party to remember.

CHAPTER SEVEN

'I might have known you'd have much more success with Duveau than I did,' Milo told me in the cab on the way back to our hotel. I had related the news of our invitation to him, and I couldn't help but feel a bit smug that I had gained us entrée to an event that might prove the key to forming a connection with the Belanger family.

'There are times when persistence wins the day,' I said.

'Yes, I'm sure it was your persistence that did the trick,' he said dryly.

'And what, exactly, do you mean by that?'

'You know what I mean. Men have only to look deeply into those dove-grey eyes of yours to fall under your spell. I saw how very much he seemed to enjoy holding you in his arms.'

Milo, completely secure in his own charms, had never minded my interactions with other men, and I knew perfectly well what this was about, why he was feigning jealousy when there was no cause for it.

'If you expect me to apologise for his attentiveness, I have one word for you,' I said.

'Oh?' he asked, and I could feel him smiling in the darkness. 'And what might that be?'

'Nadine,' I answered succinctly.

He laughed. 'Yes, I thought you might have something to say about that.'

I had to admit that I didn't find it quite as amusing as he did. Despite the indifferent show I had put on for Mr Duveau, Nadine's enthusiastic greeting had begged the question of just how close she was to my husband. I hesitated, trying to decide how best to phrase my enquiry. Finally, I came out with it: 'Is there anything I need to know about her?'

'Nothing more than what I've told you.' There was no hint of guilt in his tone, but, as he never seemed to feel guilty about anything, this was not particularly telling.

'Do you really expect me to believe she is merely the younger sister of one of your friends?'

'Whatever you choose to believe, that's the truth,' he replied easily. 'Her brother Francois Germaine and I were at school together. I visited him on holiday many times, and she has made a nuisance of herself for as long as I can remember.'

'She's a very pretty nuisance,' I noted. 'Just the kind you like, I believe.'

'Come now, darling. You didn't really mind her?'

Had I? I considered. After a very rocky patch in our marriage, I was learning to trust my husband, despite the reputation he had earned for himself. Though there were still times when the nagging doubts resurfaced, I understood that a great deal of what had been printed about Milo was untrue or grossly exaggerated. There was no denying the way women flocked to him, but I could accept the careless

71

way he welcomed their attentions as long as his heedless words did not lead to heedless actions.

'No,' I replied. 'I suppose I didn't mind her. In any event, I have more important things to consider.'

'Oh? Such as?'

'Such as what I'm going to wear to that party tomorrow night.'

I wasted no time the following morning in beginning my preparations for the Belangers' party.

While I felt that the gowns in my wardrobe were fine for a night out in Paris, something a bit more extravagant might be in order for a grand event like the Belanger party.

I realised that it might be difficult to secure a gown on such short notice, but I had an excellent relationship with a couturier called Madame Lorraine, whose evening gowns were always exquisite, and I believed there was a good chance that she would have something for me.

If I was going to go shopping, it was important that I looked as though I was not in need of anything newer or more fashionable than what I already owned. That was the way to the heart of Parisian modistes – the appearance of complete indifference to their fashions. To get the best of their clothes, I needed to dress as though adding to my wardrobe was the last thing on my mind.

To this end, I wore one of my newest acquisitions, a smart white suit with an attached capelet and a white hat that came down at an angle over my forehead. It was a very fetching ensemble that I had purchased from a well-known fashion house, and I expected Madame Lorraine would be eager to trump it if she could.

I made my way to the shop on the rue de Rivoli. I frequently purchased gowns there while in Paris, and Madame Lorraine also sent a good many evening gowns to me at home. I gave my name to the salesgirl, and a moment later Madame Lorraine came to meet me. 'Good morning, Madame Ames. It is good to see you again.'

'And you, too, Madame Lorraine. I hope you have been well.'

'Yes, thank you.' Her eyes swept over me with a critical glance, but it seemed that my ensemble met with her approval. 'Your suit is quite elegant,' she said begrudgingly.

'Thank you.'

'Is there something in particular that you are searching for?'

'As a matter of fact, there is,' I said. 'I know it is short notice, but I have an event to attend tonight, and I wondered if you might have something for me.'

She hesitated, and I wondered if the suit had done the trick. Then she nodded slowly. 'For you, Madame Ames, always. Have a seat, will you? I'll have the models put on some of my newest creations.'

I sat on the blue velvet chair and a salesgirl brought me a tray with rich, creamy coffee and chocolate biscuits. I nibbled contentedly while I waited.

Madame Lorraine had excellent taste and knew what items would best suit my colouring. I was looking forward to seeing what she had in store for me. At last she came and stood beside the door to the dressing room. The show was about to begin.

A few moments later, the first model came out. She was wearing a gown of deep red silk with sheer ruffled sleeves. It was a very pretty gown, but I was not really in the market for something red as I had purchased a red evening gown not long ago.

There was a gown of sapphire blue, one of a deep emerald green, and another in a pale grey satin. They were all lovely, but I couldn't help but feel that they were not precisely what I was looking for. I would know when I saw it.

The next model came out with a very tempting option. It was a stunning black silk gown with a fitted bodice and a confection of chiffon for a skirt. I didn't often wear black as I felt it made me look even paler than usual. My skin tone had been somewhat improved by our time in Capri, however, and there was a subdued elegance to the dark colour. I was about to tell Madame Lorraine that I had decided when another model came out, and I changed my mind.

This one was wearing a gown of pale lavender satin that gleamed almost silver in the light. The model moved and the light rippled across the fabric so that it fairly shimmered. I couldn't help but think how well it would look with diamonds.

'This gown is in a fabric called twilight sea,' Madame Lorraine said, apparently attuned to my interest.

The description was accurate. It reminded me of the pale lilac-blue of dusk settling over the surface of a calm sea. It was practically mesmerising.

There were thin straps over the shoulders and fabric that draped down across the upper arms. The neckline formed a V and as the model turned I could see that the back dipped quite low as well. It was a bit daring and yet not too revealing. It was perfect.

This was the gown that I wanted to wear. I felt that

it was, somehow, what I had wanted all along without knowing it.

'This is the one,' I said.

'Excellent choice, madame,' Madame Lorraine said. 'It is a beautiful gown. One of my favourites.'

'Do you think I might have it sent to my hotel by this afternoon?'

'This particular model has nearly your exact measurements,' she said. 'I think it should fit you perfectly. Would you like to try it on to be sure?'

I tried on the gown and found that Madame Lorraine was right; it fit perfectly.

'Even the length is just right,' she enthused. 'It looks magnificent on you.'

'Thank you.'

'I'll have it sent to your hotel within the hour.'

I was about to leave when I decided to take the black as well. One could always use a black gown, after all.

I also decided to mention the purpose of my shopping trip to Madame Lorraine. She was acquainted with a great many society women, and I wondered if she would have any insight into the Belanger family.

'I'm attending a party at the home of Helios Belanger,' I said casually, 'and I think this dress will be just the thing.'

She raised her brows ever so slightly, but did not reply.

'I thought it a bit soon to hold a party, considering his very recent passing,' I said, playing into what I assumed was her disapproval, 'but if they mean to have it, I couldn't refuse the invitation.'

'I am sure the family will manage their grief,' she said tonelessly.

'Do you know the family?' I asked, wondering what she meant.

'No,' she said. Then hesitated a moment before adding reluctantly, 'One hears things, that is all.'

'What sort of things?'

She shrugged. 'Gossip. That perhaps the family was not completely surprised by his death, given his recent illness.'

'His illness?' I repeated. So far as I knew, Helios Belanger had been the picture of health.

She seemed to waver for a moment before proceeding. 'This is *entre nous*, of course.'

'Of course. I wouldn't dream of sharing anything confidential.'

'My niece works as a private nurse. She met one day another woman in the profession who was hired briefly to look after him.'

'What sort of illness was it?' I asked, ignoring the vulgarity of the question.

'That I do not know. His wife had tried to nurse him, but it grew severe and they brought in a professional. In a matter of a few weeks, however, the nurse was dismissed abruptly. It seems Helios Belanger was once again healthy, so perhaps it was nothing serious.'

'Yes, perhaps not,' I said thoughtfully. I wondered. 'What was the nurse's name?'

Her brow rose ever so slightly at my impertinence. 'I do not know. My niece was not well acquainted with her. They spoke only in passing.'

'I see. Well, I can't thank you enough, Madame Lorraine, for my gowns.'

We parted ways and I left feeling very satisfied with my

purchases but curious about what I had learnt. If Helios Belanger had been very ill not long ago, his sudden death might not be as surprising as Madame Nanette thought. Then again, perhaps it proved Madame Nanette right. Perhaps that illness had been the killer's first attempt.

That errand finished, I decided I didn't want to go back to the hotel just yet. I was very much looking forward to the party, but before I went, I felt that I should do some research. I wanted to better familiarise myself with Helios Belanger's perfumes.

And what better way to do that than to pay a visit to a perfume shop?

The perfume shop I chose was not familiar to me, but there was no doubt the perfumes of Helios Belanger would be a part of their inventory. I went inside and was immersed in a cloud of scent. It was pleasant, if a bit overwhelming.

'May I help you, madame?' asked a pretty blonde salesgirl.

'I'm looking for Belanger scents,' I told her.

'Oh, yes,' she said. 'They have been very popular since the death of Monsieur Belanger.'

She led me to a display on the counter and picked up a glass bottle. 'This is Séduire Rouge, one of the most popular.' She squeezed the pump, releasing the scent into the air. It was a dense fragrance, better suited for winter than spring, I thought. Still, one whiff and I was half tempted to buy it. It was exotic and alluring.

The salesgirl showed me a few more fragrances and as I breathed in the heady array of scents, one after the other, I thought again what a master of his art Helios Belanger had been. Each perfume was a new experience, carefully crafted layers of scent, subtly combined and slowly revealed as they warmed on the skin, like a flower opening its petals. It was as though each of them told a story.

If it was true that Cecile Belanger shared her father's zeal, I hoped that she would continue to play a role in the company. It was obvious that more than dry scientific process had gone into the creation of these perfumes. If Helios Belanger's passion died with him, I was very much afraid that the company would cease to be what he had made it.

I looked at the array of bottles on the counter before me. 'Which scent does Cecile Belanger wear, do you think?' I asked, hoping to perhaps glean a bit more information about the mysterious family.

'Oh, no, madame,' she said, shaking her head. 'Cecile Belanger does not wear any of these scents.'

'No?' I was surprised.

'No. She has a custom scent that she created herself. It is said to be very exotic. I have heard she smells as though the answers to all the mysteries of the East are flowing through her veins.'

I was unsure how exactly one might smell if this was the case, but the fact that she wore a perfume that no one else possessed was intriguing and might, in fact, prove useful.

After an extended period of experimenting with different fragrances against my skin, I settled on a bottle of their most recent perfume, Bouquet de Belanger, one I did not yet own. While I usually wore a gardenia scent, this one smelt of roses and lilac, and I felt as though it was the perfect fragrance for spring.

The salesgirl, Marie, wrapped the bottle up for me. 'Will there be anything else, madame?'

By this point we had developed quite a chatty little camaraderie, and I didn't think she would mind a few questions. 'I hear there is to be a new scent,' I said. 'Do you know anything about it?'

She nodded eagerly. 'There is much talk about it, their most unique scent as of yet, so they say. The ingredients are said to be very rare.'

'Oh? What are they?'

'That's just it,' she said, leaning forward in her enthusiasm. 'No one knows. It has all been very mysterious.'

'I look forward to experiencing it,' I said. Then added casually, 'It was very sad, what happened to Monsieur Belanger.'

'Yes, madame,' she said. 'The world of perfume will not be the same without him.'

'Did you ever meet him?'

'Oh, no. But I am sure he will be missed.' She said this in a way that led me to believe there was a deeper meaning to the words.

'Oh?' I asked encouragingly.

She leant forward, her elbows on the glass counter. 'I heard that Monsieur Belanger had been seen with a young woman,' she told me conspiratorially.

'His wife, perhaps?' I suggested. 'They say she is much younger than he.'

She laughed, apparently delighted with my naiveté. 'No, no, madame. Madame Belanger is not the woman I mean.'

'Indeed?' I asked.

She nodded. 'He was seen with another woman. She was very mysterious, dressed all in black and wearing a veil across her face.'

I wondered who exactly it was that had been giving information to this young woman. It sounded like they had paid one too many visits to the cinema.

'That's very interesting,' I said.

She must have sensed my scepticism, for she added, 'It was my friend Lucille who saw them, coming out of a flat across from the cafe where she works. It is on the rue de Tolbiac.'

I tucked this bit of information away for future use.

'Lucille was quite sure it was he, and he was leaving quite early in the morning, too early for a social call. I suppose it must have been his mistress.'

She studied me to see if I was scandalised and, as I was not sure what kind of reaction she was hoping for, I responded vaguely. 'Indeed.'

She nodded. 'Rich men often have mistresses,' she said with authority. 'Though it isn't as though his wife is ugly. She is very pretty, in fact. I saw her once, getting into a car on the rue de Rivoli,' she volunteered.

'I have heard that she is a lovely woman,' I said. 'And I am sure she must be very sad that her husband has passed.'

'I'm sure his mistress is also distressed,' she added.

'Yes,' I replied thoughtfully. 'I'm sure she is.'

The store manager passed just then, and Marie quickly straightened.

'Would you like this delivered, madame?' she asked, and I realised that our friendly chat had come to an end.

'No,' I said. 'I'll take it with me. Thank you.'

I left the shop in a cloud of perfume, ideas whirling in my head.

Milo was not at the hotel when I returned, but my gown had arrived. After I had bathed away the somewhat overpowering mélange of scents from my skin, I removed it from the box, and Winnelda was suitably impressed when I put it on.

'It's so beautiful. You look ever so glamorous, madam,' she enthused.

'Thank you, Winnelda.'

'That colour is unlike anything I've ever seen in a gown before.'

'It is an unusual shade, isn't it?'

'I'd even take you for a French lady,' she added significantly.

'I'm glad you like it,' I said.

'Will you need help with preparations tonight?' she asked.

'No, I can manage. I won't keep you any longer. I expect you have plans for this evening?'

'Yes, we thought we might go and see a show,' she said.

'We?'

'There's another English lady staying at the hotel, and I've met her maid. We've become friends already. She's never been to Paris before either, and we both find it so thrilling but we don't much like to go out alone when we don't speak the language. It feels much safer to travel in pairs.'

'That's very nice. I hope you have a good time.'

'Thank you, madam. I hope your party is wonderful.'

At the door she hesitated and turned back to me. 'You

will tell me all about it, won't you, madam?' she asked.

I smiled. 'Certainly, Winnelda. I can think of no one else with whom I am as eager to share gossip as you.'

She grinned. 'Thank you, madam. I'm ever so excited to hear about it. If I may say so, I hope you'll take special care to let me know if you meet Mitchell. He's the one that seems the most interesting.'

'I shall keep an eye out for him,' I assured her.

She left then, and I thought again how glad I was that she had come into my service. She was not, perhaps, an ideal lady's maid by traditional standards, but her enthusiasm was unmatched, and I was very much attached to her.

I turned and examined myself once more in the mirror. The effect of the gown was rather dramatic, but that was the impression I wished to convey to Cecile Belanger. I had begun to formulate a plan for getting to know her, and I thought it might just work. It was important, though, that I look the part.

I picked up a diamond necklace from the case and held it up to my neck, examining the effect. As I had suspected, the diamonds were the perfect accent to the silvery lavender of the gown.

It was then I caught sight of Milo in the mirror behind me. He was leaning in the doorway watching me intently.

'What are you thinking about?' I asked, fastening the necklace.

'You'd be quite shocked if I told you.'

I turned to face him. 'Do you like it?'

'I like it very much indeed,' he answered, coming to me, his arms moving to my waist. 'So much so that I'd like nothing more than to stay here tonight and remove it.'

I laughed. 'I'm afraid we have more important matters to attend to. In fact, I'd say you're rather late getting in.'

'It won't take me long to prepare. You know Parks can whip me into shape in no time at all.'

'You gave Parks the evening off,' I reminded him. 'Though he's already laid out your evening clothes.'

Milo had to put no effort at all into being handsome and very little into looking perfectly turned out. It was most unfair.

'I'll just go and shave,' he said, turning towards the bathroom.

'Where have you been today?' I asked, fastening on the matching diamond bracelet.

'Here and there,' he said. 'I'll give you the dull details when I'm not running a very sharp razor across my jaw.'

'Very well.'

'How was your day?' he asked.

'Successful, I think. I learnt some things of interest this afternoon,' I said, going to the bathroom door. 'And something I think might be of use to us in forming a connection with the Belangers.'

'Oh?' he asked, his gaze on the mirror as he ran the blade down his neck.

I gave what was perhaps the less dramatic piece of news first. 'It seems that Helios Belanger may have had a mistress.'

Milo appeared unimpressed. 'Did he?'

'He was seen coming out of a woman's flat on the rue de Tolbiac very early one morning.'

'Interesting. We'll add her to our list of suspects, shall we?' I could tell by his tone that he did not think this information very noteworthy, but that was why I had saved my more significant discovery for last.

'That isn't all I learnt today,' I said. 'I also found out that there was a young woman, a private nurse, who had been hired to look after Helios Belanger during an illness some months ago.'

'Indeed?' He remained engrossed in his shaving and didn't seem to realise the possible implication of what I had just told him.

'Don't you think it might be a clue?' I prodded. 'What if it was the killer's first attempt?'

'What if it merely points to the fact that he was ailing?' Milo replied. 'The sickness might have weakened his heart.'

'Do you suppose we might get in touch with that nurse?' I asked, ignoring his inconvenient practicality. 'If we could locate her, perhaps we could discover just what sort of ailment troubled Monsieur Belanger.'

'It might prove difficult.'

'Perhaps Madame Nanette would know how we might reach her,' I mused. I did wonder why it was that she had not mentioned this nurse to us. Then again, there was the possibility that Monsieur Belanger's illness had indeed been something commonplace, and she might have thought it insignificant.

'You mentioned something that might prove of use to us in forming a connection with the Belangers?' he asked.

'Oh, yes. I had a delightful discussion with a perfume shop salesgirl and she told me that Cecile Belanger wears a custom perfume. I was thinking that I might use this as an excuse to get to know her. I could tell her that I would like a custom perfume, and perhaps it will give me the opportunity to spend some time with her, perhaps even to get to know the family.'

'It isn't a bad idea,' Milo said.

'No,' I replied. 'It is, in fact, an excellent idea.'

'It might be,' he conceded. 'I'll admit that I'm having a hard time thinking over its merits. You look entirely too beautiful and you're distracting me.'

'Am I?'

He leant towards me, but I took a quick step back, afraid his shaving lotion would soil my dress. 'Wipe your face and then you may kiss me.'

He grinned. 'Now you sound like Madame Nanette after I'd got into the jam pot.'

CHAPTER EIGHT

The Belanger home was a sprawling mansion of white stone in the Faubourg Saint-Germain, one of Paris's more fashionable and exclusive neighbourhoods. We stepped from the car, and I looked up at the residence. It was grand and stately, a fitting symbol of Helios Belanger's climb from humble beginnings to a life of wealth and privilege.

Light pooled from the windows against the darkening spring sky, and the intoxicating scent of roses, jasmine, and mimosa hovered in the air. It was almost as if the house itself was perfumed.

It appeared a great many people had already arrived by the time we approached the front door. André Duveau had assured me that we would not need an invitation to be admitted, and I had hoped that he was not mistaken. It would be terribly embarrassing to be turned away.

Even if we were ushered into the house, I had wondered if our appearance might be a bit conspicuous considering we had no connection to the Belangers or the perfume industry. It was clear as we arrived, however, that I needn't have worried. Guests were flocking to the Belanger mansion, and we drew no notice, aside, at least, from the notice Milo typically drew.

We entered the house and were caught up in the swell of music and voices. There was an orchestra in some other room, the music flowing over the guests in waves. I was briefly reminded of another elaborate party I had attended, one that had ended in murder. I hoped this evening would prove less eventful.

In the alcove created by the bottom of the winding marble staircase, there appeared to be some sort of large object obscured by a white satin cloth. I supposed this was the model of the perfume bottle that was to be revealed later in the night. It seemed the Belangers had a flair for the dramatic.

'There are the Belangers,' Milo told me, with a subtle nod in their direction. The family in question was standing not far from the stairs. They made a striking picture as they stood together, dressed in their dark clothes. Even if Milo had not pointed them out to me, I would have been able to pick them out in the room. They looked as though they belonged together, as though they had all come from a matched set of sculptures.

The oldest son, Anton Belanger, was extremely handsome. He was tall and dark with a face that would have looked at home on a marble bust. There was something proud, almost regal, about the tilt of his dark head. I wondered how much of it had to do with the empire that was now at his command. I didn't know the man, but I could almost feel his satisfaction as he watched the guests pouring into the house. It was as though he was enjoying looking at his new domain, the subjects who had come to pay tribute. I wondered if he had waited so long for this moment that he had finally decided to seize it for himself.

Michel Belanger, the second son, was also very handsome. Like his brother, he was tall and dark with chiselled features. It was almost immediately apparent, however, that this similarity was only superficial. Even as an outsider, I could tell that the brothers were not much alike. While Anton Belanger had a serious air about him, there was a glint of mischief in Michel Belanger's eyes, and those eyes moved about the room, following various women as they passed him.

The sister, Cecile, was not what I had expected. Perhaps it was an unfair preconception, but the knowledge that she was inclined to work in her father's laboratory had led me to expect that she would be somewhat prim and studious in appearance. Instead, she was a beauty. Like her brothers, she had dark hair and eyes. She was tall and thin, and elegant. Her black dress was fitted with a high neckline and long sleeves. It was somehow both subdued enough for her situation and terribly chic.

They were a very attractive family and gave the impression of a united front. Was it possible that one of these three had killed their father? Having been involved in three different murder investigations, I knew one could never rule out anyone. All things considered, it seemed especially likely that it might have been one of his children. After all, they would be the most likely to gain from Helios Belanger's death.

But there was also the young wife, who I had yet to see. Despite the fact that the Belanger company would not fall into her hands, I assumed she had been left comfortably off by her husband's death. Perhaps not as much as she stood to benefit with him still alive. Would she have killed the goose that laid the golden egg?

Then again, there were other reasons to kill besides money. I thought of what Marie, the perfume salesgirl, had told me about Helios Belanger's purported mistress. Had his young wife killed him out of jealousy?

As I considered this, I spotted a woman coming down the stairs.

'That's the wife,' Milo said. 'I recognise her from the wedding picture that appeared in the papers when they married.'

I watched Beryl Belanger make her way down the stairs. When she reached the ground floor, she moved towards the siblings, but stopped, standing a bit apart from them, as though she did not really belong. Perhaps she didn't, in a way.

They certainly gave no indication that she was welcome. Only Anton spared her a quick glance and a nod. It seemed that there was no particular warmth between the Belanger children and their stepmother. This was not exactly surprising. I didn't imagine that the siblings could have approved of their father marrying a woman who was their age, or perhaps even younger.

Knowing that Beryl had been quite young when she had married an ageing Helios Belanger, I had been prepared for an exotic seductress and was surprised to discover that she was thin and delicate with blonde hair and wide, pale eyes. She smiled wanly at something one of the guests said, revealing dimples. The smile made her appear even younger. I wondered if it was possible that she had loved a man so much older than herself.

The guest that had spoken to her passed on, and her smile fell away. It looked as though she was trying to keep her distress at bay. She might have been putting on a show, trying not to appear too happy at a party given so soon after she had been widowed, but I couldn't help but feel that her sorrow was genuine. She was pale, and even her skilfully applied make-up could not hide the fact that she was dark beneath her eyes.

'She's not beautiful enough to catch rich men for their money,' Milo said into my ear.

It seemed that he, too, had been taking stock of the Belanger family. The assessment seemed a rather callous one.

'I think she's very pretty,' I said, and I meant it. There was something small and bird-like about the woman. She seemed a bit fragile somehow. I didn't like to think she might have done something so cold-blooded as murdering her husband.

'Yes,' he said. 'But not pretty *enough*. With his money, if Belanger had wanted a beauty on his arm, he might have had his pick of just about anyone in France. There was some other reason he wanted to marry her.'

'Perhaps they loved each other,' I said. 'Such things do happen, you know.'

'Perhaps,' he said, but he didn't sound at all convinced.

Just because she had married a much older man did not mean that she had done it for mercenary reasons. It was possible, of course, but I didn't like to think that was the case.

We moved farther into the room then, pressed forward

by the incoming guests, and I lost sight of the family.

In the next room there was a buffet overflowing with delicacies of all description arranged around an extraordinary *pièce montée*, and champagne of an impressive vintage was flowing freely. Everyone seemed to be having a wonderful time, and I felt a bit sad that Helios Belanger had not been able to enjoy his own party. It did not even seem that his absence was much felt.

'Milo, don't you think it's . . .' I turned to find that my husband had disappeared. It was not at all surprising. In all likelihood he had wandered off and would find himself the centre of some adoring crowd of women in no time. Well, no matter. I could now focus my attention on the lovely array of desserts.

I had sampled a delicious truffle when I spotted Mr Duveau at the side of the room. A moment after I saw him, he looked in my direction and made his way towards me.

'Good evening, Mr Duveau,' I said as he reached my side.

'Don't you think you might call me André' he asked. 'We have been friends for a fortnight, after all.'

'All right. And please call me Amory.'

He smiled. 'Allow me to tell you how stunning you look this evening.'

'Thank you.'

'How are you enjoying the party?' he asked, reaching out to pluck a profiterole from a tray on the edge of the table.

'It's very nice,' I said. 'Though I have noticed that no one seems much broken up over Monsieur Belanger's death.'

'I suppose the reining philosophy is "eat, drink, and be merry". Speaking of which, can I get you something to drink?'

'Not just now, thank you.'

'Then I'll introduce you to the family, shall I?'

I hesitated. 'Perhaps not yet. I still feel a bit as though I'm intruding.'

'Your husband seems to have no such qualms,' he said, his eyes trained on something over my shoulder.

I turned to follow his gaze and saw that Milo had found his way to Cecile Belanger's side and had engaged her in conversation.

'Shall we join them?' André asked.

'Yes.' Inwardly, I sighed. Milo had certainly wasted no time. It was logical that he had determined that the woman of the family was the best place to start, but I did wish he hadn't run off to talk to her alone.

André offered me his arm and we walked to where Milo and Cecile Belanger stood. I wondered, given the past relationship between our hostess and the gentleman escorting me to her side, what the conversation would be like. Then again, if André had returned to Paris after Monsieur Belanger's death, I could only assume it had been to comfort Cecile. He had said they hadn't parted on bitter terms. Perhaps they were even friendly.

She looked up when we reached her, but I could read nothing in her gaze when she looked at him. 'Hello, André,' she said tonelessly.

'Hello, Cecile. Allow me to introduce Mrs Ames. She is . . .'

'Your wife, I assume?' she enquired of Milo before André could finish.

'Yes.'

I wondered if it was my imagination that she looked a

bit disappointed. I could not fault her for that. Milo looked exceptionally handsome in evening dress.

'How do you do, Mrs Ames?' she asked. Though André had greeted her in French, she had switched to English to speak to us.

'I'm so pleased to meet you, though I know now must be a difficult time. I was so sorry to hear about your father,' I said.

'Thank you.' There was no emotion in either her expression or the words, but I did not interpret this as a sign of guilt. It was much more likely that she didn't wish to discuss her bereavement with a stranger. I could not blame her. I could only imagine how trying this party was for her.

'If you'll excuse me for a moment?' André said suddenly. He left us and I watched him as he made his way to Beryl Belanger's side. He said something to her and a brief smile flickered across her face.

My attention was drawn abruptly back to Milo and Mademoiselle Belanger when Milo spoke. 'I must admit my wife and I have ulterior motives for attending this party tonight.'

'Oh?' she asked. There was only a vague politeness in her tone, and I wondered if Milo had broached the subject too quickly.

He appeared to have no such qualms. 'Yes, though I realise this isn't the best of times to talk business. Perhaps if we came back later, or next time we are in Paris . . .'

I awaited her answer with bated breath. I was afraid that she would agree to this and we would lose what might be our only chance at forming a connection with the family. I hoped Milo hadn't ruined our chances by being so bold.

When he gambled, however, he nearly always won. This time was no different.

After a brief pause, she shook her head ever so slightly. 'No, it's quite all right,' she said. 'What is it that you want to discuss?'

'My wife has found herself interested in perfume,' Milo said, his tone the perfect mixture of mild amusement and indulgence. 'I told her she may buy all the perfume she wishes, but that wasn't enough. She wanted her own perfume, a custom scent.'

'I have heard that you make custom scents on occasion,' I said, embellishing what I had been told about her own unique perfume. The fragrance had drifted up to meet me as I stood beside her. It was a warm and spicy scent, almost hypnotic in its richness. The combined notes of balsam, vetiver, and a trace of some other exotic element I could not quite name reminded me of a delicate incense. It was less feminine than I had expected, yet alluring and mysterious. I could understand now why the perfume salesgirl had spoken of it so reverently.

It seemed to me that impatience flickered across Cecile's features, though she tried quickly to hide it. She was, at heart, a businesswoman, and it must have occurred to her that it was just possible we might be valuable customers.

'I wear a custom scent,' she said. 'That may be what you have heard. We have not made them for customers. The expenses are prohibitive.'

Milo smiled. 'Not prohibitive to everyone, I'm sure.'

She hesitated.

'We came to you because your family's name is at the

top of the industry. No price is too high to make my lovely wife happy.'

I wondered if he was laying it on a bit thick, but the words seemed to have had their effect. Some of the brusqueness left her tone.

'It is possible, I suppose,' she said slowly.

'Oh, that would be wonderful,' I enthused. 'I'm so interested in the process. Would it be possible for me to be involved?'

Again, the hesitation. She didn't particularly want to work with me, but Milo had made it clear that he was willing to pay whatever she asked.

'Let me consider how the matter may best be handled,' she said. 'Perhaps if you will come to tea the day after tomorrow and we can discuss the details?'

'That would be wonderful. Thank you.'

Another guest moved forward to speak to Cecile then, and we moved away, back into the crowd.

'Well, darling, I think we've got our foot in the door,' Milo said in a low voice.

'I wish you had consulted me before you just went ahead with it like that,' I said crossly. 'It was my plan, after all.'

'And a very good plan it was. I saw no reason not to put it into operation as soon as possible. No reason to tiptoe around things. None of them are weeping over the deceased, after all.'

'I thought the same thing. It is strange, isn't it?' I said. 'It seems as though at least one of them would have mourned him.'

Milo shrugged. 'Not everyone is worthy of being mourned.'

'That's very cynical,' I said.

'But true, nonetheless.'

'What do you think Cecile Belanger made of our request?'

'We annoyed her, but she no doubt considers us eccentric Londoners with too much time and money on our hands. It ought to work.'

'I feel as though this may have been an expensive way to go about it,' I said.

Milo shrugged. 'What good is money if you don't use it? As I see it, it's a worthwhile investment. Madame Nanette's suspicions will be either confirmed or put to rest, and you'll get a custom scent.'

There was a sudden stirring in the crowd just then, and I realised that Anton Belanger was about to speak. It seemed that it was time for the show.

Anton Belanger made his way up four or five steps of the marble staircase, turning to face the room, and the crowd hushed. His dark eyes moved over the guests for a moment before he began to speak.

'Ladies and gentlemen, we are so pleased that you could join us tonight. While it is a night of sadness, it is also a night of joy. We mourn our father's passing, but we are pleased that his legacy lives on.' His grave, handsome face and the low, sombre tone of his voice gave an oddly pleasing gravity to the situation, allowing us all to feel that this was a memorial for Helios Belanger rather than a blatantly commercial venture on the day after his funeral.

'My father had a dream, a dream that I shared, for a perfume that would reach new heights, for a scent that would be more than just another in a long line of fragrances, one that would have a life of its own.' It was a pretty speech, even prettier in French than it might have been in English, and I could tell that the crowd was fully behind him. I had to admit that I was rather impressed with his sentiments.

'We have guarded the secret of this scent and we can promise that it will be unlike anything you have ever smelt before. Soon the perfume will be available to all, but tonight we will present to you the bottle which was specially designed by the illustrious Jens Muller.'

He gestured to a man who stood at the corner of the room. He was the sort of man one might not have noticed in a crowd: of average height, fair, thin. The expression on his face was one of supreme indifference. There was a ripple of applause in the crowd at the mention of his name, but the man did not acknowledge it. Instead, he lifted his glass to his lips.

Anton turned again towards the veiled sculpture. 'My father may not be here in body, but I feel that he is here with us in spirit. And so, for my father, I give you L'Ange de Mémoire.'

He nodded at the man standing beside the draped object in the curve of the stairs.

He pulled the satin cloth and it slid to the floor in a white puddle. A murmur went up from the crowd. Beneath it was a marble sculpture, as tall as Cecile Belanger, that represented the bottle in which L'Ange de Mémoire would come.

It appeared to be the figure of a woman, but as I looked closer I realised that it was an angel, her wings wrapped around her body, creating the effect of a draped, flowing gown. It was her face that was most arresting – a soft, peaceful smile playing on her lips. The Angel of Memory, she was called, and her faraway expression indeed recalled a moment of pleasant reminiscence. It really was an impressive piece of workmanship. It almost looked as though it would have been better suited to a cathedral than a perfume shop.

The hush that had fallen over the crowd faded as applause broke out. It appeared that L'Ange de Mémoire was a success and we had not even smelt it yet. I tried to imagine what sort of scent might be suited to so ethereal a vessel.

I glanced at Jens Muller to see his reaction to the crowd's approval. The bland expression remained on his features, but I thought there was a hint of something less restrained in his gaze as he watched the spectacle at the staircase. I could have been wrong, but it almost looked to me like anger. I wondered at whom it was directed.

I looked back at Anton Belanger, who still stood on the steps above the room. Despite his subdued expression, there was a look of triumph in his dark eyes.

He started to step down, but hesitated. 'I would like to say one more thing,' he said as the applause died away. 'My father made a name for himself, building an empire from nothing. There have been questions regarding the direction in which his company will go now that he is dead.'

I glanced at the other members of the Belanger family as he spoke. It was Cecile's face that made it clear to me that this part of his speech had not been planned. A barely concealed expression of surprise had crossed her features and then had hardened into a mask of something very much like contempt.

'I want you all to know that Parfumes Belanger will

continue to grow and thrive,' he went on. It seemed to me that his eyes flickered to his sister as he spoke. 'I hope there will no longer be any questions about the future of Parfumes Belanger or in whose hands that future rests.'

It seemed that the crowd was slightly confused by this impromptu addendum to his speech, but I recognised it for what it was. Anton Belanger had made a very public proclamation of power. Whatever her role at their father's side had been, it was clear that Anton did not intend to share his new-found control with his sister.

Helios Belanger had been rumoured to cut his enemies down before they could form their defences. If this was true, this move by Anton Belanger would have done his father proud.

Milo, it seemed, had the same thought, for he turned his head to murmur in my ear, his tone sardonic. 'The king is dead. Long live the king.'

CHAPTER NINE

The night wore on, and I found that, while I was enjoying the party, I was not learning as much as I had hoped. In fact, I had begun to wonder about the feasibility of our entire plan. I was doubtful there would be anything else to be learnt tonight. The Belangers had been surrounded for most of the evening, and I did not foresee the opportunity to speak with them again.

I was ready to go back to the hotel, but Milo had again disappeared into the crowd. So long as I was able to find and extract him by the evening's end, it would be all right. In the meantime, I needed a bit of air. It seemed to me that every woman there had decided to pay tribute to the late Helios Belanger by drenching themselves in his perfumes. I had made my own contribution by wearing the Bouquet de Belanger that I had recently purchased. As lovely as the scents smelt individually, the conglomeration was a bit overwhelming. I was beginning to get a headache.

I wandered into one of the less crowded rooms and found the doors leading out onto the courtyard. I stepped out and found myself alone. I would have expected that more people would have wanted fresh air, but perhaps the party was too enthralling to tear themselves away from. The air was filled with music and laughter and I had noticed that the liquor had begun to flow rather freely.

There was no light in the courtyard, save for that of the moon, and I took a deep breath of the cool night air, enjoying the solitude. The scent of flowers I had smelt on arrival was thicker here, and I suspected that the courtyard garden was in full bloom.

I was about to venture farther into the courtyard when a light was suddenly switched on in one of the rooms along this side of the house, casting rectangles of light out into the darkness through the panes of the French doors.

Out of curiosity, I moved in that direction. I had not yet reached the source of light, however, when I heard voices. It seemed the doors were slightly ajar.

'What is so urgent that we must leave our guests, Anton?' The voice belonged to Cecile, and, despite her measured tone, I could tell she was displeased.

'Where is the key to the safe?'

'What do you mean?' she said impatiently.

'He always kept the key with him, but I have not seen it since his death.'

'Perhaps it is in his room,' she said. 'He had taken to hiding it. It must be somewhere among his things. If we cannot locate it, Monsieur Dofour has a key. What is this about?'

'I wanted to look at the formula.'

'Now?' she demanded.

'I want to be sure it is there. You saw the enthusiasm of

the crowd, Cecile. We must make sure that we deliver that perfume.'

'The formula is in the safe. Where else would it be?'

'Are you sure you do not have the key?' he asked, the accusation plain in his voice.

'I am quite sure,' she replied coolly.

'I hope you are not attempting things behind my back, Cecile.'

There was a moment of silence and when she spoke, her voice fairly crackled with suppressed anger. 'Whatever you may think, you do not rule me, Anton,' she said. 'No matter what speeches you have made, the will has yet to be read. And you may believe that if I do anything, it will not be behind your back but to your face.'

There was nothing else after that, and I assumed she had left the room. I moved away as quietly as possible, considering what I had heard. It seemed Cecile had reason to believe that Anton might not inherit Parfumes Belanger, after all.

Not wanting to risk being seen, I followed a little path through the foliage that eventually led back around to where I had started. I stopped for a moment to admire the aroma floating up from the rosebushes.

The voice spoke in my ear suddenly from behind, startling me. 'There you are, my darling.' The words might have been Milo's, but they were spoken in French in a voice I didn't recognise.

Before I could turn, his arms slid around my waist and I was pulled against him. 'I have been waiting for you a very long time. It was agony.' Then warm lips pressed against my neck, and I realised that I had better make his mistake known to him before things progressed any further.

I removed the hands from my waist and turned to face my amorous companion. 'I'm afraid you have the wrong person,' I said in English.

Somehow I was not surprised to see that it was Michel Belanger who crept up behind me in the dark.

He did not look in the least embarrassed by his mistake. 'A thousand pardons, Mademoiselle . . . ?'

'Madame,' I corrected, not giving him my name.

The fact that I was married did not faze him any more than kissing a stranger's neck had done.

'I was to meet a lady here, a lady in a silver dress. From the back, you . . .' – he shrugged, a smile tugging at the corners of his lips – 'resemble.'

'Women look very much the same in the dark, I suppose,' I said, not quite managing to suppress my sarcasm.

His smiled broadened. 'This is true, perhaps, but they feel different. Another moment, and I would have realised.'

'Well, I shall leave you before your friend comes and finds that you have been feeling me by mistake.'

'Madame, wait . . .'

But I had already slipped past him and back into the house. I did not intend to stay alone with Michel Belanger any longer than necessary.

The crowd inside seemed to have grown thicker since I had stepped outside, and I had a difficult time making my way through the throng of people. I was just passing a group of three women who stood close together drinking champagne and conversing in French, when something one of them said caught my attention.

'Michel looks remarkably calm tonight, all things

considered,' she said. She might have been referring to his father's death, but her tone was sarcastic not sympathetic.

I stopped, trying not to be too conspicuous as I listened.

'Do you really think his father went through with it?' asked a second woman in a bright red dress. She took a deep draw on a cigarette in a long black holder. 'Monsieur Belanger was forever threatening him, but I think Michel never really believed him.'

'My father told me Monsieur Belanger had arranged to meet with Monsieur Dofour, his solicitor, shortly before his death,' said a third woman in a gown of gold satin. 'Whether or not it happened, I don't know, but I would, perhaps, be a bit nervous if I were he.'

'His latest affair might have pushed the old man too far,' said the first woman. 'Perhaps Monsieur Belanger should have thought twice about insisting that Michel end things with Angelique. She was notorious, perhaps, but at least not married to a government official.'

'Notorious is too kind,' said the woman in gold. 'Angelique is a dangerous woman. I'm surprised Michel survived her. I would have thought he would be the one to end up dead when he broke it off, not his father.'

They tittered a bit at this, but I suddenly wondered who exactly this Angelique was and if it was possible she harboured a grudge against Monsieur Belanger for having forced his son to break off their romance.

'Anton looks well,' said the woman in gold. 'In fact, I have never seen him look better.'

The woman in the red dress blew out a slow stream of smoke. 'So Anton inherits Parfumes Belanger and poor Michel will end up with nothing except his amusing personality.'

'Yes, and if he was disinherited, he will perhaps not be quite so amusing,' said the first.

They laughed and began to talk about something else, and I moved away.

So Helios Belanger had threatened to disinherit Michel. He would not be the first serious-minded father to grow tired of his son's bad behaviour and threaten such a thing. However, not all such fathers ended up dead under suspicious circumstances. I wondered if Helios Belanger had ever kept that appointment with his solicitor. It was certainly something to keep in mind.

I made my way farther into the room and suddenly spotted Herr Muller, the sculptor, standing at the corner. His arms were behind his back, and he was observing the crowd with a contemptuous expression. I supposed that he was not the sort of man who enjoyed parties. Perhaps he would rather be in his studio working than standing in formal clothes among a room full of people who had very little understanding of his art.

I thought of going over to congratulate him on the piece. It really was impressive. I made my way through the crowd and had almost reached him when I saw Anton Belanger step towards him. I moved closer, hoping I would be able to hear what they were saying.

'You needn't have come tonight, if the party is so repellent to you,' Anton was saying. I was a bit surprised by his words. Though it was apparent that Herr Muller was not enjoying the evening, this was not the sort of remark I would have expected from Anton Belanger. Then again, it seemed he was making a habit of antagonising people this evening.

'It is the way these people stand in awe of your father's name that repels me,' Herr Muller replied. Strong words indeed.

Anton did not appear as surprised as I to hear such words. 'It was a business transaction,' he replied tonelessly. 'You were not required to approve of my father.'

Herr Muller lowered his voice, but I could still make out the words. 'Never before have I met such opposition when sculpting a piece. Never before have I taken such insult. "You are in league with my enemies," he told me! Imagine it!'

'My father was a passionate man,' Anton said calmly. 'He did not always mean what he said. As his friend, you should have known that.'

'We were friends once, but that is long past. I would not have finished the sculpture after his behaviour, had I been left a choice.'

'It is an excellent sculpture,' Anton said. 'Your reputation is secure.'

I glanced at the sculpture. The face of the woman stood tall above the crowd, her serene composure immune to the revelry around her. I had to agree with Anton Belanger. There was nothing in it that might prove damaging to Herr Muller's reputation as a sculptor. If anything, I would have thought it rather a triumph.

'I tell you, your father proved to me that he was not the man I thought he was.'

'My father is dead, Herr Muller,' Anton said tersely. 'There is no need to discuss it further.'

'I have no wish to discuss him ever again,' Herr Muller replied. With that, he moved past Anton and disappeared into the crowd.

This was certainly an interesting development. So Monsieur Belanger and the sculptor who had created the bottle had once been friends but had ended things on decidedly bad terms. I wondered what had caused the rift between them. Had it merely been the design of the bottle? If so, what had Monsieur Belanger meant when he said that Herr Muller was in league with his enemies?

'There you are, darling,' said Milo, coming up behind me. 'I was afraid you'd been swept away into the night.'

He had no idea how close I had come. Had I not moved quickly, I might still be in Michel's clutches in the courtyard.

'What have you been doing all night?' I asked him. 'I've not seen you for ages.'

'Making conversation, seeing what I could learn. It's a dull lot, mostly. I managed to speak for a few moments with Anton Belanger earlier in the evening.'

'Did you?' This was something I had not managed to accomplish, though I had heard more than my share of his conversations with others. 'What did he have to say?'

'He rather droned on about the perfume. He's determined to play his part tonight, though I think he's secretly bored to pieces by perfume. It's the money he's after, and the power that comes with it, not carrying on in the grand tradition of the Belanger name.'

I nodded. 'Cecile has the passion, but Anton has the power.'

'There's something else,' Milo said. 'Apparently, people are wondering if the perfume will be revealed on schedule.

It seems Helios Belanger was very secretive about its formula, and there is speculation that it might take longer to complete, now that he is dead. I have heard people discussing the subject tonight, and many of them thought the perfume would be revealed at this party along with the sculpture. Perhaps that's why Anton gave his "all will continue as before" speech.'

'Yes,' I said thoughtfully, thinking of the heated conversation between Anton and Cecile. That might explain why Anton had suddenly been so eager to review the formula, to assure himself that they would be able to put the perfume into production.

'I heard something, too,' I said. 'It seems that Helios Belanger had threatened to disinherit Michel.'

'That is nothing new,' Milo replied. 'He was doing that ten years ago.'

'But he had apparently arranged to meet with his solicitor shortly before his death.'

'It may be worth considering,' he conceded. 'Perhaps I can ask around.'

'I also heard three women discussing Michel's former mistress, a woman called Angelique. One of them said she was dangerous.'

'So Michel was involved with Angelique, was he?' Milo said.

'You know her?' Somehow this did not surprise me.

'I know of her. She's a singer and dancer, something of a celebrity among the cabaret set.'

I tucked this information away for later.

'I learnt something else,' I said. 'Monsieur Belanger and Herr Muller were on very bad terms, it seems. Herr Muller said that Monsieur Belanger accused him of being in league with his enemies.'

'Interesting.'

'What of Madame Belanger? Did you speak with her?' I had hoped to have a chance to speak with the young widow, but I had not seen her since Anton Belanger's speech. It was so frightfully crowded I didn't see how anyone might have a decent conversation.

'No, I think she went back upstairs.'

I wasn't surprised. She had looked as though she hadn't wanted to be here at the party. I couldn't blame her. It must have seemed terribly callous for all these people to be enjoying themselves so thoroughly when her husband had been laid to rest only yesterday.

'Speaking of Michel, he's the only Belanger sibling I have left to speak to tonight,' Milo was saying. 'He usually gravitates to the most beautiful woman in any room. I'm rather surprised he hasn't made his way to you yet.'

'Oh, I've met Michel,' I said with deliberate casualness.

'Have you?'

'Yes. He kissed me in the courtyard.'

Milo's brows rose. 'Did he indeed? I know Michel works very quickly, but how did he manage that, exactly?'

'He came up when my back was to him. I believe he mistook me for another woman. We look rather alike from behind, it seems.'

It seemed to me that his eyes narrowed ever so slightly. 'No such thing. In all likelihood, he saw you and followed you into the courtyard.'

'Do you really think so?' I asked, not sure if I should be alarmed or amused. It was rather an outrageous way to meet a woman, but I could concede that the ploy of a stolen kiss might be successful on a lonely lady looking for romance.

'It seems very like something Michel would do.'

I shrugged. 'There is something rather exciting about a strange man kissing one in a dark courtyard, I suppose.'

'I'm rather surprised you fell for his lie.'

'If I had fallen for it, I might still be in the courtyard,' I replied. I was unable to resist teasing him just a little. After all, there was the matter of Nadine. It would do him good to know he was not the only one who could go about getting kissed by near-strangers. 'I imagine a kiss on the neck was just brushing the surface of his repertoire.'

'Yes, well, you'd do well to stay away from him.'

'You needn't worry,' I said. 'I would never consider an affair with a man like Michel Belanger.'

'That's reassuring,' Milo said dryly.

It wasn't meant to be reassuring. 'Yes,' I added. 'Michel isn't at all my style. If I were going to take a Belanger as a lover, it would be Anton. He's the man with all the power, after all.'

The party showed no signs of slowing as Milo and I slipped from the house well after two o'clock in the morning. I was tired and somewhat discouraged. While we had formed a tenuous connection with Cecile Belanger and overheard a bit of gossip that could potentially prove useful, I felt much less optimistic about our prospects than I had earlier today. The more I considered it, the more complicated things seemed to be. As Madame Nanette had said, any of them might have done it.

'You're unusually quiet,' Milo said, intruding upon my morose reflections, as we took a cab back to the hotel. 'What are you thinking about?'

I sighed, leaning my head back against the leather seat. 'I am beginning to realise the impossibility of our task,' I admitted. 'It's going to be difficult to prove anything.'

'You're just tired. You'll feel more optimistic in the morning.'

I wasn't sure that I agreed with him on that score. I had the uneasy feeling I was going to find it as hopeless then as I did now.

We reached the hotel and went up to our suite. It was dark and quiet, soothing after the heat and noise of the Belanger home.

The headache I had developed earlier in the evening had not abated, and all I wanted to do was go to bed. I walked through the sitting room and into the bedroom and Milo followed.

'I've been thinking it over,' he said as I sat at the dressing table to remove my jewellery and make-up, 'and I believe the best course of action is to divide and conquer.'

I glanced at him warily over my shoulder. 'In what way?'

'You shall pursue your sources, and I shall pursue mine.'

I understood perfectly what that meant. Milo had no interest in perfume or in spending long stretches of time with Cecile Belanger in her laboratory. Instead, he intended to spend his evenings in gambling clubs and cabarets with companions of questionable character.

'I'm not sure I approve of this plan,' I said. 'It seems to me that our most viable lead is Cecile Belanger. I don't know what you can possibly glean from nights spent gambling and drinking with your friends.'

'I think you underestimate my capabilities,' he said.

'I never underestimate what you are capable of,' I replied dryly. That was the problem.

He shot me a smile as he removed his dinner jacket and then loosened his necktie.

'You'd be surprised what I might learn. A man like Helios Belanger was sure to have vices that would betray his character. There are any number of things that might have led to his murder.'

'Perhaps,' I conceded. There was, after all, the rumoured mistress to be considered. It was certainly not unheard of for illicit relationships to lead to violence. And if Helios Belanger had been keeping that secret, there might be others to be uncovered.

Whether or not Milo would learn anything in the course of his nocturnal pursuits remained to be seen, but I would not press the matter further. It was just possible that he might. Besides, he was likely only going to be in my way if he accompanied me to tea with Cecile Belanger. I had found that Milo often proved a distraction when ladies were present. Furthermore, I knew he was going to do as he pleased, so there was no point in arguing about it.

'Don't look so glum, darling,' he said. 'We learnt more tonight than you think.'

'Such as?'

'Well, the question of the will may be useful to us. And we've seen first-hand the tension between Anton and Cecile. Perhaps that is something you may use to your advantage when you go to tea. Cecile may be in need of a confidante.'

'Yes, but I have seen what the family is like. They will not be the sort to share confidences with a woman they barely know. Whatever squabbles they may have between themselves, I believe they'd close ranks rather quickly if they suspected that they were being investigated.'

'Then we mustn't let them suspect,' Milo replied.

CHAPTER TEN

The bright sunlight was streaming through the window when I opened my eyes the following morning, and I could hear the birds chirping cheerfully outside my window. Though I had gone to bed very late, I felt well rested. In fact, I felt as though I had slept later than usual. I glanced at the little gold clock on the table beside the bed and was startled to see that it was past ten o'clock.

I sat up on my elbows, disturbing Milo, whose arm was flung across me. He stirred. 'What's the matter?' he mumbled.

'It's so late. I planned to rise hours ago.'

'Parisian mornings were made for lounging in bed,' he said, his arm tightening around my waist. 'Lie down.'

I complied, though I was still perplexed. 'I can't think why Winnelda didn't wake me,' I said. 'Do you suppose something's happened?'

'Winnelda and Parks were both rewarded very handsomely yesterday to stay out of my sight this morning,' Milo replied. 'I knew we would be out late, and I didn't want to be disturbed.'

So that was it. Well, I couldn't blame Milo for wanting a bit of peace and quiet. He was not a creature of the morning, and it did seem as though Winnelda was forever popping in and out of rooms at frightfully early hours.

'I suppose it was nice to sleep a bit late,' I said, settling back into my pillows, 'but I have a great many things to tend to.' There were several things I wanted to do before having tea with Cecile Belanger tomorrow.

'No, you don't,' he said. 'I don't know why you must always be in a rush, darling. Take a few moments to enjoy the simpler things in life.'

He did have a point, I supposed. We were in Paris on a beautiful spring morning. My very handsome husband lay beside me in bed. There was no reason why we should not enjoy our solitude. And yet . . .

'I keep thinking of the party last night,' I said.

He sighed. 'Somehow I knew that was what you were thinking about. For pity's sake, Amory, can't you forget the matter for a few hours at least?'

'Not as easily as you can, apparently.'

'There are more pressing matters on my mind at the moment.' He leant to kiss my neck.

'From what Madame Nanette said, Anton has wanted to run his father's company for years, but Cecile has already been running things behind the scenes. But where does Michel fit into the picture? Is he as indifferent to it all as he seems?'

'Amory, do pay attention,' he said.

'I'm sorry,' I said mischievously. 'But when you kissed my neck, I couldn't help but think of Michel.'

'Is that so?' Milo asked, pulling me onto my side to face him.

'He made quite an impression,' I told him with a credibly straight face.

'Then I shall have to do everything in my power to make you forget him.'

He kissed me deeply, and it was not long before all thoughts of Michel Belanger had fled.

Alas, a few moments later we were interrupted as the telephone began ringing shrilly in the sitting room. Milo did not seem to hear it, or at least made a good show of ignoring it.

'We had better see who that is,' I said at last.

'They'll ring us again.'

'It may be important,' I said. 'What if it's Madame Nanette calling to tell us something that she's learnt?'

Though Milo didn't want to admit it, he knew I was right. He sighed heavily and threw aside the covers, depositing them in a heap atop me, and rose from the bed.

He went out into the sitting room and answered the telephone. I could hear the low murmur of his voice, but I could not make out what he was saying. I found myself hoping that it was something inconsequential and we might resume our interlude.

Unfortunately, it was not to be.

'You were right. It was Madame Nanette,' he said, coming back into the room.

'Is everything all right?'

'It seems to be. She's on her way up.'

'Here?' I asked, shoving aside the satin bedspread that Milo had so unceremoniously dumped upon me and sliding from the bed. 'We're not even dressed!'

'I imagine Madame Nanette has seen nightclothes in her time,' Milo said.

I hastily pulled on a robe over my rather revealing satin nightdress. 'Yes, but it looks as though we've been . . .'

'Cavorting?' Milo supplied as he unhurriedly put on his dressing gown. 'Imagine, a man and his wife taking pleasure in each other's company in the privacy of their bedroom.'

I wasn't a prude, but somehow the thought of Milo's former nanny finding us in our current state of dishabille was discomforting.

Milo, on the other hand, had never cared in the least what other people thought. It was a very convenient sort of attitude to have, for him at least, but I had never been able to adapt it.

'Call for some coffee, will you?' I asked him.

'Certainly.' He went back out into the sitting room, and I went to the dressing table and attempted to tame my hair. Madame Nanette had said that she would call on us on her day off. I wondered what it was that had caused her to visit earlier than intended.

By the time I heard Milo greeting Madame Nanette, I had managed to smooth down my dark waves and tie the belt on my robe. I still felt woefully unprepared for company, but there was no helping that now.

I went out into the sitting room where Madame Nanette sat on the sofa. Milo sat across from her, perfectly at ease in his dressing gown. I took a seat on the edge of a chair, wishing I had had the time to dress. I was unaccustomed to receiving guests in my bedclothes.

Madame Nanette either did not notice or graciously pretended not to. Instead, she apologised for having dropped in unexpectedly.

'You're always welcome,' I assured her.

'I imagine there is something new you have to tell us?' Milo asked, pouring coffee into a cup and handing it to her.

'Yes, I had not meant to come until tomorrow, but I have learnt something else that I wanted to share with you.' She did not tell us right away. Instead, she said, 'You met the family at the party.'

'You heard that we were there?' Milo asked.

'Yes,' she said, her eyes twinkling. 'I heard Mademoiselle Belanger mention to Monsieur Michel that she had met an English couple who was very interested in perfume.'

'And you knew it must be us,' I said.

'Yes, but that is not why I've come. There is something else that has happened that I thought perhaps you should know about.'

'Another item of news you weren't meant to hear?' Milo enquired.

'I am not an eavesdropper, if that's what you mean to imply,' she told Milo archly.

'Not at all, madame,' he said, soothing her. 'I only meant that you are in an ideal position to learn of the workings of the family.'

I was intrigued by the relationship between this woman and Milo. There was a gentle courteousness in his treatment of her that I had never noticed in his interactions with anyone else. There were moments when he flashed his grin at her and gave her those quick, acerbic retorts to which I was accustomed, but there was also something different that she brought out in him, a warmer and less guarded side of his nature. It was a side I wanted to know more about.

Her expression softened. 'Yes, that is true. The family

sometimes forgets there are other ears than theirs in the house. What I have learnt has to do with both Helios Belanger's final flight as well as L'Ange de Mémoire.'

'The new Belanger scent?' I asked.

'Yes. As you know, Monsieur Belanger went to Grasse two days before his death. I have learnt that the purpose of that trip was not solely to visit his factory. He was to have had a meeting there to finalise some aspect of the scent.'

'Yes, we heard he was very secretive about it,' Milo said.

She nodded. 'It caused some discord, I believe, for he had always shared his formulas with Cecile.'

'But not this time?' I asked.

'No. More than once I heard them discussing some aspect of it, and always he seemed to dance around the answer and refused to tell her what it was she wanted to know.' She hesitated then added, 'It almost seemed as though he didn't trust her.'

I wondered if this had something to do with her relationship with André Duveau. Perhaps Monsieur Belanger had suspected Mr Duveau meant to venture out on his own and had worried that she might divulge too much, intentionally or not.

'What do you know about the formula?' I asked.

'From what I understand, there were meant to be two copies of it. One that was kept in Monsieur Belanger's safe, a safe to which only he and his solicitor had the key. The second copy was brought by Monsieur Belanger to the factory the night of his accident. It was to be kept in the safe there so that they might begin production.'

'And have they begun production?' I asked.

She shook her head. 'The manager of the factory,

Monsieur Gauthier, has been at sea and only just arrived back in France last night. He was to have begun work on the perfume when he returned. This morning Monsieur Anton mentioned that he was going to contact Monsieur Gauthier. He decided to telephone him after breakfast and see if everything was all right.'

I wondered where this was leading. We were on the precipice of discovering something important. I could feel it.

'After a few moments, Monsieur Anton came out of Monsieur Belanger's study – Monsieur Anton's study now, I suppose – looking very grave indeed. He spoke in a low voice, but it carried to where I was standing and I distinctly heard him say, "He does not have the formula, Cecile."'

'It wasn't there?' I asked, my heart beating a bit faster.

'That is the strange part,' she said. 'Monsieur Anton told Cecile that Monsieur Belanger had indeed gone to the factory. One of the employees reported that, as he had always done, Monsieur Belanger had delivered the necessary documents in an attaché case and put them in the factory's safe. However, when Monsieur Gauthier went to retrieve them this morning, he found that they were incorrect.'

'Incorrect in what way?' I was growing more intrigued by the second.

'It was difficult to tell from what Anton said, but I gathered that, though they closely resembled what the formula should be, key elements were replaced with nonsensical words. It was no longer a correct formula for L'Ange de Mémoire.'

'So they couldn't make scents of it?' Milo asked dryly.

Madame Nanette and I both frowned at him for his ill-timed pun.

'But that means . . .' I said, my words trailing off as the significance of this news sank in.

Madame Nanette nodded. 'It seems that someone must have switched the formulas deliberately.'

'What of the copy in the safe?' I asked, remembering I had overheard Anton telling Cecile that he couldn't find the key. A suspicion was beginning to form in my mind.

'It seems that he cannot open the safe, for he told Cecile that he had rung up the solicitor to come and open it. However, the solicitor was not available until tomorrow, which caused much distress. He asked his sister, his voice very strained, "What if the formula in the safe is also incorrect?"'

'Now we seem to be getting somewhere,' Milo said, leaning back in his seat. 'I assume that the perfume can't be completed without the correct formula?'

'That is my assumption as well. Monsieur Anton seemed extremely distraught about it.'

I could imagine he might be. His success in taking over from his father might hinge upon the ability to produce L'Ange de Mémoire. The world was awaiting it with bated breath, and it would likely be a severe blow to the reputation of Parfumes Belanger if they could not produce it now that Helios Belanger was dead.

'Did anyone else have access to the factory's safe?' Milo asked.

'No. Only Monsieur Belanger and Monsieur Gauthier.'

'Then it seems the formulas must have been switched before Monsieur Belanger left Paris.'

Madame Nanette nodded. 'That is what Monsieur Anton said. By this point, he was very angry and talking loudly. He told Cecile that someone must have taken the formula from Monsieur Belanger's attaché case before he left for Grasse. He seemed convinced that the copy in the safe would be compromised as well.'

'And what did Cecile say?' I asked.

'She said it was nonsense. That there must be some mistake. She told him she was sure the copy in the safe would be the correct one.'

I wondered. If someone had taken the formula from the attaché case, it seemed likely the copy in the safe had also been taken, especially given the fact that the key to the safe had gone missing. After all, how would it profit the thief to steal one copy and leave the other?

Another thought occurred to me. 'Cecile is very capable,' I said. 'Would a missing formula really mean so much? Even if the copy in the safe is incorrect, she might develop a new scent as she will presumably do from now on.'

'I do not know much of such things,' Madame Nanette said, 'but it seems as though Mademoiselle Cecile had mentioned something about a new process that Monsieur Belanger was developing. He had been working on it for some time. That was one reason he was so secretive.'

'I see,' I said. 'Then, if the formula contained some process that could not be duplicated, surely it would be in the best interest of all the Belangers for the formula not to have disappeared.'

Milo smiled. 'Unless one of them meant to sell it.'

Madame Nanette nodded slowly. 'The exact conditions of the will seem to be in question. Perhaps one of them took it as a means of insurance.'

'I imagine there are also a good many competitors who

would pay a pretty penny for such a thing,' Milo said. 'Whoever does not inherit might be willing to sell the formula to the highest bidder.'

'One of them might have switched the formula, providing an inaccurate formula in case Monsieur Belanger happened to glance at it, and then given him poison before he flew to Grasse,' I said, warming to the theme. 'Perhaps they had hoped he would crash his plane on the way, erasing what they had done. If an incorrect copy was later found in the safe, they would simply assume that there had been a mistake and that the correct copy had perished with Monsieur Belanger in the crash.'

'This is assuming, of course, that the copy in the safe is incorrect,' Milo pointed out. 'It might very well be that a viable formula is there, safe and sound.'

Somehow I doubted it.

'If the formula was the motive, it may exclude the sculptor,' Madame Nanette said.

I shook my head. 'I overheard him tell Anton that Helios Belanger had accused him of being "in league with his enemies". He appeared indignant, but it might have been for show. Perhaps Helios Belanger was right and Herr Muller had been after the formula all along. Which means our list of suspects has not been narrowed in any significant way.'

I thought suddenly of André Duveau. If anyone might have had a motive to steal the formula, it was he. The fact remained, however, that he had been in Como for at least a fortnight before Helios Belanger's death.

'What do you know about André Duveau?' Milo asked, giving me that uncanny sensation that he had been following my thoughts.

'He was engaged to be married to Cecile Belanger,' Madame Nanette said.

This was new information. He had spoken casually of their relationship. I had not realised that they had been engaged.

'Why did they call it off?' I asked.

'I don't know, but I do not think it was one incident. I suspect that perhaps Mademoiselle Cecile realised how fond she is of her independence.'

'But they parted amiably?' I asked, though I had seen first-hand that there did not appear to be any bad blood between them.

She nodded. 'It seems so. They appear fairly cordial towards one another, though there is a reserve in their interactions now.'

I wondered what it was that had really caused their parting. It could be, as Madame Nanette suggested, simply a difference in personality. Cecile seemed a woman who enjoyed control, and a relationship with a man of easy and abundant charm could be a difficult thing to manage. This was something I knew first-hand.

'Aside from that,' Madame Nanette was saying, 'I know that he was a pilot in the war. Decorated for heroism, I believe.'

'Yes, he told me a bit about his time in the war,' Milo said.

This was something I had not heard, but I was not exactly surprised. There was something of the daredevil in André's manner, and I could easily picture him taking to the skies without fear or hesitation.

Knowing he was a war hero seemed a point in his favour. There was also the seemingly casual way he had decided to enter the perfume industry. It was a hobby, not a grand passion. I found it difficult to believe that he would kill for such a thing.

And there was something else to consider. Though all clues seemed to point in that direction, I realised there was still the possibility that the missing formula was unrelated to his death. Perhaps Monsieur Belanger had simply brought the wrong papers to Grasse by mistake. It was unlikely, but possible. There were, after all, other motives we had not yet explored. I thought about the woman the perfume-shop girl had mentioned, the one she had assumed was Helios Belanger's mistress. I wondered who she might have been, if there was some other relationship in which Helios Belanger was involved that might have led to his death.

'Did Monsieur Belanger keep a mistress?' I asked.

Again, it seemed as though there was something akin to hesitation in Madame Nanette's manner. 'I cannot say for certain.'

I studied her face, wondering how she felt about Helios Belanger. She had claimed that there were no feelings lingering between them, but I wondered if that was entirely true.

'Then you suspect something,' Milo said, also picking up on her hesitation.

She nodded slowly. 'Yes, I have had my suspicions. Small things. He has gone out and come back in at odd hours. And there have been hushed phone conversations. I know, of course, this is not proof of guilt, but it did make me wonder if perhaps . . . well, if he had found another companion.'

'It sounds plausible,' Milo said.

'Did Madame Belanger suspect anything, do you think?' I asked.

'That I do not know. They have always seemed to be kind and affectionate towards one another, but I could not tell you the true nature of their relationship. She has seemed happy enough. But things have been difficult for her, I would say.'

'In what way?'

'She does not know many people in Paris. Her French is not, perhaps, as good as she would like it to be. Besides that, she is not really from their world. Her family was, from what I have heard, a good one but not wealthy. She was not raised to make her way in society, and I think it has been somewhat trying.'

I could well imagine how difficult it must have been for a young woman to move to a new country and adapt to a different language with a family that was not particularly welcoming. What was more, the idealism of the first bloom of romance often faded quickly when the realities of life intruded. The consequences of a whirlwind marriage were also something I knew first-hand.

She hesitated and I knew that there was something more. 'What is it?' I asked.

'It might be nothing,' she said slowly. 'I don't like to say things without proof.'

'If it made an impression on you, it may very well be something,' Milo said.

'As I said, I don't know if there is any truth in it. I have seen no proof. It is only a feeling that I have.'

'Yes? What is it?' Milo pressed.

'I think that Beryl Belanger may be hiding a secret relationship of her own.'

'Really?' I asked. This I found surprising. I had had the distinct impression that Madame Belanger was mourning the loss of her husband. Then again, I supposed having a lover and regret at being widowed were not mutually exclusive.

'What makes you think so?' Milo asked.

'There has been something in her manner lately, something a bit secretive. I came in on her one day writing letters, and she took care to put her hand across the page so that I could not read it, not that I would have tried. She often seemed jumpy, on edge, as though she was afraid of being discovered doing something she oughtn't.'

'It seems there are a great many secrets in the Belanger household,' I said.

'Yes,' she said thoughtfully. 'Though it is possible that I am seeing suspicious behaviour where there is none.'

'There is one more thing I have been wondering,' I said. 'I heard that there was a private nurse hired to look after Helios Belanger during an illness some time ago. Do you think the illness might have been the killer's first attempt?'

'I do not know much about that illness,' she said, to my disappointment. 'He kept to his room a good deal at the time, and the family did not mention it. Helios was not a man who liked his weaknesses known.' With that, she stood. 'And now I must go. I have been gone too long already.'

Milo rose to see her out.

'You will let us know if there is anything else?' he said as they reached the door.

'Yes,' she replied. 'I may be contacting you sooner than you know. Tomorrow is the reading of the will, and I have a very uneasy feeling about it.'

'Why should you?' Milo asked.

'I don't know. It is just a feeling I have.'

I couldn't resist telling her what I had learnt. 'I overheard a woman at the party say that Monsieur Belanger had contacted his solicitor about making a new will. She indicated that Michel may have been disinherited.'

Madame Nanette's dark brows rose. 'That I know nothing of, but it confirms my suspicions that there may be trouble.'

'It may be all right. Perhaps there will be some happy resolution to all of this,' I said, though I'm afraid my tone was unconvincing.

Madame Nanette smiled a bit sadly and shook her head. 'No, I'm very much afraid all of the unpleasantness has just begun.'

CHAPTER ELEVEN

Madame Nanette gone, I went back to the bedroom with renewed purpose. Milo followed me at a much more leisurely pace.

'What are you doing?' he asked as I took a dress of rose-coloured silk from the wardrobe.

'Getting ready to go out,' I replied, walking past him towards the bathroom.

He stopped me by reaching out to catch my arm and pulled me against him. 'Why would you want to do that? I very much hoped we might go back to bed.'

I smiled, disentangling myself from his embrace. 'As tempting as the offer may be, Madame Nanette's visit has only convinced me that it's important to learn what we can as quickly as we can. There is not much we can learn about the missing formula today, perhaps, but we can look into other motives. If Monsieur Belanger did have a mistress, it might have led to his murder. Even if an affair wasn't the cause of his death, his mistress might know something that the family doesn't, if he confided in her.'

He sighed. 'What do you intend to do?'

'I'm going to the cafe that the girl at the perfume shop mentioned to speak to the waitress who allegedly saw Helios Belanger with another woman. If at all possible, I'm going to try to speak with the alleged mistress. Would you like to come with me?'

He took a seat on the edge of the bed. 'I don't think so. I might go to Longchamp this afternoon.'

Though mildly annoying, it was no great surprise that Milo would find a trip to the racetrack more preferable to sitting in a cafe with me. 'Very well,' I said, turning towards the bathroom. 'Will you be back for dinner?'

'I'll ring you and let you know. What time will you be back?'

'I don't know. Leave a message at the desk if I'm not here.' I certainly did not intend to sit around waiting for his call. Milo might be willing to spend his time in Paris out gallivanting, but I had a mystery to solve.

Milo went off to the races, and I took a cab to the cafe on the rue de Tolbiac, that Marie, the perfume salesgirl, had told me about. It was located on a corner with red awnings, pots of flowers, and little tables set up on the walk outside. It was a quaint place, but not much different from any of the other hundreds of cafes scattered across Paris. I glanced at the building across the street. It was grey stone and was apparently comprised of several flats. It, too, was unremarkable.

Marie had mentioned that her friend's name was Lucille, and I debated on the best way to approach her. I had often found that casual conversation was much more effective for gaining information than outright questions were, but I could think of no way to guarantee that I could speak with Lucille unless I asked for her directly. Thus I decided to be direct.

'Is Lucille here today?' I asked the waiter who seated me.

'Yes, madame,' he answered. 'I will send her to you.'

Lucille turned out to be a pretty young woman with brown curls and large, dark eyes. 'You asked for me, madame?' she said when she arrived at my table.

'Yes,' I said. 'I recently met your friend Marie; she recommended this cafe to me.' This was not exactly a lie, as it was the shopgirl's story that had sent me here.

'Marie? Yes, she and I are very good friends.'

I glanced at the building across the street. 'She told me that you have seen a certain illustrious gentleman leaving that flat.'

Her eyes seemed to brighten at the prospect of sharing a secret with me, and she leant forward slightly, lowering her voice. 'Yes, madame. I saw Helios Belanger one morning. Oh, I do love his perfumes. When I go to visit Marie at the shop she lets me try them on. One day I will buy the biggest bottle they have.'

'They do have lovely scents,' I said. 'I expect it was very exciting to see the man in person.'

She shrugged. 'It is more exciting to see cinema stars. I have seen them in my time. And there is a cabaret not far from here. Many of the performers come here to eat. It's very exciting.'

'Yes,' I agreed, hoping I could steer the conversation back on course. 'But it was Helios Belanger that you saw visiting the flat across the street?'

She nodded. 'I saw him come out of the building very

131

early one morning.' As Marie had intimated, very early in the morning did not seem to indicate a business call.

'He came out with the woman who lives in the corner flat on the second floor, the one with the window box,' she said, indicating it with a nod of her head. 'I have seen her tending the flowers in the window.'

'You're sure it was Helios Belanger?' I asked.

She nodded. 'Oh, yes. Very sure. I read all the society columns and have seen his picture many times. I was very surprised that he should come from the building so early in the morning, for I knew that he did not live there. He has a very grand house in the Faubourg Saint-Germain.'

So far I could not argue with her logic. She seemed a clever girl, and everything she said stood to reason. I thought she was what might be called a credible witness.

'And that was when I saw her come out behind him,' she said. 'She was wearing a veil, but I recognised her just the same. She is very tall and thin, and I knew at once that it was her.'

'She came out directly after he did?'

'Yes. I thought it strange that he should be there, but when I saw that he was with a woman I understood.' She smiled as she said this, seeming to enjoy the hint of scandal in her words.

'You're certain they were together?'

'They got into his car together,' she said. That seemed to settle it.

'Was it a cab?' I asked.

She shook her head. 'No, madame. It was a private car. A long, shiny black car. Very elegant.'

So Monsieur Belanger had apparently spent the night at

132

the flat of a woman who was not his wife and left with her early the next morning. I wondered why he had made no effort to hide his appearance but she had chosen to wear a veil. It was also interesting that he had had his own car pick him up. Apparently, he had not tried very hard to hide his relationship with this woman.

'When was this?'

'Two or three weeks ago.'

'I see. Well, you have been very helpful, Lucille.'

I suddenly realised that I was very hungry. All I had had today was the coffee I had shared with Milo and Madame Nanette. I picked up the menu.

As Lucille took my order, my eyes flickered back to the building across the street. Perhaps after I ate, I would pay a visit to the flat and see if there was some way that I could gain information about the mysterious woman who lived there.

The building had a cool, dimly lit foyer with two lifts across from the front door. A lift operator stood beside them, looking rather unenthusiastic about his post.

I walked across the less-than-immaculate floor and noticed that the paint on the walls was scuffed in places. It was not a bad place, really, but I had definitely seen better. I somehow thought that if the woman Lucille had seen with Helios Belanger was involved with him, she was not a long-term mistress. Though my knowledge of such things was admittedly limited, I did not believe this was the sort of flat in which an extremely wealthy man would house his lover. At least, it certainly was not the sort of flat I would expect if I were a rich man's inamorata.

Though I very much wanted to talk to the woman in question, I had not yet come up with a method of doing so. The lift operator seemed an ideal place to start. He would, after all, have first-hand knowledge of the people coming and going from the building.

I approached him. 'Good afternoon.'

'Good afternoon, madame,' he replied without enthusiasm. 'What floor?'

'I don't wish to go up just now,' I said. 'I wanted to ask you about a woman who lives here.'

'What is her name?'

I hesitated. I had been afraid that he would ask me that. 'Well, that's another thing,' I said. 'I don't know exactly what name she might be using.'

If this was surprising to the man, he did not show it. 'What does she look like?'

I realised how very poorly planned this venture had been. The woman had, according to Lucille's description, been heavily veiled. I didn't even know what colour her hair might be, let alone what she looked like.

I leant forward conspiratorially, hoping to avoid answering any questions. 'I think she may be involved with a wealthy gentleman. He comes to visit her here sometimes.'

I was careful not to say the name of Helios Belanger. For one thing, it was just possible that there was no scandal here, and I didn't want to start one needlessly. For another, it was likely that the lift operator did not know the gentleman's name, and it would be useful to be as vague as possible.

This seemed to do the trick, for recognition came into his eyes. 'Ah, yes. I know the lady you mean. Mademoiselle Yvonne. She lives on the second floor,' he said. I felt my spirits rise only to be crushed by his next words. 'But you won't find her in. She left town two days ago.'

'Left town? Are you sure?'

He nodded. 'I helped her bring her bags to a big black car waiting on the corner.'

I wondered if she had gone for good. It seemed very strange to me that she should have vacated her flat. It was another mysterious disappearance that coincided with Helios Belanger's death.

I tipped the lift operator and made my way back out into the warm afternoon sun. I had come away from this venture with more questions than answers, but I felt somehow that I was on the right track.

I was not surprised to find that Milo had not returned by the time I arrived back at the hotel. Winnelda had returned, however, and was eager to tell me about her adventures the previous night.

'We went to La Nuit Noire, and it was ever so scandalous, madam. The costumes they wore left very little to the imagination, and I have never seen such dancing. There was a dancer called Lorenza who learnt to dance in a sheik's harem.'

'Did she indeed?'

'Yes, she travelled the world learning all manner of dance, but it was the harem ladies who taught her best. Trudy says that it would be ever so romantic to live in a harem.'

'Trudy?' I asked, a bit confused.

'My friend who is the maid for the other English lady.'

'Ah, yes.'

'Trudy says she may run away someday and hopes she ends up in a harem.'

I wondered a bit about the suitability of Winnelda's new friend, but then I was Winnelda's employer, not her mother.

'I don't think you should like harem life,' I ventured.

She shook her head, a bit mournfully it seemed. 'No, madam. I don't think I should like the food over there.'

I let it go at that, and, in light of her extreme enthusiasm, sent her off again to see what other excitement was to be had.

There was no call from Milo and no message at the desk when dinner time arrived, so I had dinner in the hotel dining room. Afterwards, I went to the cinema and watched a film. Or tried to watch it. My mind was much too preoccupied to pay close attention.

I had pondered all day what I should do about the woman living in the flat across from the cafe. If it was true that she had left Paris, I found it doubtful that there would be any way for me to contact her. What was more, it was entirely possible that she played no part in the grand scheme of things. Even if she was Helios Belanger's mistress, her leaving town immediately after his death was not necessarily suspicious. Perhaps she had wanted to get away, find time to face her grief. Such things were not uncommon.

Besides, the fact remained that we did not even know for certain that Helios Belanger had been murdered. This nagging doubt continued to plague me. What did we really know? All we had for certain were Madame Nanette's suspicion, the questionable behaviour of his family members, and a misplaced formula. None of these things

136

were proof positive, and unless we had such proof we were going to have a very difficult time indeed doing anything.

Feeling rather unhopeful, I returned to the hotel.

I had not left word for Milo, and I half hoped that he would be in our room waiting and worrying for me when I arrived back. I should have known better. The room was dark.

I switched on the light and removed my coat, dropping it on the chair near the door. Then I went to the telephone and called down to the desk. 'Were there any messages left for me?'

'No, madame.'

I set the telephone on the receiver, tamping down my annoyance.

It was not unlike Milo to have forgotten to ring me. In fact, it was rather typical. I could not help but feel, however, that now was an extremely inopportune time for him to revert to typical behaviour.

I was awakened sometime in the middle of the night as the door to the bedroom opened. I was not a particularly light sleeper, but I think some part of me had been listening for my husband's return.

'Milo?' I asked.

'Yes,' he said, closing the door behind him. 'I'm sorry to wake you.'

'What time is it?' I asked.

'I'm not entirely sure.'

I sat up, squinting to see him in the dark and was surprised to be hit with a rather strong smell of alcohol. 'Are you drunk?' I asked. He had never come home drunk before.

'Certainly not. You know that I've long held gambling and drinking to be an exceedingly poor mix.' He didn't sound drunk, and I knew it was true that he took his gaming rather seriously.

'You smell as though you've taken a bath in it.'

'An unfortunate side effect of a rather exuberant young crowd at this particular nightclub. A young woman lost her footing and spilt the contents of her glass. I expect Parks will be most put out with me.'

I switched on the lamp near the bed and looked at the clock. It was nearly four o'clock in the morning. It was definitely not the first time that he had come home at such an hour, but I found it particularly annoying that he had disappeared for almost an entire night when I had very much been wanting to discuss what I had learnt with him.

'You must have had a very successful evening,' I said, not bothering to hide my irritation.

'It was, in fact, a rather dull evening,' he said as he undressed, either oblivious to my displeasure or purposefully ignoring it. Probably the latter. 'But I have some news that may interest you.'

'Perhaps you may tell me about it at a more decent hour,' I said. 'You need a bath, and I think I shall go back to sleep.'

'Sleep if you must, darling, but I'm certain you shall be very interested in what I have to say.'

With that he went off to the bathroom and began to run a bath. I switched off the light and lay down again, staring at the dark ceiling.

I didn't begrudge my husband his bit of fun on his own. After all, we had been in each other's constant company for the past month in Italy, and I had never been the type of woman who expected her husband to remain at her beck and call. In fact, for the first five years of our marriage I had been extraordinarily broad-minded when it came to my expectations for Milo's involvement in our relationship.

What I did resent, however, was the lack of communication when it came to the matter of Helios Belanger. He had introduced me to this mystery, but it seemed that he was determined to investigate it on his own.

Then again, I didn't see what type of useful information he could have gleaned in a raucous nightclub. He was very clever, and it was just possible that he had learnt something important, but I wanted very much to doubt it.

Naturally, I was still awake when he came out. I would have liked nothing better than to have fallen back into a restful sleep in his absence, but my curiosity got the better of me.

As he came out of the bathroom, I switched the light back on and sat up again.

'Ah, so you didn't fall asleep,' he said.

'You knew I wouldn't,' I retorted, annoyed. 'What did you learn?'

'You said we needed to discover more about Helios Belanger's death. Well, I may have accomplished just that.'

He had my full attention now. It was just the thing that I had been contemplating earlier this evening, our lack of actual evidence. Was it possible that he had been able to discover something?

He was rubbing his hair dry with a towel and seemed in no hurry to share what he had learnt. I was fairly certain he was doing it to annoy me. If so, he was succeeding.

'Well?' I demanded. 'Go on.'

'Always so eager,' he said with a smile. He tossed the towel aside and came towards my side of the bed. He took a seat on the edge near me.

'At the nightclub, I had a conversation with one of the medical staff who was at the morgue when they brought in Helios Belanger's body.'

'How did you manage that?' I asked. If it had been anyone but Milo I might have been incredulous that they had accomplished this feat. Knowing my husband as I did, I did not find it at all surprising that he had been able to not only locate such a person but manage to talk to him.

'It's not important,' he said. 'This gentleman, René, after I had treated him to several drinks, became very friendly and eager to talk. He said that the body was brought in and that the coroner who examined him said he exhibited many symptoms of heart failure.'

I found this highly dissatisfying. We were looking for signs of murder.

'Helios Belanger's own doctor was also summoned,' Milo continued. 'My friend René said the doctor intimated that Belanger had no history of heart trouble, but he did not seem particularly troubled by the death. These things can happen suddenly, he said, and though Monsieur Belanger always had been extremely healthy, the heart is an unpredictable thing.'

'Was any sort of post-mortem done?' I asked.

'I gather there were some external signs that seemed to live up to what they expect from people who die of heart attacks, mottled skin and bluing of the fingertips and lips or some such thing.'

'That sounds as though it could also be poison,' I said. 'They didn't . . . examine him internally.'

'No,' he said. 'It seems rather as though they took one look at him and decided his death appeared natural. In fact, his doctor recommended against a post-mortem.'

'That seems unusual.'

Milo shrugged. 'He did not want to cause further grief to the family. It's not so unusual.'

'So if they were to look for poison or some such thing, they would have to exhume him,' I said. 'It doesn't seem very likely that the police would agree to that without some sort of definite proof.'

'No,' Milo agreed. 'And that's not likely to happen when his own doctor believes he died of natural causes.'

'How very frustrating this all is,' I said.

'Darling, have you considered that perhaps we have our answer?'

I looked up at him. 'What do you mean?'

'He was an old man known to have a high temper, and he was recently ill. It's entirely possible that he suffered a heart attack, especially given the recent close call he had in his aeroplane. Perhaps the simplest explanation is the true one.'

His words surprised me. 'Do you really think that?'

'I'm beginning to wonder.'

For some reason, I found it difficult to believe. What was more, I was not certain that Milo really believed it himself.

'I wish we could find a way to talk to the nurse they hired for him,' I said. 'She might be able to tell us if his first illness was suspicious.'

Something like exasperation crossed his expression. 'Or perhaps he was simply an ill older man whose life had run its course. You know, darling, you're positively ghoulish, hoping with all your heart that it is, in fact, a murder.'

'No such thing,' I protested. 'But if it was a murder, we don't want a killer to go free.'

'Well, I suppose I've done my part for the evening.'

'Yes. But you might have rung me,' I said, lest he think that I approved of his independent endeavours.

'It was a very tedious night, all told. You can believe me, darling. I would much rather have been here with you.'

I did not believe this for one moment. Try though he might to deny it, I had no doubt that Milo had enjoyed every moment of his evening. Old habits die hard, and I knew that the pull of his favourite amusements was strong. I was still a bit irritated with him for waking me up in the middle of the night, but, as he had acquired such useful information, it was difficult for me to remain cross with him.

'So we have a nurse whose whereabouts we do not know and a mysterious woman who may have been involved with Helios Belanger.'

'You located your mystery woman, did you?'

'Not exactly.' I quickly related to Milo the events of my day. 'And so she has disappeared.'

'*Cherche la femme* seems to be the theme of the evening,' he said.

'Yes, it's all most troublesome.'

'Don't you think we might dispense with thinking of it, at least until the sun comes up?' he asked. He leant forward, his arms on either side of me on the bed. He smelt of soap now rather than stale alcohol, and a lock of his damp hair brushed my forehead as he bent to kiss me.

'Yes, Milo, you're right,' I replied after a moment. I reached up to sweep the strand of hair back from his face. 'It's dreadfully early. I am going back to sleep.'

'Minx,' he said. He dropped another kiss on my lips and then rose, going around to his side of the bed.

'I do feel as though we've made some progress today,' I said, attempting to be optimistic.

'I told you not to fret,' he replied as he pulled back the covers and slid into bed beside me.

My mind played over the events of the day. We had discovered several interesting leads that might bring us to significant evidence if we followed them.

Despite Milo's efforts to convince me otherwise, I still believed that Helios Belanger's death had not been due to natural causes.

'It does seem as though there are a great many people who might have had a motive to kill Helios Belanger,' I said aloud. 'And if we can seize upon the culprit and find proof, perhaps the police might be willing to re-examine his death. Don't you think?'

My musings were met with silence.

'Milo?'

With a rush of indignation, I recognised that deep, steady breathing. He was already asleep.

CHAPTER TWELVE

I took no particular care to keep from waking Milo the next morning, but he slept soundly and was undisturbed by my preparations.

I bathed and dressed and was just about to leave the room when I noticed his dinner jacket had slid to the ground from the chair where he had carelessly tossed it when he had come in this morning. As Parks was already likely to be highly annoyed that the jacket had been soiled, I thought it best that I keep it from getting rumpled further.

I scooped the jacket up and noticed a piece of paper on the floor beneath it. Likely it had fallen from Milo's pocket. Picking it up, I saw that it was a train ticket. That struck me as curious. Milo certainly had not been wearing evening clothes on the train from Italy, and I knew that a ticket would not have escaped Parks' eagle eye for any length of time. What, then, was it doing in Milo's pocket?

I looked closer at the ticket. As I had suspected, it was not the train from Milan. In fact, it was a ticket from Paris to Beauvais. I frowned. We had not been to Beauvais, nor could I think of any reason we should want to go there. What on earth was this doing in Milo's pocket?

The realisation hit me suddenly, followed by chagrin that it had taken me so long to come to it. Milo had come in so late, not because of the time he had spent gathering information at a nightclub, but because he had taken the train to Beauvais and back. The liquor he had been doused in had probably been spilt on him by an unsteady rider on the train and not an inebriated woman.

I went over in my mind what he had told me last night. Thinking about it now, I didn't see how the conversation he had had with the morgue employee, René, could have taken more than half an hour. Whatever Milo had been doing last night, it was clear that he had not spent the entire evening in a nightclub.

I recognised that familiar sinking feeling accompanied by a surge of indignation. My husband had lied to me.

I dressed carefully for my meeting with Cecile Belanger that afternoon. I wanted to continue to cultivate the impression of a woman of leisure with money to spare. The Belangers might be from humble origins, but they were decidedly discerning in their tastes now.

I selected a black suit with a loose jacket over a black silk shirt with white polka dots. I chose my pearl necklace and bracelet to accent it, as well as a plain black hat with a feather. It was a subtle choice, but one that I thought would fit well with Cecile Belanger's understated elegance.

I bid Milo goodbye without asking him about the ticket I had found in his pocket. I needed time to decide how I wanted to address it. I was sure there was a perfectly good explanation, or at least one that seemed good to him. Whatever it was, something told me to bide my time. That didn't mean, however, that I did not ponder the matter for my entire cab ride.

The Belanger home seemed just as imposing as it had on the night of the party. I hoped that today would prove more useful to the investigation than the party had been.

I was admitted and led into a small sitting room. It was exquisitely decorated in shades that reminded me of a flower garden in the spring. The furniture was pale violet satin, the curtains rose-coloured velvet. Oil paintings of decadent bouquets hung in heavy silver frames. Even the paper on the walls was a muted floral design. The room spoke of taste and luxury, and the scent of lavender hung in the air.

A moment after I had entered the room and taken a seat near the marble fireplace, Cecile Belanger came in. I was surprised to see that she was followed by the elder Belanger brother, Anton. They were both dressed in black and looked solemn and striking in contrast to the soft colours of the room. I was glad I had chosen a similarly subdued ensemble.

'Thank you for having me today,' I said to Cecile when we had exchanged pleasantries. 'I realise there must be a great many other pressing matters you have to attend to.'

'There are many details to discuss, and I was unsure of how long you intend to remain in Paris,' she replied. 'My brother Anton has decided to join us. As you know, he is acting as the head of Parfumes Belanger now.' There was a tightness about the words, as though she was almost unwilling to say them. I wondered if she would continue to accept his rule without question. Given what I had overheard between them on the night of the party, I didn't think so.

'How do you do, madame?' he said in a tone that made it clear he was not at all interested in how I did. Anton Belanger, it appeared, did not have his brother's outward charm. Instead, he looked as though he was trying very hard to tamp down his impatience. There were better things to do than to cater to an Englishwoman seeking to indulge her vanity.

I suspected that he was annoyed with his sister for agreeing to do business with me. I was certain the Belanger family was not in particular need of our money, and I couldn't help but wonder if Cecile had done it expressly to annoy her brother.

It could very well be, of course, that Anton Belanger was grief-stricken and resented the intrusion so soon after his father's death. Under normal circumstances, that would have been my assumption. Having seen, however, the somewhat callous way he had staked his right to the Belanger throne at the party, I did not think that it was the case.

It would be difficult, I thought, to play to both of them in the same room. After all, they were vying for power and I couldn't very well support both of them at once. Then again, I supposed there was a way I could offer something both of them wanted. Anton craved respect, and I thought Cecile would respond to sympathy. It was only a matter of finding a balance between the two.

We settled ourselves and the maid brought tea to us. I noticed that the food was much more British than French.

'We have become accustomed to taking English tea,' Cecile said, as though following my thoughts. 'Beryl is very particular about her teatime.' I could not infer from her words what she thought about her stepmother.

I glanced at Anton Belanger, wondering if his feelings on the matter might be apparent, but there was nothing on his features.

'We drink Turkish coffee and Indian chai just as often,' Anton said, and I was a bit surprised that he had joined the conversation. 'Our father was a man of the world and embraced all it had to offer. He adopted many foreign customs and spoke seven languages. He raised us to speak several as well, making it usually possible for us to converse with our clients in their own languages.' I had noticed that both of them initiated their conversations with me in English, despite my willingness to converse in French, and now I understood why. It was a part of the Belanger technique, another small way to indulge their clientele. Helios Belanger had been a smart man.

'Your father sounds like a fascinating man,' I said.

'He was,' Cecile replied, her tone softer than I had yet heard it. Anton did not comment.

The fragrance of the tea floated up to me, and I took in the aroma. 'This tea smells wonderful,' I said. 'Jasmine?'

'Yes. The nanny who looks after my young sister created it for us. She spent many years in England and said she knew a lovely recipe for tea. My father was especially fond of it. He took a cup every night.'

'How nice,' I said, hoping to shift the conversation away from Madame Nanette. I didn't want to risk revealing a connection between her and Milo.

'I have enjoyed Belanger scents for many years,' I said, taking a sip of my tea. 'I am quite excited to have a scent of my own.'

Cecile nodded. 'I hope that we will prove worthy of carrying on his legacy.'

A hint of a frown flickered across Anton's handsome brow, but he said nothing.

'I'm sure you shall,' I said quickly.

'My father was a great man,' Cecile said. I glanced at Anton, wondering if he had noticed that she had not said 'our father'. It seemed as though Cecile had decided to proceed as if her brother were not in the room.

If he had found the phrase insulting, he did not show it. In fact, I was not entirely sure that he was listening to us. He had lit a cigarette and was smoking it, his eyes off in one corner of the room.

'He was a man unlike anyone I ever met,' she said. 'He told me once that as a young man he had dreamt of far-off places. When he was little more than a child, often sleeping on the cool ground, he would look up at the stars and imagine that he was in some far-flung country. He was a man who made his dreams come true.

'He later travelled the world from Egypt to Persia to India. He saw their wonders and he gathered their scents. I think that was one reason that he loved perfume. He said that each perfume was a combination of memories for him. He turned the things, the experiences he loved, into a tangible object. I don't know of any other man who could have done it as my father did.'

She spoke eloquently, and I felt a pang of sadness that so rich and vibrant a life had come so abruptly to an end. What a waste, that all that knowledge, the passion that came with taking fragrances and turning them into a physical substance, was gone. I was glad that Cecile Belanger seemed to have inherited that passion from her father. Parfumes Belanger would be in good hands. Provided Anton allowed her to take part in it.

'I expected that your husband would be here to discuss the details,' Anton said suddenly, breaking into Cecile's sentimental reveries. I understood, of course, what he meant. He had expected Milo to handle the financial aspects of this particular transaction. Well, I was well versed on that score.

'My husband knows that I am perfectly capable of discussing the details myself,' I told him pleasantly.

Again, he did a poor job of hiding his annoyance. 'Very well. Then let's discuss the price, shall we?'

We did, and I found that Monsieur Belanger drove a hard bargain. I had expected the price to be high, and it was. As Milo had pointed out, however, it was a small price to pay if it helped us to solve a murder. I could really think of no other means of spending considerable time with the Belanger family. After all, if I had not come up with this scheme, I would certainly not be having tea with them now.

The negotiations finished, Anton seemed to have lost all interest in the proceedings. 'I will leave you two now, to discuss the details,' he said, rising. 'I am pleased to have met you, Madame Ames.'

With that, he turned and left the room. I was, admittedly, glad to see him go. It was not that he made me uneasy – I had interacted with dour personalities often enough – but I was glad for the chance to speak with Cecile alone.

'You must excuse my brother,' she said when he had gone. 'Anton has never been very good at social niceties. I suppose he is somewhat like my father in that sense.'

'Which of you is more like your father?' I asked.

The question seemed to catch her off guard, and for a moment I was worried that I might have said the wrong thing. Then she seemed to consider the question.

'We are both like him, I suppose. I have my father's passion, but Anton has his determination, his desire to succeed.'

'I imagine he was very proud of both of you.'

A shadow crossed her eyes. 'I believe that he was, yes.'

I wondered if it had occurred to Anton and Cecile that they would have a much better chance of success if they worked together. The traits they had inherited from their father would best be used in combination. It was not my place to say so, however. That was something they would have to work out on their own.

'Well,' she said, seeming to rouse herself. 'Now we will get to the pleasant part. We will discuss scents.' There was a sudden light in her eyes.

'I'm afraid I don't know very much about the way perfume is made,' I said. 'I am relying on you.'

'The science of scent,' she said, seated on the edge of the satin chair, her hands folded in her lap, 'is something which cannot be explained in a few moments. Indeed, it is really something that requires a lifetime to master. I have studied a long time and there is still much I have to learn. I imagine many people believe that it's just a shake of orchid and a dab of rosewater that creates perfume in the bottle. It's nothing at all like that. It's

151

much more mysterious. It is chemical and yet magical.'

She looked up as though she suddenly felt that she had been talking too much, but her smile was not an embarrassed one. Rather, she looked a bit amused at the idea that anyone might not care as much for the subject as she. 'You must excuse me. I do tend to run on about perfume.'

I smiled. 'I find it fascinating.'

She studied me for a moment, as though looking for falsity in my words, but I had been perfectly sincere. I admired both her passion and the skill that was required to pursue it.

Cecile stood, then, smoothing out her skirt. 'Neither of my brothers has what it takes to become a master parfumier. Anton, perhaps, has the brains for it, but not the heart. Making perfume is like making music. One can know all the right notes, but if there is no true feeling, the piece is missing something. It doesn't capture the senses.'

'I've never thought about it in that way,' I said, 'but I suppose you're right.'

'My father understood this. Many people thought he was a hard man, and he was in some ways, despite his kindness. But there was something else in him, the heart of an artist. We understood one another.'

She stopped again. 'But I talk too much. Never mind. Would you like to see my scent garden?'

I hesitated ever so slightly, unsure of what she meant.

'It started as a small garden in the courtyard, a collection of flowers and herbs that I thought would help me to hone my sense of smell. I wanted to really be able to differentiate between the notes in the perfume. My garden grew, and then I began to become interested in some plants that were not exactly suited to our climate. My father gave me the old greenhouse and helped me choose plants for it. As my collection grew, so did the greenhouse. My father expanded it for me several times. I'm very proud of it.'

'I'd love to see it.'

I followed her from the sitting room and through the house, out into the little courtyard where I had encountered Michel the night of the party. The scent of flowers was as strong here today as it had been then, and I could see what I had not been able to see that night. The little courtyard was part of a garden, awash in colour and scent. Forsythia, lilac, and mimosa were in bloom, and the branches of the cherry blossom tree along the stone wall swayed in the breeze. Along the walk grew a profusion of flowers: daffodils, peonies, irises, nasturtiums, and the delicate bell-shaped lilies of the valley.

'It's beautiful,' I said sincerely.

'Not all of the plants here are suitable for perfumery, of course, but it is nice to surround oneself with flowers. Do you garden, Madame Ames?'

'I have a small flower garden at our country home, though it is rather a paltry effort compared to this.'

She shrugged. 'I do not spend much time outside of Paris. My plants give me something to occupy my time. If you'll come this way.'

We rounded a flowering bush, and came face-to-face with Beryl Belanger.

'Oh,' she said. 'Hello.'

She looked even smaller up close than she had from afar, standing on the staircase at the party. Again I had the impression of a delicate little bird, her eyes fluttering from Cecile to me and back again.

I was not sure why, but I felt that there was something almost guilty in her expression. I wondered if it had to do with the fact that she held a basket with freshly cut roses in it. Perhaps she had been poaching in Cecile's private reserve.

'Hello, Beryl,' Cecile said. 'Allow me to introduce you to Madame Ames. Madame Ames, this is my father's widow, Beryl Belanger.' She made this unfaltering introduction without emotion, but I thought Beryl flinched a bit at the word 'widow'. Cecile was a difficult woman to read. I tried and failed to determine what her feelings for her young stepmother might be. Whatever she felt, she was very careful not to make it apparent.

'I'm pleased to meet you, Mrs Ames,' Beryl said. 'Cecile mentioned that she is creating a perfume for you. I'm sure it will be wonderful. My husband was very proud of her talents.'

'Have you been in the greenhouse?' Cecile asked. Her tone was pleasant, but I felt almost as though it held a note of scolding. I wondered what the dynamic in the house had been with Cecile, who had been her father's protégée, and the young woman who had been his wife. It seemed that Cecile's personality was much stronger, and I could believe that it would not be easy for Beryl Belanger in this house now that her husband was dead.

'I . . . no,' Beryl said. 'These are the roses from the other side of the garden. I thought they would be nice in a vase in the sitting room.'

'Yes,' Cecile said. 'I only wanted to make sure that, if

154

you had been there, that you had made sure to secure the door. I found it ajar a few days ago, and I should hate for Seraphine to wander in one day. There are a great many dangerous plants, not to mention my chemicals.'

'I don't go into the greenhouse,' Beryl said.

'Well, someone was there,' Cecile said. 'Perhaps I ought to get a lock.'

'Yes, perhaps you should,' Beryl replied agreeably.

So the greenhouse contained dangerous plants and chemicals and was left unlocked. It seemed, then, that anyone might have access to poisons necessary to kill Helios Belanger.

'Well, if you will excuse us,' Cecile said. 'I am going to show the greenhouse to Madame Ames.'

'It was very nice to have met you,' I told Beryl.

'Yes, I'm so pleased I was here when you came,' she said. 'It has been a very long time since I was in London. Perhaps we will meet again before you go home and you can tell me the news.'

'I would like that,' I said.

She went on her way then and Cecile turned to me. 'My stepmother is very fond of plants, though she chooses them more for the way they look than the way they smell.'

I suspected that, in the world of the Belangers, this was a very disparaging assessment indeed.

CHAPTER THIRTEEN

Cecile Belanger led me to a white-framed greenhouse, the panes of glass glinting brightly in the afternoon sun. We stepped inside, and I was immediately hit with a potent bouquet of fragrance. For a moment, I was lost in the heady, almost dizzying, combination of scents. However, after a moment passed, I began to make out some of the individual smells that hovered in the air. Jasmine, rose, and violet were the most discernible. Other, more exotic scents were also familiar, but I could not name them offhand.

I looked around. Flowers and plants grew everywhere: on climbing trellises, in pots on the floor and tables and planters hanging from the ceiling. There were also trees growing in huge earthen vessels. I spotted orange, lemon, and acacia, among others. Everywhere one looked there was some other lovely flower or shrub to draw the eye. It was a glorious jumble of plants, but I could sense that there was definite order to the seemingly untamed verdure. This was no common greenhouse. It was as though I had stumbled into some exotic and well-kept jungle in the middle of Paris.

'It's magnificent,' I said.

She smiled, and it was the first time I had seen what looked like genuine happiness in her face. 'It has taken me a long time to get it just as I wished. I am very proud of it.'

A flagstone path lead through the foliage, and I followed her along it through the warm, sweet air as she pointed out different plants.

'Here I have herbs,' she said. 'Marjoram, mint, patchouli, rosemary, lemongrass, just to name a few. I had to keep them here rather than in the potager so Cook would stop stealing them to put in our dinners.'

I laughed.

'I have over twenty varieties of roses,' she said, nodding towards a large section of the greenhouse where roses grew in tangled abundance. 'Several of them are hybrids I've developed myself, mostly to enhance the aromas.'

I was very much impressed. Cecile Belanger was clearly a master of her craft.

We reached the back of the greenhouse and there was a door in the wall. Cecile opened it and led me into a room that, though attached to the greenhouse and possessed of large windows open to let in the sunlight, was not made entirely of glass like the rest of the building. It looked as though it might be the office of a scientist. There was a large portion of the room with scientific equipment on tables and a wall of shelves full of carefully labelled jars. A thin rope was strung across the ceiling and held bunches of dried flowers. The smell was subtler here, less fresh than the greenhouse but still very pleasant.

'This is the laboratory that my father created for me,' she said. 'Of course, it was rather rudimentary to start.

I don't know if he really believed at first that I meant to dedicate myself to it. Once he saw that I loved it as much as he did, he began to buy me more equipment. Some of it rather expensive. He had his own scientists, of course, but there were times when I solved my own little olfactory dilemmas.'

She pointed to a shelf of leather-bound books. I looked closely and saw that there were no titles on the spines. 'These are my scent journals,' she said. 'I started writing them at a very young age, under my father's guidance. I began taking special care to study scents and write them down. I was always stopping to smell the flowers, an English expression, is it not? I would keep a log of what plants smelt like and how they smelt after different amounts of time, how they smelt when mixed together. They called him Le Nez, the nose, for his renowned sense of smell, and he called me his petite nez. Later, of course, my notes became much more scientific. My father would often read over them and add remarks.'

'I think it's wonderful that he encouraged you to follow in his footsteps,' I said.

She nodded. 'I was always very happy that he did not view women as incapable of doing the things that men do. Instead of pointing me towards more jejune pursuits, he did everything possible to nurture my fascination with scent and develop my skills.'

She was fortunate in that respect. I knew a great many women who had been discouraged from such pursuits by parents who thought their main objective was to marry well and produce heirs.

She led me to the table that held her equipment. There

was a large metal press and an array of beakers, droppers, spoons, and a great many other things I didn't recognise. She pointed to a curious-looking contraption. 'This is for steam distillation,' she said. Her hand moved to another piece of equipment, what appeared to be a stack of frames on the floor, not unlike a wooden beehive in appearance. 'Are you familiar with the process of enfleurage?' she asked.

'Only vaguely,' I admitted. I had determined it would not do any good to pretend that I was in any way knowledgeable about the process of perfumery. Better to say that my interest was newly developed than fumble my way through feigned familiarity.

'Enfleurage is used to extract the fragrance from flowers.' She picked up a plate of glass in a wooden frame. 'In cold enfleurage, these chassis are coated with fat, and flower petals are pressed between them. The fat absorbs the fragrance from the petals over the course of several days. The process is repeated until the fat has absorbed enough of the fragrance.'

'I see,' I said. 'How very interesting.'

'I have always thought so,' she said, a smile forming at the corners of her mouth. 'In fact, I first attempted it many years ago. I had seen the process done at my father's factories and here in his laboratory as a young girl. He made his own lavender pomade that he was never without, and I was fascinated by the method and most eager to try it myself. When I was perhaps ten years old, I located some broken window panes in the garden shed, coated them with leftover grease I had secreted from the kitchen, and picked some roses from my mother's garden, pressing them with some old bricks for several days. Unfortunately,

I lacked the correct technique. The grease went rancid and the flowers rotted. The resulting pomade was putrid in the extreme, as I'm sure you can imagine.'

We laughed, and I could tell the memory was special to her. 'I put it in a jar anyway,' she said. 'My mother accepted the present graciously, and my father took me back to the shed to show me what I had done wrong.' Her smile faded ever so slightly as a look of sadness came into her eyes. 'I learnt everything I know about perfume from my father, and everything about being a good woman from my mother.'

'They must have been very special people,' I said.

She nodded. 'My mother was a beautiful woman.' There was something unspoken in the words, and I wondered if she was thinking about her stepmother, comparing the young woman who had married her father to the woman who had raised her.

The soft silence of the room was suddenly broken by the ringing of a telephone I had not noticed on the wall. 'We had it installed for the sake of convenience, but it is sometimes a nuisance,' she said, going to answer it.

'Yes?' She listened for a moment and then glanced at her wrist. In keeping with her generally understated appearance, the only jewellery she wore was a watch. Granted, it was a watch set in diamonds and emeralds. Displaying both great wealth and eminent practicality, it suited Cecile Belanger perfectly.

'Very well,' she said. She hung up the phone and turned to me. 'I'm sorry, Madame Ames, I'm afraid I have lost track of time. In order to create your custom scent, we really should talk more. I need to learn more about you before

I can determine what will best suit you. Unfortunately, I have another engagement this afternoon.'

I remembered what Madame Nanette had told us. Today was the reading of the will.

'Perhaps we might set up another appointment?' I asked.

'Yes . . .' It seemed that she hesitated ever so slightly and then said suddenly, 'Would you and your husband like to come to dinner tomorrow night?'

I couldn't help but be a bit surprised at the invitation. This was more of a social engagement than a business transaction. I thought perhaps that she had warmed to me throughout the course of the day. I certainly felt as though I knew her better than I had.

'That would be lovely,' I said.

'Good.' She smiled. 'I shall look forward to it.'

I couldn't help but feel a bit guilty. I had approached Cecile Belanger under false pretences, but now I felt that what might have the potential to blossom into a genuine friendship was tainted with my treachery. Of course, there remained the possibility that Cecile was a killer, in which case I was certainly not the one who should feel guilty.

We walked back through the garden and into the house. Just as we reached the foyer, Anton stepped out of the office that he had inherited from his father, the one from which I had heard their conversation at the party. 'Cecile, may I speak with you?'

'Yes, after I've walked Madame Ames out.'

'I can show myself out,' I said. It was, after all, only a few steps to the door.

'Very well,' she said. 'Good afternoon, and we shall see you tomorrow night?'

161

'Yes. I shall look forward to it.'

With a dismissive nod in my direction, Anton motioned for her to precede him into the room and he followed her, closing the door behind them. As much as I was tempted to press my ear against the door, my sense of propriety won the day and I turned to take my leave.

It seemed my opportunity for eavesdropping had not been lost, however, for just as I reached the front door I caught the sound of voices in the drawing room, and I couldn't help but hear what they said.

'What a lovely bouquet. And you look positively blooming yourself.'

'Thank you,' came the hesitant reply.

I recognised both voices. It was Beryl and Michel Belanger. It seemed Michel must have just come in and found Beryl arranging her roses from the garden. There was something in the interaction that gave me pause. This seemed to be more than a friendly conversation. His next words confirmed it.

'One might never know that you were recently widowed.' His tone held a jesting, almost mocking, note. 'I have no doubt you will find comfort in your grief.'

'I wish you wouldn't say such things, Michel.' Her voice was strained, almost distressed.

He laughed. 'You needn't feign grief with me, my dear stepmother.'

'Please,' she whispered. 'Don't . . .'

'I do not judge you, not at all. Nor do I begrudge you your little afternoon walks in the Jardin du Luxembourg. I think tomorrow would be a good time for one, yes? He is anxious to be alone with you, I am sure.'

There was a sudden thump and the shatter of glass followed by a startled cry.

'How clumsy of you, Beryl,' Michel said.

I slipped out the front door before one of them came from the room to summon a maid to clean up the broken vase.

So the tensions in the Belanger household had not diminished with the death of Helios Belanger. What was more, it seemed that Madame Nanette had been correct in her suspicion. Beryl Belanger had a lover. Was that motive enough for murder? People had killed for less.

I returned to the hotel and was a bit surprised to find that Milo was there. He was reclined on the sofa, his feet propped up on the arm, smoking a cigarette.

'Hadn't you anything amusing to do this afternoon?' I asked. It was only by the strongest of efforts that I kept from asking him if he had a train to catch. Throughout my entire afternoon, that ticket in his pocket had been at the back of my mind. I wanted very much to know why he had lied to me, but I was putting off asking him. Perhaps some part of me was afraid to discover the answer.

'Not particularly,' he replied. 'I had thought about it, but then I realised Madame Nanette was likely to ring us after the reading of the will if anything of interest occurred.'

It was uncharacteristically thoughtful of him to have decided to await her call.

I went to the sitting area and took a seat on the chair across from him. 'Cecile Belanger left me for an appointment. It must have been the reading of the will. I suppose we are likely to hear something before dinner.'

'How did you succeed with the Belangers?' he asked. 'Did you learn anything?'

'A few things, I think,' I said thoughtfully. 'The most telling, perhaps, is that the door to Cecile's greenhouse, which contains a number of deadly plants and chemicals, is left unlocked. It also seems Madame Nanette was right about Beryl Belanger having a lover. I overheard Michel taunting her about it.'

'Has she risen to the top of your suspect list, then?' Milo asked.

Despite his somewhat flippant tone, I gave him my honest answer. 'It's difficult to say. It seems to me that Cecile was very fond of her father. Of course, that might have been an act. It's difficult to tell about Anton. He didn't say much, except for what he plans to charge to make my custom perfume.'

I named the price that Anton Belanger had quoted me, and Milo shrugged. I ought to have known that he would have been unimpressed with the exorbitant cost of procuring a custom perfume along with information.

'And we've been invited to dine with the Belangers tomorrow night.'

'Excellent, darling. You have made progress,' he said.

'I hope so. It seems as though things have been frightfully difficult to uncover thus far.' I glanced at him. 'There are so many secrets. One never knows what people are hiding.'

'No, one doesn't,' he said, with no hint of guilt.

I opened my mouth to confront him about the train ticket, but was prevented from doing so by the ringing of the telephone.

Milo and I glanced at each other. I would have thought

it was too early for Madame Nanette's call, but perhaps the reading of the will had not taken as long as I thought it might.

I started to rise, but Milo sat up and was on his feet before I was. 'I'll get it,' he said, dropping his cigarette in the ashtray.

He crossed to the telephone and picked it up.

'Hello,' he said. There was a slight pause and I could tell from something in his manner that it was not Madame Nanette. 'Yes. What did she say?' Another pause. 'Indeed. You have done very well.'

This was rather a curious conversation. I wondered to whom he was speaking.

'No,' he said. 'No, I don't think . . . Yes, thank you.'

He put the telephone back on the receiver and turned to me, a hint of a smile playing on his lips. 'I have garnered us a valuable opportunity,' he said.

'Oh?' I asked.

'I've found a way for us to speak to Herr Muller.'

I had to admit this was good news. I had been trying to think of a way I might approach him but, short of commissioning him to make a sculpture of some sort, I had not had any good ideas. And I did not particularly want to pay for both a custom perfume and a sculpture in the space of one visit to Paris.

'It turns out that he has come to Paris to meet with a model,' Milo said.

Something about this bit of information struck a chord of suspicion in me. I suddenly had the distinct impression that he was being evasive.

'Who was that on the telephone, Milo?'

165

'That was Nadine,' he said, very casually.

It was just as I thought.

'Dear little Nadine,' I said. 'What did she have to say?'

'It occurred to me earlier that she might prove of use to us.'

'Did it?' I replied, quite interested to know his logic. 'How so?'

'I told you that she works as a model. I rang her this afternoon and asked if she might ask some of her friends if any of them have posed for Herr Muller before. It turns out he's rather a well-known figure here in Paris. Nadine has been acquainted with several of his models, including the one he is going to sculpt next. She made plans to meet them at a nightclub tonight and has invited us to join them.'

Though I hated to give any credit to Nadine, I couldn't help but feel it would be a good opportunity. Herr Muller had behaved rather strangely at the party, and I would like to see what else I could learn about him.

On the other hand, I was already very annoyed with my husband for keeping secrets from me, and the prospect of a dinner with him and a table of young models was not entirely appealing.

I realised suddenly that he was waiting for a response. 'Very well,' I said. 'I think that may prove very useful.'

'I thought it was rather clever of her to arrange it.'

'Yes. Perfectly enchanting,' I replied. 'How shall we ever repay her?'

My inability to keep the edge from my voice annoyed me. I had nothing against Nadine, and she had indeed been quite helpful. The problem was that I could not forget that ticket I had found in his pocket this morning, but nor did the time seem right to confront him about it.

All of this crossed my mind in a matter of seconds. When I looked up, Milo's eyes caught mine, and it was too late for me to mask my expression.

'What's the matter?' he asked.

'Nothing,' I replied lightly. 'I told you, I don't mind Nadine.'

'I don't mean Nadine,' he said. 'There's something else.'

I hated moments like these, when he could read my emotions with minimal effort and I could tell nothing of what was going on behind those blue eyes of his.

With great effort, I smoothed my features and offered him a smile. 'I suppose I'm a bit tired after meeting with the Belangers today. It's nothing.'

CHAPTER FOURTEEN

Madame Nanette had not rung us by the time we left for the nightclub. Milo had been a bit reluctant, I think, to leave the hotel without hearing from her, but I was not especially concerned. It was likely that she had been caught up caring for the child and had not yet found the time to contact us.

We met Nadine and her party at a nightclub in Montparnasse. This was the sort of place that was more likely to appeal to the younger set. The dances on the floor were much more lively than the ones to which I was accustomed, and the women all seemed to be wearing clothing that was a good deal more ostentatious than mine. Then again, I was no longer one of the flashy younger generation. I had chosen a heavily beaded gown of sapphire blue, which I felt was quite gaudy enough.

We were shown to a table where Nadine sat with two other young women, two young gentlemen, and Herr Muller. The gentlemen rose when we reached the table, as did Nadine. She was, as I had expected, extremely glad to see Milo. She stopped just short of embracing him as we arrived. To her credit, she greeted me almost as warmly.

'Your gown is magnificent, Madame Ames. When I have seen you in the society columns, I have always thought how very lovely you look. *Très* chic.'

'Thank you,' I said. Her own gown was a bright shade of pink that quite suited her.

She introduced us to her companions. The two young women were fellow models, one of them had come with Herr Muller, the other with one of the young men. The second young man was, if the way he glared at Milo was any indication, a special friend of Nadine's.

As luck would have it, Herr Muller's seat was next to mine at the table. He greeted us without enthusiasm. I took no offence, as he did not seem particularly interested in anything about the evening. I expected that learning anything from him would prove a difficult task, but I was up to the challenge.

We ordered dinner, and I made my first attempt at conversation.

'We were at the party at the Belangers' home,' I said. 'I had hoped to get a chance to speak with you, but the crowds were very large.'

'Yes, it was very crowded.' It seemed to me that his eyes had darkened ever so slightly at the mention of the Belangers' party. It was not surprising, given what I had overheard. I would have to tread carefully with my questions.

'I was very impressed with your sculpture,' I said. 'It will make a beautiful perfume bottle.'

'Thank you,' he said tightly. He seemed very much

disinclined to discuss it, and I thought it best to let the topic drop for the moment. Perhaps he would be a bit more conversational after a few glasses of wine.

Dinner was relatively uneventful. Nadine and her friends were pleasant, and we found common ground in discussing the current fashions. Herr Muller did not contribute much to the conversation. I did notice that his features, though expressionless, did not carry the same haughty disdain that had been in evidence at the Belanger party. He merely seemed bored.

It seemed that the wine had indeed improved his temper, however, for, the meal finished, he rose and turned to me.

'Will you dance with me, madame?' he asked.

'I should like that very much,' I replied.

He pulled back my chair and we made our way towards the dance floor. When we reached it, he stepped back from me a moment, his eyes running over me. 'I remember you,' he said at last. 'You were wearing a lavender gown.'

I smiled. 'Yes. It was a new gown.'

'It was not the gown that interested me,' he said. 'You have a lovely body, madame.'

I paused only slightly at this unusual compliment. 'Thank you,' I replied.

He took me into his arms, then, and we began to move around the floor.

'I hope you do not mind me saying so, but I notice the bodies of women. It is my business to do so.'

'Yes, I suppose it is. Was Mademoiselle Montreau the model for the bottle sculpture?' I asked, referring to the young woman who had accompanied him to dinner.

'No,' he said, and I thought I detected a hint of a story

in the single word. I was glad when he continued. 'Helios had wanted me to model the bottle after his late wife, but I cannot work from an old photograph. I need living flesh.'

I wondered what Beryl Belanger had thought of her husband calling his perfume the Angel of Memory and intending to model the bottle after his deceased wife.

'I thought perhaps his new wife would suffice,' Herr Muller went on, 'but then I was introduced to a young woman named Angelique, and I knew at once that I wanted to sculpt her. I wanted, in fact, to make her my permanent model, but she said that she would model for the bottle but nothing more.' He sounded irritated by this fact. I supposed it was not usual for women to refuse him.

So Angelique, Michel Belanger's former mistress, had been the model for the bottle. I wondered how that had come about.

'She is a friend of Michel Belanger, I understand,' I said.

'She was, yes.' Again, I had the impression that there was more than what he was saying.

'I heard that Monsieur Belanger did not approve of the relationship and drove them apart,' I said, hoping to nudge him along. It seemed to have done the trick, for his eyes flashed.

'Helios Belanger was a fool,' he said hotly.

Under other circumstances, I might have been a bit surprised that he should speak so vehemently about a man who had recently died. Given what I had overheard at the party, I had not expected warm sentiments.

'You think that Michel Belanger and Angelique were a good match?'

'No,' he scoffed. 'Michel did not deserve her. I say Helios

was a fool because of the way he acted. He did not want Angelique to be the model for the bottle. We had many rows over it. He ought to have trusted my judgement rather than fight me. He was behaving very strangely about the matter. After all, the sculpture is an angel, who better to model for it than a woman named Angelique?'

'Had you known him long?'

'Too long it seemed to me.'

I wondered if there was some particular event that had driven the two of them apart or if it had simply been a clash of artistic personalities.

'I would have thought it might have strengthened your friendship, working together so closely,' I ventured.

He shook his head. 'We were friends once, but not at the end. I should never have agreed to create the bottle, but I have admired his perfumes, given them to my wives and mistresses, and I thought that a bottle would be an interesting form of art. I have never done something like this before, something that will be reproduced in glass. I was not entirely sure that I wanted to do it, but I was finally convinced. It did not take me long to realise that I would not be able to tolerate his interference. He was constantly changing his mind, questioning my decisions. He insulted me more than once. In the end, I could work only with Monsieur Anton.'

This was what I had gathered from the conversation I had heard at the party. It was not entirely surprising that two men of creative temperament should have had difficulty working together.

'What did Monsieur Anton say about Angelique serving as the model?' I asked. 'I have the impression he does not much approve of Michel.'

'It was no one's concern but mine. I decided that I wanted Angelique, and I had her.'

'I see. No doubt she was flattered to have been made into the bottle.'

He smiled a bit ruefully. 'Angelique is not an easy woman to flatter. And she was a terrible model. Always she was wanting to move. "I must have something to drink." "I want to smoke a cigarette." "This room is too hot." I have never had a model who was as difficult as she. Never again will I work with such a woman.' Despite the heat of his words, his mouth had softened around the edges, and I could not help but think that Angelique had cast her spell over him.

This speech seemed to have tired him, for he stopped as we reached the edge of the dance floor and pulled a handkerchief from his pocket, wiping his brow.

I thought it would be a good thing to speak with Angelique at some point. She might have some interesting insight to offer about the Belanger family. Granted, she was much more likely to be interested in speaking to Milo than she would be to me.

I glanced to where Milo was dancing around the floor with Nadine's friend, Mademoiselle Montreau, the woman who was Herr Muller's current model. I hoped that he would attempt to glean some sort of useful information from her, but the way she threw her head back and laughed at something he said made me doubt it.

I turned my attention back to the matter at hand. 'I am sure that Monsieur Belanger would have loved the sculpture and would have been glad that it will carry on his legacy.'

'I think, if he had lived, he would have chosen a different bottle,' Herr Muller said.

This I had not expected. 'I find that very surprising,' I said. 'Was it because of Angelique?'

'It was because Helios Belanger was a fool,' he said. 'He saw enemies where they did not exist.'

'But surely, if you had a contract, he would not have been able to refuse it?'

'We did not have a contract because I had done the sculpture as a favour. It was an agreement between gentlemen, before I realised that Helios Belanger was no gentleman. I was to receive my compensation when the bottle went into production.'

Then he stood to lose if Monsieur Belanger had changed his mind. It was a very good motive. I wondered if I should press him further.

Nothing ventured, nothing gained. I would have to be blunt. 'I suppose it is vulgar to say so, but it seems that Monsieur Belanger's death was beneficial to you.'

It seemed to me that his gaze narrowed ever so slightly, and I wondered if he suspected that there was more to my comment than simple observation. Whatever he thought of my remark, he did not deny it. 'Yes,' he said. 'His death has saved me a great deal of trouble. Monsieur Anton will use my bottle, and I will receive my compensation. I did not hate the man, but nor do I mourn him.'

'I see.'

So Herr Muller had been reluctant to do the sculpture in the first place, and might have been out a good deal of money if Monsieur Belanger had lived. I wondered if it might be reason enough to kill.

The dance ended and we went back to the table. Milo was not there, nor did I see him on the dance floor.

Nadine must have noticed that I had looked for him, for she smiled. 'He has gone to use the telephone, I think.'

I suspected that he had gone to see if there had been any messages left for us by Madame Nanette. It was obvious that he cared for her a great deal, for there was no other aspect of his life in which he was so solicitous.

'Do you know,' Nadine said, leaning towards me, 'that when I was a child, I was very much in love with your husband.'

'Oh?' I asked, not entirely sure where this story would lead.

'Yes, he came home with my brother Francois for Christmas, and I told my mother, "One day I shall marry him." My mother told me she would forbid it, considering the way he and Francois and Michel Belanger behaved.' She laughed. 'And so I planned an elopement. He never knew it, of course. I was heartbroken when I heard that he had been married. I have grown up now, of course. I see that he made a very good match.'

I smiled. 'Thank you.'

'When two people are meant to be together . . . well, nothing can stop it.'

I thought this seemed a good opportunity to broach the subject that had been on my mind. 'You mentioned Michel Belanger. Do you know Angelique?'

'Nearly all of Paris knows Angelique,' she said. 'But I have never met her. She is very famous. Or perhaps infamous is the better word.'

'She sings, I believe?'

'And dances, without many clothes, so they say. At La Reine Bleue.'

I was deprived of further gossip as Milo made his way

back to the table just then and stood behind my chair. 'I'm terribly sorry, but I'm afraid we'll have to leave,' he said. 'Something has come up.'

He must have been contacted by Madame Nanette. Milo appeared perfectly at ease, but I could sense a certain tension in him. There must be something wrong.

He pulled out my chair, and I rose.

As we said our goodbyes, I wondered if I would have another opportunity to speak to Herr Muller. There had been much in our conversation that seemed promising in the way of making him a suspect. I couldn't say that I felt strongly that he was a killer, but I didn't doubt the potential was there.

He looked at me then, almost as though he had read my mind, and offered me a small smile. I felt a bit of a chill as his cool eyes met mine. And then the sensation disappeared, and I wondered if I had imagined it.

'It was very nice to meet you, Herr Muller,' I said. 'I shall be looking forward to seeing more of your work in the future.'

He looked as though he was about to say something, but then thought better of it. Instead, he nodded. 'Thank you.'

Milo took my arm, and we walked towards the exit.

'Madame Nanette?' I asked.

He nodded. 'She left a message at the desk. She said only that she would come to see us at midnight unless she was able to ring again before then.'

'There may not be anything wrong,' I said.

'Perhaps not, but the desk clerk said she sounded distressed.'

That seemed an ominous sign. I thought perhaps the

will might provide some interesting bit of news, but I didn't think that it would be cause for distress.

'Did the clerk say anything else?'

'No. I assume she didn't want to say much over the telephone. Likely she was still at the Belanger residence and would need to put the child to sleep before she could get away.'

I sighed. 'Then there's nothing we can do but wait.'

It was nearly midnight when we reached the hotel. I was glad. I didn't feel like I could stand much suspense. For some reason, I was very on edge about Madame Nanette's news, whatever it might be. Milo, as usual, gave no outward indication of alarm, but I knew that he must be concerned.

It was a relief when at last we heard her knock at the door.

Milo went to answer it, and Madame Nanette came into the room, her face very grave.

'Come and sit down, madame,' Milo said, leading her to the sitting area. 'We could have met you at a cafe or some such place. You needn't have come here to see us.'

She shook her head. 'No, I didn't want to chance being seen in public. I am more certain now than ever that someone had a hand in Helios Belanger's death.'

'You're very pale,' Milo said. 'Would you like a drink?'

She shook her head. 'No, no. I am well, thank you. It is just that I have had a very trying afternoon.'

'Why don't you start at the beginning,' Milo said. 'Today was the reading of the will?'

'Yes, that was the first thing that upset me. You see, Helios left me money. Quite a lot of money.'

'And this is cause for distress?' Milo asked wryly.

'Well, yes, in a way,' she said. 'I never dreamt that

he would remember me in his will. We have not meant anything to each other in thirty years. I think the family wonders why it was that he did such a thing.'

'It doesn't much matter what the family thinks,' Milo said. 'That was Monsieur Belanger's decision. Besides, I'm sure there is more than enough money to go around.'

She sighed. 'I suppose. But there is something else. The will stated that Anton and Cecile should maintain equal control of Parfumes Belanger.'

'I see,' Milo said. 'That does seem to be an interesting development.'

'I don't suppose Anton was very pleased about that,' I said.

'No. They had a very great quarrel about it, in fact. Anton said that his father had told him that he would be given control of the company. He even claimed to have seen a draft of a different will.'

'A different will?' Milo questioned.

'Yes. He said it was in his father's desk drawer. He offered to produce it, but the solicitor said that, even if a later will had been drafted by Monsieur Belanger, it had not been witnessed and was not legally binding.'

'And Monsieur Belanger was dead before that newer will could be formalised,' Milo said.

Madame Nanette nodded.

'What did Cecile say?' I asked.

'Not much. She did not seem surprised. I can only assume that Monsieur Belanger had told her his true intentions.'

'What of Michel?' I asked.

'That was another surprise. Michel was left a very large sum of money, though Monsieur Belanger had frequently quarrelled with Michel and even threatened to disinherit him on occasion. In fact, I wondered if that second draft of the will had said as much, for Anton looked livid about his brother's inheritance, as though he had not expected him to receive it.'

'So he left Michel a small fortune with no strings attached,' I mused. 'Perhaps as much money as his siblings with no responsibilities.'

She nodded again.

'That seems rather a strike against Michel,' Milo said.

'Perhaps,' I mused. 'But if Monsieur Belanger had indeed drafted a second will that gave complete control of Parfumes Belanger to Anton, it is possible that Cecile saw it as well as Anton. She might have heard that he had asked his solicitor to come and realised that, despite her role in Parfumes Belanger, he meant to leave the company to her brother.'

'In which case, Cecile might have had motive to kill her father before the second will could be witnessed,' Milo said.

'Yes,' Madame Nanette said. 'Cecile might have wanted to prevent his changing the will to disinherit her, if indeed that is what the second will would have done.'

'It's also a good motive for Anton, if he thought he was going to benefit,' Milo pointed out. 'If he believed that the second will was legally binding and that he would have control of the company, that might be a very good reason to kill his father.'

'Anton might also have been afraid that Belanger might change his mind again and give Cecile an equal share of the business,' I said slowly. 'Perhaps he decided to act quickly and kill his father before it could be done.'

'It's possible,' Milo said.

'I wish we could see the second draft of the will,' I mused. 'It might give some insight into Monsieur Belanger's frame of mind before his death. I find it rather strange that he would draft any will that did not give Cecile some share in the company. After all, she is the one who cares most for perfume.'

'He would not be the first father to overlook a daughter for a less competent son,' Milo said.

'No,' Madame Nanette admitted. 'But Amory is right. It is unlike him. So many things about this Helios Belanger were different from that man I knew.'

'What about his widow?' I asked, remembering Beryl Belanger. 'And the child, Seraphine. I assume he left them something?'

She nodded. 'A very sizeable sum of money went to Madame Belanger, and even more was set up in a trust for the child. They will be well looked after.'

I suddenly thought of something. 'I understand that Beryl often goes for walks in the Jardin du Luxembourg. I suspect it may be where she meets her lover. If she goes out tomorrow, will you ring me? I'd like to meet her there.'

'Yes,' she said. 'I will let you know.'

'So Beryl has a secret lover and was left with plenty of money,' Milo said.

He looked over at me, and I sighed. 'I had hoped the will might give a clear motive to one of the Belangers in particular,' I said. 'Instead, it seems it has given an excellent motive to all of them.'

'I haven't told you the strangest thing,' Madame Nanette said.

'Good heavens, there's more?' I asked.

She nodded. 'It has to do with the formula. You remember that a copy was expected to be in his safe?'

'Yes,' Milo said. 'I imagine Anton Belanger was most anxious to have it opened.'

'Yes. He had a difficult time containing his impatience. The solicitor brought his key after the reading of the will and they all gathered round, waiting to see if the formula was secure.'

I felt a growing sense of anticipation as she spoke, as though what she was going to say might be the key to the whole mystery. I had no idea how right I was.

'And was that copy of the formula incorrect like the one in Grasse?' I asked.

'There was no formula,' she said. 'When they opened the safe, they found it was empty, save for a key.'

CHAPTER FIFTEEN

'A key to what?' I asked.

'That is just it,' Madame Nanette said. 'No one knows. The house was in an uproar after that, for Monsieur Anton said they will not be able to create L'Ange de Mémoire without the formula.'

'So either Monsieur Belanger placed the documents elsewhere, or someone has his copy of the key to the safe and has moved the formula,' Milo said.

'Then it seems the missing formula is the likely motive, after all,' I said. 'If we can find who stole the formula, we will likely have our killer.'

Madame Nanette nodded. 'So it seems.'

She glanced then at the clock. 'I should be getting back before I'm missed,' she said.

Milo rose. 'I'll accompany you back.'

'You needn't do that,' she protested. 'I don't want to risk being seen together. It might spoil everything.'

'Very well,' Milo said, 'but I shall at least put you in a cab.'

'You'll still come for tea tomorrow, won't you?' I asked, remembering that it was her day off.

She hesitated. 'I do not wish to intrude. I realise I have been coming here rather a lot.'

'Nonsense,' I replied. 'We're always delighted to have you. I do hope you will come. I'd like very much to have a chance to talk to you . . . about other things than this.'

She smiled. 'Very well. I shall see you tomorrow.'

They went downstairs, and I sat down to consider what we had learnt thus far. It all kept coming back to that formula. Someone had taken the copy from both Monsieur Belanger's attaché case and his safe. It must have been one of the family members, but why had they taken it? To sell it? To keep it until the fate of Parfumes Belanger was determined?

My instinct told me the missing formula was somehow connected with the rumoured second draft of the will. It was just possible that it might reveal who had the best motive for killing Helios Belanger. I wished I was able to look at the draft to see just what it contained, but it seemed very unlikely.

In any event, there was little I could do about it tonight.

I went to the bedroom and changed into my nightclothes. A few moments later, I heard Milo come back in. I walked to the sitting-room door.

'What do you make of all this?' I asked him.

'It's certainly something to consider,' he said.

'Something to consider?' I repeated. 'I'd say it's rather good evidence.'

'Evidence that someone might have taken the formula, yes. But you'll remember, darling, that we don't know for certain he was murdered.'

I didn't know why it was that he had suddenly become so resistant to the idea. It was, after all, his suspicion that had brought us to Paris.

I stopped in the doorway when I realised that Milo was filling up his cigarette case from the box on the table.

'What are you doing?' I asked.

'I'm going out,' he said, putting the case back into his pocket. 'You needn't wait up for me.'

Though I should not have been, I was startled by this announcement. It was after one o'clock. I had certainly thought he meant to stay in with me tonight.

I wrestled inwardly with the best way to reply. After finding the ticket, I knew that he was hiding something. I supposed that I ought to be glad that for once I wasn't concerned that it was a woman. I was beginning to trust him on that score. Besides, if it had been an illicit liaison he was after, he needn't have travelled to Beauvais; there were plenty to be had in Paris. No, it was something more than that. I suspected that it had to do with Helios Belanger, and if that was the case, I didn't know why he should want to keep it from me.

I debated on what might be the most effective tactic and decided to appeal to his baser instincts. I was, after all, still clothed only in my lacy nightgown.

'Must you go?' I asked lightly. I walked to where he stood and slid my arms around his neck. 'I was rather hoping we might retire for the evening.'

He smiled down at me, his arms encircling me. 'It's a very tempting idea, darling, but I'm afraid I have a prior commitment.'

'With whom?' I asked.

'Francois Germaine,' he answered readily. 'When he

heard I was in Paris, he rang me up and I agreed to meet him tonight.'

'But it's terribly late.'

'Gamblers never sleep, my lovely.'

'I was hoping to discuss things with you,' I said.

'Darling, as you've pointed out, it's late, and I'm quite sure that you're tired. Might we discuss things in the morning?'

It seemed I would need to be more direct. I stepped back, letting his hands fall away from my waist. 'Milo, I know you've been keeping things from me,' I said.

I waited for him to deny it, or for him to give some sign that he was even considering telling me the truth, but there was nothing. He merely watched me and waited.

It was time to confront him with the evidence. 'I found the ticket to Beauvais in your pocket,' I said.

Perhaps nothing in life was more infuriating to me than Milo's absolute lack of remorse when confronted with his own wrongdoing. No matter what he had done, how apologetic I thought he ought to be, he always managed to make me feel as though he thought I was being unreasonable. This time was no exception.

'Searching my pockets, were you?' The words were spoken lightly, but there was some hint of accusation in them that I didn't like.

'The ticket fell out onto the floor,' I said coldly, 'but that is beside the point. Why did you go there?'

'It was a business matter,' he said. 'Nothing for you to worry about.'

'I don't believe you,' I said.

His gaze met mine unflinchingly. 'That's entirely your prerogative.'

'Then you're not going to tell me why you went there?'

He didn't hesitate, didn't even blink. 'No.'

I didn't know what was more irritating: that he was being evasive or that he was making no effort to hide that fact.

'Why not?' I demanded.

'Some things don't concern you, darling,' he said.

I don't think he could have possibly said anything that would have made me angrier. I felt my face flush hot and, for a moment, I was absolutely speechless.

'Does it ever cross your mind to think of anyone other than yourself?' I asked as steadily as I could manage, doing everything in my power to keep from crying in fury. As I said it, I realised it was a question I had wanted to ask him for most of our marriage.

'Amory . . .' He sighed.

'Never mind,' I said. 'I know perfectly well what the answer to that is.'

Suddenly, I knew that I would not be able to hold back the tears any longer, and I refused to cry in front of him. Let him do as he pleased. Wordlessly, I went into the bedroom and closed the door behind me.

Though I didn't want to admit it, even to myself, some part of me hoped that he would come in, that he would admit that he was wrong.

But he didn't, and a moment later I heard the front door close behind him.

He had not returned by morning. I had spent half the night lying awake in my bed, listening for the sound of the door, half expecting him to come in late again, but, after staring at the darkened ceiling for what seemed like hours, I had at last given in to a restless sleep.

As a result, I felt tired and rather grim when I rose the next morning. A quick glance in the mirror confirmed that I did not look at all well.

Winnelda had come to see about helping me dress, but I had sent her off on an errand. I didn't feel up to company this morning. I needed time to think. It had been a long time since we'd had a good row, and I was not entirely surprised that it had happened. Nevertheless, it was infuriating that he had gone out and had chosen not to return home.

Though I felt like doing nothing but pulling on a silk robe over my nightgown and sulking about all day, I bathed and put on a becoming dress of red silk.

Feeling at least adequately prepared to meet the day, I went out into the sitting room. A hotel maid had brought a tray with coffee and pastries, but I had a headache and very little appetite.

Perhaps what bothered me most was that I had spent years concealing my emotions from Milo and now that I had become comfortable enough in our relationship to reveal my feelings, he had disregarded them. I wondered if my marriage would always be like this: a step forward and two steps back.

I poured my coffee and stirred in extra sugar for good measure.

I was halfway finished with the cup when the door opened and Milo came in, still in evening dress. He closed the door behind him, but didn't move towards me. Instead, his eyes searched my face. I met his gaze for only a moment before turning my attention back to my coffee cup.

'Good morning,' he said in a tone that was not at all apologetic.

'Good morning,' I replied, not looking up at him. I was not in the mood for pleasantries this morning. In fact, I was suppressing a very strong inclination to throw the coffee pot at his head. Alas, theatrics were not in my nature any more than repentance was in his.

'You're up rather early.'

'I think we may dispense with the civilities, Milo,' I said.

'I thought we might be particularly in need of them this morning.'

'We are apparently in need of a great many things,' I said, 'none of which I wish to discuss at present.'

I wondered where it was that he had spent the night, but I didn't feel inclined to ask him at the moment. Perhaps a part of me was afraid of the answer.

'I suppose you're wondering where I've been all night,' he said, with that irritating habit he had of knowing what I was thinking.

'No,' I retorted. 'I haven't the least bit of interest.'

'Well, I've brought you a present.'

'Have you?' I asked disinterestedly. Milo did not, as a general rule, buy me gifts when we had quarrelled. He wasn't the type of man who felt the need to atone for his mistakes.

'Yes, wait here for just a moment.'

He walked to the door and opened it, motioning to someone outside.

The door opened wider and a bellboy came in, struggling under the weight of a large brass cage. I had to look twice to make sense of what was in it, and I was struck by a mixture of incredulity and, against my will, amusement.

'A monkey,' I said, my gaze shifting from the cage to Milo's face. 'You've bought me a monkey.'

He smiled. 'Surprised?'

Surprised was not actually an accurate description of what I was. Milo had given me unusual gifts before, the latest of which had been a pearl-handled revolver. However, if you had given me a year to guess what this particular gift might be, I would never have thought of a monkey.

It was a very small monkey with large dark eyes. He was perched in the cage, his head tilted to the side. He seemed to be studying me just as I had studied him.

'How did you happen to come by him?' I asked, impressed at how calm I sounded. This entire situation was so bizarre; I had no protocol to follow.

'It was all part of a rather elaborate wager. I wasn't exactly sure what I'd even won until he was presented to me.'

I was trying very hard to maintain my composure. I was terribly angry with Milo and hurt by his behaviour, but this was all so ridiculous that I was sorely tempted to laugh. How very like him it was to throw me off so completely.

I rubbed a hand across my eyes. I was suddenly tired.

'You don't like him.' Milo's tone was designed to induce guilt, as though he had presented me with a piece of jewellery I didn't like and not a small mammal.

An exasperated sound somewhere between a sigh and a laugh escaped my lips. 'I'm sure he's a very nice monkey, Milo, but what are we to do with him?'

Milo shrugged. 'Bring him home, I suppose.'

'We cannot keep a monkey in our flat. I can only imagine what Winnelda would have to say about that.' She was sure to come into the sitting room at any moment, in fact, and go into hysterics at the sight of him.

'Well, we'll send him to live at Thornecrest.'

'Surely you don't mean to keep him?'

'Certainly, I do.'

I studied his face and found that he was perfectly in earnest. There was amusement in his eyes, but no hint of jesting. 'Milo, we cannot possibly keep a monkey.'

He smiled. 'There you're wrong, my love. We can do anything we like.'

'Milo . . .'

'I'm going to freshen up,' he said, turning towards the bedroom. 'Perhaps you can keep Emile company.'

'Emile?' I asked.

'The monkey is called Emile.'

Of course he was.

The monkey, hearing his name, chirped excitedly. He looked almost as though he was smiling at me.

'He is rather a fetching little thing,' I said. 'What does he eat?'

'Fruits and the like, I imagine.'

'His previous owner didn't tell you how to care for him?'

'I think he was happy to get the absurd little thing off his hands. I've only had him for the space of a few hours, and he is proving to be quite a nuisance.'

'You shouldn't say such things. You're liable to hurt his feelings,' I said, my tone heavy with sarcasm.

'Don't be ridiculous,' Milo said as he disappeared into the bedroom. 'He can't understand me. He only speaks French.'

CHAPTER SIXTEEN

Winnelda was absolutely no help when she returned from her errand a few moments later. She was delighted to see the monkey. It seemed only by the barest of margins that she kept herself from jumping up and down with excitement at the very sight of him.

'What a cute little thing you are,' she said. 'I do hope we shall be friends.'

'He doesn't speak English,' I said, feeling utterly ridiculous even as I said it.

Winnelda looked crestfallen. 'Not at all?'

'I don't believe so,' I replied, 'but perhaps you can teach him.'

'Oh, do you think so, madam? I will try it!'

As I walked back to the bedroom, she leant down towards the cage. 'Hello, Emile,' she said very slowly. 'My name is Winnelda.'

Emile replied by chattering brightly, and Winnelda laughed.

I knew in that moment that I would never be able to rid myself of this monkey.

The telephone rang and I went to answer it.

'Amory?' The voice on the other end spoke quietly, but I recognised that it was Madame Nanette.

'Yes.'

'I thought you might like to know. Madame Belanger has gone for her walk.'

'Thank you,' I said. I would go to the park directly. If I could arrange to encounter her, I might be able to learn something.

I rang off and turned to see that Milo was coming out of the bedroom. He had bathed and dressed and was just tying his necktie.

'Why are you dressing?' I asked. 'Aren't you going to sleep?'

'I'm not particularly tired,' he said. 'Who was on the telephone?'

I was tempted to be as evasive with him as he was with me, but things would become too confusing if we were both duplicitous.

'It was Madame Nanette,' I said. 'Beryl Belanger has gone for her walk. I'm going to see if I can intercept her in the park.'

'Would you care for some company?' he asked.

I hesitated for just a moment. I was still angry and didn't particularly feel up to his company this morning. However, there was nothing to be gained by being spiteful.

'You may come if you like,' I said.

It was a beautiful morning for a walk in the park. The sun was bright and the air was cool. Milo and I strolled along beside each other, neither of us saying much.

If it had been a few days ago, I would have taken his

arm, enjoyed the sensation of ambling along in the sunshine with him beside me. As things stood now, I felt we were on the verge of losing much of the progress we had made in our marriage, and I didn't want that to happen.

I had seldom been so happy as I had been as of late, and I didn't intend to give that up. We needed to talk about what had occurred.

'Are we just going to pretend as though last night didn't happen?' I asked at last.

'I would much rather proceed that way,' he said lightly, 'but I don't suppose that's what you have in mind.'

I stopped walking and turned to face him. 'You realise I'm still angry with you. The fact that you've given me a monkey doesn't change anything.' Had that absurd sentence really come from my mouth?

'I'm sorry you're angry, darling,' he said. 'I promise not to leave your side this evening.'

'That isn't the point,' I said. 'I don't need you to dance attendance on me. I don't care if you go to your gambling clubs or make ridiculous wagers, but there's something that you're not telling me, and I want to know what it is.'

'You're very beautiful,' he said, a smile tugging at the corners of his lips. 'Especially when you're angry.'

'Milo, I will not be condescended to.'

'I need you to trust me, Amory,' he said, his expression suddenly much more serious than it had been a moment ago. I looked into his eyes, wishing as I always did that I could tell what he was thinking.

I sighed. 'You make it very difficult.'

'I know. But I promise I shall tell you everything in good time.'

'But I . . .'

It was just then that I saw Beryl Belanger turn the corner and begin walking our way, pushing a pram.

'There she is,' I whispered, my grip tightening on his arm. 'Act naturally.'

'I always act naturally,' he said.

'Yes, you're right,' I replied. 'That's the trouble.'

I walked away from him before he could reply.

'Good afternoon, Madame Belanger,' I called.

She looked up sharply, her expression slightly wary, but she smiled when she saw that it was me. 'Oh, hello, Mrs Ames. It's good to see you again,' she said with what seemed to be sincerity.

'It's good to see you, too,' I said. 'May I introduce you to my husband, Milo?'

'How do you do?' she said. I noticed that, even newly widowed, she was not immune to the impact of Milo's good looks. I thought she flushed a little as he smiled at her.

'It was such a lovely morning, my husband and I thought that we might just take a stroll around the garden,' I told her.

'Yes, this is a lovely park,' she said. 'I come here often.' It seemed to me that she was a bit uneasy. Though she was facing me, her eyes occasionally swept the park behind me. Was she, as I had suspected, waiting for her lover? It didn't seem likely that he would approach us when we were talking to her.

'This must be your daughter,' I said, looking down at the child in the pram. The young girl was the image of her mother, but with dark hair and large, dark eyes like the Belangers.

'Yes, this is Seraphine,' she said, smiling easily for the first time.

'Hello, Seraphine,' I said.

'Hello, madame,' she replied sweetly.

'She's lovely,' I told Beryl.

'Thank you.'

'I want to walk, Maman,' the child said, raising her arms to be lifted from the pram. Beryl picked her up and set her down on the ground and Seraphine took a few steps down the path.

'Don't wander far, Seraphine,' Beryl told her, as she turned back to us. 'I do hope you're enjoying your stay in Paris.'

'Oh, yes, it has been wonderful,' I said. 'I'm very fond of Paris.' I looked at Milo with what I hoped might pass for an adoring gaze. 'We honeymooned here, so I feel rather sentimental about it.'

'Yes,' she said. 'I, too, thought it very romantic when I came here as a new bride.'

'Oh, I'm sorry,' I said. 'I hope I haven't brought up distressing memories.'

'No,' she said, smiling a bit sadly. 'I enjoy thinking of those days. I like to talk about Helios. It makes me feel close to him. I have clung to the memories these past few days.'

'How was it that you met your husband?' I enquired. I supposed it might be a bit intrusive of me to ask, but she seemed in the mood to talk about it and I was very curious to know about her relationship with her much older, wealthy husband.

'We met at the beach in Southsea,' she said. 'I lived

there, you see, and Helios was in town meeting with someone. I liked to take long walks along the shore, to think about things. One day I was walking, not paying attention where I was going, and I bumped directly into him.' She smiled a little at the recollection, and I thought again how pretty she was when the sombreness left her face. 'I might have gone on walking, but there was something about him that captured my interest. It's difficult to explain. Helios was so very alive. If you had ever met him, you would know what I meant. There was something so dazzling, so passionate about him. One had only to spend a few moments in his company to know that he was something very special.'

It was much the same that I had heard from Madame Nanette about Helios Belanger. I found myself wishing, not for the first time, that I had been able to meet him.

'He was not the type of man I expected to marry,' she said bluntly. 'As a girl one doesn't picture oneself married to a man so much older. But the more that I began to know him, the more I began to realise that he was a man with whom I could be very happy.'

I was a bit surprised to hear this. From what Madame Nanette had told us about his strong-willed, even domineering, ways, I would have thought that such a thing would not make a young woman happy.

It was almost as though she had read my mind. 'Oh, he was difficult at times,' she said, 'but there was a kindness in him that never wavered. I loved him dearly.'

It was not perhaps a declaration of passion, but I could not help but believe that there had been some sort of love between them.

'Excuse me a moment, will you, ladies?' Milo said suddenly. 'I think I've seen someone I know.'

He walked away, leaving us alone, and disappeared around a bend in the path. I didn't think it likely that he had spotted anyone. More likely he had wanted to give me time to speak to Beryl Belanger about her marriage.

Beryl watched him go. 'You'll forgive me for saying so, but I had always thought to marry someone charming and handsome like your husband. When I met Helios, however, it ceased to matter to me that he was older than I was. I suppose our romance was viewed as unusual to some, but that never bothered me. I have always found it is useless to worry about what people say, don't you think so?' It might have been a rhetorical question, but I suddenly wondered if she had seen Milo's name in the gossip columns.

'Yes,' I agreed. 'It really is useless to worry about such things.'

It seemed now that she had begun confiding in me, she was finding it difficult to stop.

'It hasn't always been easy. My . . . stepsons are difficult at times.' She flushed. 'And I think that Cecile resents me for taking her father from her. They were very close. I don't suppose it helps matters that I am a year younger than she.'

No, I thought. I didn't suppose that helped at all.

'I think she is quite lovely,' she said. 'It's just that she is so very hard to talk to. We don't have much in common at all. I'm afraid I had a rather traditional upbringing. Cecile was raised to think like a man. She doesn't enjoy any of the same things I do.'

I imagined Cecile felt much the same way. This quiet, mild-mannered woman could be of very little interest to her.

'I know she compared me to her mother. Perhaps Helios did, too. More than once he called me "Elena" by mistake. I sometimes wondered if he wished I was she.'

Beryl laughed suddenly, a bit self-consciously. 'You must forgive me for going on so. It's just lovely to speak to an Englishwoman,' she said. 'There are days when I miss speaking in my native tongue. France is a lovely country, but nothing compares to one's homeland.'

'Have you been to England recently?' I asked.

She shook her head. 'No. Helios didn't much care for England. He preferred that we remain at home. I wanted to show Seraphine my native land, of course, but he said that we would do that when she was older.'

'Well, if you are ever in London, I should love to have you for tea,' I said.

She smiled, seemingly with more gratitude than the simple invitation merited. 'I hope that I shall be able to travel to London again someday soon.'

It was then I noticed Milo was coming back in our direction and carrying Seraphine. I felt a strange little flutter in my stomach at the sight of it. In all honesty, I had long had reservations about Milo's suitability for fatherhood, but he looked quite natural with a child in his arms.

He was conversing with her in a pleasant tone, and she seemed completely absorbed in what he had to say, nodding her head and pointing to something in the distance.

'Seraphine decided to go for a walk alone,' he said when he reached us, setting her down. 'We happened to cross paths on my way back and she agreed to accompany me.'

'Thank you, Mr Ames,' said Beryl. 'I'm afraid that I was so engrossed in conversation that I wasn't paying attention.'

'Seraphine and I are quite good friends already,' Milo said.

She beamed up at him. I was not at all surprised that he had been able to charm the child. It seemed he was a favourite with women of all ages.

'Yes, well, I suppose we should be getting along now,' Beryl said. 'It's nearly time for luncheon.'

She picked up Seraphine and put her back in the pram. 'It was lovely to see you again, Mrs Ames. Perhaps our paths will cross again soon.'

Then Cecile hadn't told her that we were coming to dinner.

'As a matter of fact,' I said. 'Cecile has invited us to dine with you this evening.'

'Oh,' she said, doing a poor job of concealing her surprise. 'That will be lovely. Until tonight, then.'

She turned and walked unhurriedly away, but I almost had the feeling that she was trying desperately not to look around, as though she didn't want us to know that she was looking for someone.

I turned to Milo as we left. 'What do you think of her?' I asked.

'I don't believe for a moment that she loved him,' he said.

I couldn't entirely agree. 'She seems very much touched by his death,' I said. 'I can't help but feel that he meant something to her.'

'I'm sure he did,' Milo said, his tone holding more than a hint of sarcasm.

'What do you mean by that?' I asked.

'I mean that she seemed rather overanxious to share her feelings with you, a perfect stranger. Laying it on a bit thick, I'd say.'

It was a possibility. But it was also possible that she was what she seemed to be: a young, lonely widow without anyone in whom she could confide.

'I believe she cared for Monsieur Belanger. I'm quite sure that there is sorrow in her eyes.'

'It isn't sorrow,' Milo said. 'It's guilt.'

I was surprised by this assessment. I wanted to argue, but the more I thought about it the more I thought that he might be right.

'Don't forget she came here to meet her lover,' he added.

'So perhaps she fell into a relationship with someone and feels guilty about it. That doesn't mean she killed him,' I said. 'I don't think her as mercenary as you do. In fact, she told me that she was at first rather reluctant to marry him.'

'A lie, of course,' Milo said.

'You don't know that.'

I considered myself a very good judge of character, though, admittedly, Milo had perhaps been exposed to more of the darker side of human nature. I supposed it was possible that he could see something in Beryl Belanger that I did not.

'I don't know it,' he admitted. 'But I certainly don't believe she's all that she seems. Granted, she makes a pretty picture, all wide eyes and dimples.'

'You distrust her because of the way she looks?'

'I distrust her because of the way she uses her looks,' he corrected. 'She is very aware of her best features and knows how to use them.'

'The same may be said of you,' I replied.

He flashed a smile at me. 'Some would say I am not to be trusted either.'

I rolled my eyes. 'Besides the fact that she has dimples, what evidence is there that she and Helios Belanger were not happy in their marriage?'

'They kept separate rooms. Remember: she was not with him when he died.'

I did not remind him that there had been a time when we had kept separate rooms. Then again, perhaps that was a point in his favour as far as his argument went. Our marriage had not been in a good state at that point.

The fact remained that she was rumoured to have a lover and had been left quite a lot of money.

'There's one more thing of note,' he said.

'Oh, what's that?'

'When I said I spotted a friend, it was, in fact, a familiar face who turned and left when he rounded the corner and saw us.'

'Her lover, perhaps?' I asked. 'Who was it?'

'That's the interesting part. It was Herr Muller.'

CHAPTER SEVENTEEN

Was it possible that Beryl Belanger was having an affair with the sculptor who had been designing the perfume bottle for her husband? If so, it might be an added motive for both of them. Herr Muller had seemed quite taken with Angelique, but he had also mentioned that he had thought of sculpting Beryl. Could it be that they had formed a relationship? I had a hard time picturing the two of them in a torrid affair, but stranger things had happened.

That didn't address one aspect of the mystery, however. If they had done it, where did the missing perfume formula come into play? Had they planned the murder so they could be together and then seized the opportunity to take the formula? It seemed unlikely. The two motives just didn't fit together. There was still, I supposed, the vague possibility that the missing formula was unrelated to the murder. One thing was certain: no matter which way I turned, there were more questions than answers.

I didn't share these thoughts with Milo as we returned to the hotel. We had not had the opportunity to sort out our differences, and, though I felt we might have discovered something important on our walk in the park, I was not feeling especially communicative.

We entered the lobby and Milo stopped at the desk, and the clerk handed him a slip of paper, which he read and put in his pocket. There might have been nothing to it, but my suspicions were already aroused by his recent behaviour, and his words once we reached our room confirmed that something was afoot.

'I need to go out for a while, darling,' he said. 'Do you mind?'

'No,' I replied. 'But you do remember that Madame Nanette is coming to have tea with us.'

'I may not be back by then,' he said. 'You'll make my excuses?'

'Certainly,' I said lightly, though I was a bit surprised that he would so easily dismiss plans with Madame Nanette, given how highly he regarded her. I hoped this didn't mean he meant to neglect our other plans as well.

'You haven't forgotten that we're having dinner with the Belangers this evening?' I asked.

'Of course not,' he said. 'I am hoping that one of them will let slip that they killed their father and we can lay the thing to rest.'

I wasn't sure what had brought on this flippancy. It wasn't unlike him to be glib, of course, but I had the growing impression that he was much less concerned about the case than he had been. Whether it had to do with whatever he was hiding or if he was merely losing interest, I had yet to determine.

'What will you do until tea, darling?' he asked.

'I daresay I'll find something to amuse myself,' I replied. I felt his gaze on me and met it with a smile. After our conversation this morning, he had likely expected to encounter more resistance.

'Very well,' he said. 'I shall see you this evening.'

He left, and I wasted no time. If Milo was going to do things on his own, there was no reason that I should not. I went to the telephone and picked up the receiver.

'Can you please place a call for me? I'm trying to reach a gentleman named André Duveau.'

We met at a cafe not far from the hotel. He was waiting at a table inside when I arrived.

'I was pleased that you rang me up, Amory,' he said when we had settled into our seats. 'It is not often I have luncheon invitations from beautiful women.'

This I did not believe for a moment. I was fairly certain that André Duveau was not lacking when it came to the attentions of women.

'I'm pleased you were free,' I said. 'Milo had other business to attend to today, and I do hate to eat alone.'

He smiled. 'It is much more pleasant to eat with pleasant company.'

We ordered our meal and fell into comfortable conversation. As always, I found André to be charming company. There was something very unguarded about him, an easy friendliness that one did not often encounter. I felt as though I had known him much longer than a fortnight.

'Are you enjoying your stay in Paris?' he asked as our food arrived and we began to eat.

'Oh, yes, I'm always very happy to be here.'

'How long do you intend to stay?' I suddenly had the impression that there was a reason he was asking me these questions beyond polite interest. I realised that it was entirely possible that, given their continued friendship, Cecile Belanger had mentioned my interest in perfume to him. Did he think it suspicious, given the timing? If so, I needed to try to set his mind at rest.

'Perhaps a week or so. I have commissioned Cecile Belanger to make a custom perfume,' I said.

'Yes, she told me,' he said. So I had been correct. It seemed to me as though there was something watchful in his gaze as he looked across the table at me. I almost felt as though he was waiting for me to confess something to him.

'I suppose you think it's rather frivolous of me,' I said with what I hoped was a rueful smile.

'Not at all. I understand very well the allure of perfume.'

'I heard only recently that Cecile Belanger wears her own unique perfume, and the novelty of the idea struck me. I thought it would be wonderful to have a scent all of my own.'

'I see,' he said. I could tell that he did not believe me. I wondered if there was any way he suspected my motives. I didn't see how he could, but I could not rule out the possibility. I would have to tread carefully.

'Perhaps it was not an ideal time to approach the matter, given Monsieur Belanger's death, but I have always been one to seize opportunities.'

He smiled, leaning forward ever so slightly. 'I am also one to seize opportunities. I agree that sometimes one must strike while the iron is hot.'

'Precisely.'

'Besides,' he said. 'It will be good for Cecile to have something to focus on. She was very close to her father, and I know his death has shaken her.'

'Yes, she has spoken very fondly of him,' I said.

'He taught her well, and she will do him proud. She'll run things as well as he ever did. I've offered to fly her to Grasse to tend to things at the factory when she's ready.'

'I'm sure she will be glad to have the company.'

I wondered if I should steer the topic away from Monsieur Belanger's death. I didn't want André to think I was unduly curious. I had already asked him a great deal of questions over the course of our short acquaintance. He seemed as though he wanted to protect Cecile, and I imagined that protective instinct was what had made him wary of my enquiries.

'I just don't know that I could ever be comfortable in an aeroplane,' I said, taking a bite of my lovely bouillabaisse. 'But perhaps it takes getting used to. Have you been flying long?'

'Yes, I signed up for the war and became a pilot. It made for an eventful war. I was shot down over Germany, in fact,' he said. 'I parachuted and made it out safely, but it isn't something I would care to repeat.'

'No, I imagine not. I think it's wonderful that you continued to fly after such an experience.'

'Once flying gets in one's blood, I'm afraid there's no cure,' he said with a smile.

I laughed. 'Then I shall blame you if my husband contracts that particular disease.'

'I should hate to be in your bad graces, Amory.'

'Well, you have given me your lovely perfume, so I feel

206

as though it will be difficult for me to be angry with you for long.'

'It will be nothing compared to L'Ange de Mémoire, I'm sure.'

'Oh, I don't know,' I said. 'I think your perfume speaks of quality.'

'I hope so. Monsieur Belanger taught me quite a lot. In fact, he was annotating a book on perfumery for me. I was anxious to learn some of his techniques.'

This piqued my interest. I wondered if André was aware that Helios Belanger had been developing a new, highly secret process for L'Ange de Mémoire. I could not help but feel that André was an ideal suspect when it came to the missing formula. The fact remained, however, that he had not been in Paris the night of Monsieur Belanger's accident. It would have been impossible for him to switch the formulas in the attaché case.

'It sounds selfish, I suppose,' he said, 'but I do hope I can get the book back. I'm sure it will prove very valuable. When the time is right, I need to ask Cecile if she can locate it.'

I thought this might be as good a time as any to shift the topic towards Beryl and Herr Muller. Given his former ties to the family, it was just possible he might have some information to share.

'The L'Ange de Mémoire bottle is very lovely,' I said. 'I recently met Herr Muller. He was at a nightclub when Milo and I went to dinner, and I was able to speak with him.'

'He seems to be quite a character,' he said. 'I don't know him well, of course, but it appears to me that he thinks rather highly of his art.'

'He seemed rather taken by his model, Angelique,' I said, hoping that this might prod him to tell me more about the affairs of the Belangers.

He laughed suddenly. 'Well, I can't say I'm surprised.'

'I understand she's very beautiful.'

'Yes, among other things,' he said dryly.

'And she was Michel Belanger's mistress?' I knew that such things were not exactly polite conversation, but sometimes there was no other way to get the information one was seeking than to be blunt.

'She was something of the kind,' André said. 'Despite the fact that I was very close to Cecile, I saw little of Michel and Angelique. They preferred their company a bit livelier, I'm afraid.'

'Their romance was doomed to failure, then?'

'If you could call it a romance. They seemed to enjoy getting into public rows more than anything else. Once she threw a knife at him, so the story goes.'

'Oh dear,' I said. 'It does sound like rather a contentious relationship.'

He smiled a bit grimly. 'Michel seems to enjoy that sort of thing. He has rather a violent temper. He's constantly getting into rows. Nearly killed a man once.'

'I didn't realise,' I said.

'I'd say Angelique, troublesome though she is, was well rid of him.'

'It seems there has been a great deal of unrest in the Belanger home,' I said mildly.

'Yes. But I'm surprised your husband didn't tell you all of this,' he said.

I frowned. 'Why should Milo know about this?'

'I told him. We've spent evenings gambling together, and I'm afraid I indulged in a bit of gossip. It seems your husband isn't inclined to tell tales.'

'No,' I said as lightly as I could manage. 'I suppose it must have slipped his mind.'

So Milo had been gathering information all along and hadn't shared it with me.

André had confirmed what I already knew. First, the motives for Helios Belanger's murder were plentiful. Second, my husband was an absolute wretch.

CHAPTER EIGHTEEN

Madame Nanette arrived punctually for tea, and I showed her to the little sitting area where the hotel maid had laid things out.

'I'm afraid Milo was called away on some business,' I said as I poured the steaming liquid. 'He asked me to make his excuses.'

'We can do without him,' she said with a smile. 'To be honest, I am glad we have the opportunity to talk alone, you and I.'

'Yes, it will be nice to get to know each other better,' I said. I handed her a cup and saucer and took my own to the seat across from her. 'I'm very glad we've had the chance to visit with you, despite the circumstances.'

'So am I. I feel already as though I have learnt a great deal about you.' Her warm eyes met mine. 'You are just the type of woman I hoped Milo would marry.'

'Oh?' I asked, a bit surprised.

'Yes, I knew he would marry a beautiful woman, but I had hoped she would also be a good woman. I am pleased that you are both.'

'Thank you,' I said, touched by her words.

'I am not surprised that he also chose someone strong and intelligent with a good head on her shoulders, a woman who would challenge him; he would have tired easily of anything less.'

'What was Milo like as a child?' I asked. I wasn't sure where the question had come from, but I was suddenly very eager to know. Perhaps no one was in a better position than Madame Nanette to help me understand him.

She smiled. 'He was much as he is now – charming and full of mischief.'

I couldn't help but laugh. 'I should have known, I suppose, that he has always been that way.'

'Hold on a moment. I have something for you.' She picked up her handbag and reached inside. A moment later she pulled out a small, square leather-bound book and handed it to me.

I opened it to the first page, and my heart clenched a little at the face that looked up at me. I had never seen a photograph of Milo as a child – he had kept very few mementoes of his early life so far as I knew – but it was somehow exactly as I might have imagined he would have looked. I could see the man he had become in the child's face, the line of his jaw, the blue gaze showing pale in the sepia photograph, the glossy black hair. But it was the precocious smile that tugged at the corners of his mouth and the glint in his eyes that I recognised most clearly. For some reason I felt tears come to my eyes.

'He was an adorable child,' I said.

She nodded. 'A very handsome boy. He was smart, too, and good-natured. He developed his charm very young and always knew how to work it to the best advantage.'

I had expected no less. I had always believed Milo had been born with the knack for convincing people to do as he wished.

Madame Nanette smiled, confirming my thoughts. 'It was very difficult to refuse him anything he wanted.'

I could well imagine it.

'I kept this book of photographs and other souvenirs of his childhood,' she said. 'When I left, I brought it with me to give to him later.'

I flipped through the pages. There was a photograph of a very young Milo astride a horse, looking as though he had been born for riding. Another showed him standing in front of Thornecrest, our country house. I felt an unexpected twinge of maternal longing as I looked at them. Perhaps one day I would have my own dark-haired child standing with Milo in that very spot.

The book also contained an array of seemingly inconsequential things: pressed flowers, dried leaves, and feathers – the little things that would have been important to a young boy. There were also a few letters he had written to her, ranging from a childhood note with large, misspelled words and slanted script to a strong, confident hand he had developed as he went away to school. On the last page there was a clipping of our wedding announcement.

'It's a wonderful book,' I said. I was reluctant to hand it back to her, for I could not help feeling that some key to unlocking at least some of my husband's secrets lay in its pages.

'I'd like you to keep it,' she said. 'I was saving it for Milo.'

I was deeply touched. 'Thank you. I shall treasure it.'

'Has he ever told you how I came to be his nanny?' she asked, taking a sip of her tea.

'No,' I said. 'He hasn't told me much about his childhood.'

Milo was not the sort to indulge in nostalgia. Aside from a few fond references to Madame Nanette, I had heard very little about his life before we met.

'I was engaged by Mrs Ames before Milo was born,' she said. 'I was young, French, and inexperienced, so I did not think I had much of a chance at the position. But she took a liking to me at once. She said I had a kind face and that was what most mattered to her.'

'What was his mother like?' I asked.

'She was a beautiful woman. Black hair and the bluest eyes I had ever seen. I didn't know her long, but I was very impressed with her. She was not like many women, ready to send the child out of sight to the nursery. She was very keen to be a mother.'

I wished Milo had been able to know her.

'She sounds lovely.'

'You know that she died when he was born.'

I nodded.

'It was something of a shock to everyone. The delivery went well, but she died suddenly of a haemorrhage the following day. Mr Ames, Milo's father, was devastated. He was quite mad about his wife, and there was some worry after she died that he might do something drastic.'

This was a new piece of information. I had always wondered about Milo's father. It had been obvious in the way that Milo referenced him that they had not been close. I had attributed their lack of a good relationship to Milo's youthful wildness, but perhaps the rift ran deeper than that.

'Mr Ames had very little to do with him. Milo tried, I think, to win his father's affection at a young age, but he soon realised that it was useless. Perhaps that was when he decided to win the affection of everyone else.'

'Yes,' I said. 'Perhaps so.' I was glad that she had shared this with me. I sometimes felt as though I knew almost nothing about my husband. It was enlightening to learn something about his childhood.

'I'm glad he had you as a child,' I told her.

'I very much enjoyed raising him. He has not always behaved properly, but he was a good boy at heart. So, you see, it was lucky that things went as they did with Helios Belanger.'

I had wondered about the details of her relationship with Helios Belanger, and now that she had brought it up, I felt that I could ask.

'What happened with you and Monsieur Belanger?'

She let out a soft breath that might have been a sigh. 'It is hard to say, I suppose. We were very young. One feels so sure of one's feelings at that age. With youth there is a feeling of invincibility. It is only when you get older that you begin to realise that life is not always going to be the way you expect it to be.'

'You grew apart?' I asked.

'Not exactly that,' she said. 'Helios had begun to excel at his amateur perfumery. The apothecary for whom he worked saw his potential and began to send Helios to gather ingredients, first throughout France, then across Europe, then farther. Before long, Helios was travelling the world. Still, I thought our love would last. He sent me letters frequently and brought me back gifts from strange and exotic places.'

'Did you ever talk about marriage?' I asked.

'Not in so many words. Of course, a young woman always thinks of such things. It was after one trip, however, that everything changed. He came home and told me that we could no longer be together, that our lives were taking us on different paths.'

'You had no inkling that he was thinking such things?'

'No, I thought . . . well, I thought wrong. I didn't ask questions. If he wanted his freedom, I would let him have it. And so I wished him well and went on my way.'

'And you hadn't spoken to him in all these years?'

She shook her head. 'He had moved on with his life, and I had moved on with mine. There was no reason for us to speak.'

'Why do you think it was that he asked you to come and look after his child?'

'I have considered that,' she said. 'His letter was formal, polite. He gave no particular reason for his request. As I said, I had recently left a post, and, of course, I was curious about what had become of Helios. I saw no reason to refuse the opportunity.'

'Did you never discuss the past?' I asked.

She hesitated. I realised that it was a personal question, but I was very curious to know the answer.

'We did. Only once. It was late one evening not long ago. I had put Seraphine to bed and was passing along the corridor when he came up the stairs. 'Good evening, monsieur,' I said, thinking to say no more. But he put his hand on my arm. He looked at me strangely, and suddenly

I felt that all the years had slipped away and I was looking at him as he was then. "I hope you are happy, Nanette," he said. "I cared greatly for you."'

I felt as though I was holding my breath, waiting for her to go on, but she merely shrugged. 'I said, "Thank you." And then it seemed as though he came to himself and he dropped his hand from my arm and went along without another word.'

'What did you do?' I asked.

'Nothing. I didn't really know what to make of it. Within the month he was dead. I wish, in a way, that I had said something in return.'

She shifted the conversation then and we talked of other things, but I felt the shadow of it remained. Though she was not the type of woman who would want sympathy, I couldn't help but feel a bit sorry for her. To lose love once was a difficult thing; she had loved and lost the same man twice.

After Madame Nanette had gone, I sat contemplating the details of the case. It seemed as though the mystery of Helios Belanger's death was constantly revealing new facets, and it was difficult to make sense of the resulting shape of things.

I was roused from my reverie by a good deal of chattering coming from Emile's cage. I went to open the door and he leapt at once into my arms. I was a bit startled as he climbed to my shoulder, but he made several amiable noises and gently patted my hair.

'You're a good little fellow, aren't you?' I said.

He seemed to agree with me.

I took him to the sofa, and was feeding him bits of apple when Winnelda came in to help me dress for dinner.

'Oh, you've taken him out!' she cried excitedly. She moved to the sitting area and absently picked up the leather memory book that Madame Nanette had given me from the chair, before taking a seat there.

Emile chattered loudly and, jumping into Winnelda's lap, took the book from her and brought it back to me.

'I beg your pardon,' Winnelda said with every appearance of sincerity. 'I didn't mean to take what didn't belong to me.'

I supposed it was one of the monkey's quirks. I had heard of such animals being trained as pickpockets, but it seemed that mine was extraordinarily conscious of the personal belongings of others.

For the next several minutes Emile entertained us with his repertoire of tricks, the pièce de résistance of which was a backward flip from the arm of the sofa to the floor. That seemed a good time to return him to his cage, and I began to prepare for dinner.

It was getting quite late, and there was no sign of Milo. He had been gone for the better part of the day, doing heaven knows what, and I was growing increasingly cross with him. Not just for today, but for his behaviour over the course of our stay in Paris.

I was sitting at my dressing table in my slip, Winnelda smoothing out the waves in my hair, when I at last heard him come in.

I didn't look away from the mirror as he came into the bedroom. 'Hello, darling,' he said.

'So you've seen fit to come back, have you?' I replied.

'I told you I wouldn't miss dinner.'

'You've told me things you didn't mean before.' Try as I might, I could not keep my anger at bay. I felt very much as though I wanted to quarrel with him, but if we were to have a successful evening, now was not the time.

'You're annoyed with me,' he said.

'How astute you are, Milo,' I replied, spraying on a cloud of my new Bouquet de Belanger perfume. 'Perhaps you should be a detective.'

Winnelda gave my hair a final brush and stepped back. 'Will that do, madam?' she asked.

'Yes, Winnelda, thank you,' I said.

She went over to the bed where my new black evening gown was laid out for the evening. Her eyes darted to the doorway as Milo came farther into the room.

'A night at the Belangers' should prove interesting,' Milo said.

'Do you think so?' I rose from the dressing table, turning to face him. 'I'm sure it will prove rather dull in comparison to the evenings you've been having.'

From the corner of my eye I saw Winnelda shifting uneasily. No doubt she was beginning to become uncomfortable. The poor girl had not been trained as a lady's maid, and she had not yet mastered the art of feigning deafness in the face of connubial quarrels.

'I'll put that on now,' I told her.

She brought the gown over to me and helped to slip it over my head, careful to avoid mussing my hair.

'You will be interested to learn where I've been,' Milo said.

'I doubt it,' I replied as the gown fell into place. 'If I had to guess, I'd say it involved gambling or horses. Or perhaps a woman. None of which you need any more of.'

'You are feeling rather prickly this evening, aren't you?'

Winnelda's face had grown pink, and she was practically jostling me in her haste to finish doing up my gown and excuse herself. 'I can take care of this, Winnelda,' I said. 'You may go.'

'Thank you, madam,' she said with great feeling. She bobbed a little curtsey and hurried from the room.

'Now you've frightened her off,' Milo said. 'Whatever's the matter with you?'

I drew in a breath. 'I am annoyed, Milo. While I've been trying to help Madame Nanette, you've been running all over Paris doing . . .' I waved a hand impatiently, 'whatever it is you've been doing.'

I turned and went to my jewellery case, picking up a necklace of diamonds and onyx on a silver chain.

'For the record, I've gained neither money, horses, nor additional women this afternoon. I've been out to the airfield.'

I stopped, the necklace dangling from my hand, and turned to look at him. 'The airfield?'

'Yes. I went to talk to the men who were there when Helios Belanger crashed his plane.'

I sighed. 'Why didn't you tell me?'

'I wasn't sure anything would come of it.'

'Well, did it?'

'I'm not entirely sure,' he said. 'The mechanic at the airfield assures me that there was nothing mechanically wrong with that plane.'

'Of course they would say that,' I said.

Milo nodded as he came up to me and turned me around so he could finish fastening up my dress. 'They won't, of course, want an aeroplane accident laid at their feet. But assuming they are correct, that means that there are two other options: weather and pilot error.'

'What was the weather like that night?' I asked, holding up the ends of my necklace so he could fasten it.

'Cold and clear,' Milo said.

'Then it seems it must have been something to do with Monsieur Belanger's condition.'

'Yes. They also assured me, however, that there was nothing wrong with Monsieur Belanger when he arrived at the airfield. He seemed much the same as usual. It was only after he had crash-landed that he seemed somewhat dazed.'

I frowned. 'How can that be? If he was poisoned at home, wouldn't the symptoms have been evident sooner?'

'It seems likely that they would have,' Milo agreed.

'What if it was a heart attack?' I said suddenly, turning to face him again. 'What if he wasn't murdered at all, and this is all a wild-goose chase?'

'I had the same thought,' he said.

Somehow I knew that there was something else, something he hadn't told me. 'But what?' I asked. 'There's more, isn't there?'

He went on with what seemed to be a bit of reluctance. 'It seems that after Helios had crashed his plane, they all ran to help him. The young man I spoke with was the first to get to the plane and as he helped Helios out of the wreckage, he said something rather curious to him. He said, "Can't let them end me. I must remember to see to the will."'

I gasped. 'He knew that someone was trying to kill him. Who do you suppose he meant?'

'I'm afraid I couldn't venture a guess,' Milo replied, with much less enthusiasm than I would have demonstrated upon presenting such a startling piece of information.

'If he wanted to instate the new will, he must have known who his killer was and wanted to stop them before he was killed.'

'Don't get carried away, darling,' Milo said. 'It might only have been that he felt he was near death and wanted to be sure his affairs were in order.'

'Oh, you don't believe that for a moment, so do stop trying to convince me otherwise,' I said impatiently.

'I don't know what to believe,' he said. 'But I'd rather not make outlandish suppositions without proof.'

I ignored him as I considered the implications. It seemed fairly clear that Helios Belanger had suspected that someone was trying to kill him, thus his desire to change the will. But how was this related to the missing formula? Had someone attempted to steal the formula and kill Helios Belanger in his plane? Perhaps he had uncovered the treachery and that was why he had wanted to change his will. He had not had the time to do so, but perhaps he had even challenged the person, prodding them to try again. And this time they had succeeded.

'That second draft of the will must reveal who he trusted and who he didn't,' I said.

'Perhaps, darling,' he replied, turning towards the bathroom to wash up before dressing, 'but I'm afraid we may never know.'

That was what he thought. If I had anything to do with

it, I was going to get a look at that copy of the will. Madame Nanette had mentioned that Anton said the draft was in his father's desk drawer. I knew what that meant, of course: I was going to have to find a way to get into Anton Belanger's office.

CHAPTER NINETEEN

We arrived back at the Belanger mansion and were shown into the drawing room. It had seemed a large room at the party, but it looked so much larger tonight, with only a few people in it. In fact, the only occupants now were Cecile and Anton Belanger. They stood near the window, speaking in low, urgent tones, their expressions dark. It looked as though they were having an argument.

I wondered if it had to do with their joint involvement in Parfumes Belanger. Even having known them a short time, I knew that it was not going to be easy for the two of them to find a way to work together.

With all that had happened, I imagined that the family was not thrilled to have us here tonight. After the death of their patriarch and the startling revelations of the will, I supposed the last thing they wanted to do was make pleasant small talk with strangers. Perhaps this was the source of their tense exchange.

Before I could catch anything of what they were saying, however, Cecile noticed us and stepped away from her brother.

'Ah, Monsieur and Madame Ames. Good evening.'

She came towards us with a smile. She was wearing a long-sleeved dress of dark grey silk, and once again I admired the simplicity and elegance of her attire. I was learning that, though her clothes were very much in fashion, she was not particularly drawn to the trends. It was as though her elegance had a quality of timelessness.

I was glad I had worn my new black gown, for it, too, was understated and chic.

'I am so glad you've come,' she said.

'Thank you for having us.'

'You've met my brother Anton,' she said to me.

'Yes, good evening,' I said.

'And this is Monsieur Ames. Monsieur Ames, my brother.' Anton Belanger nodded somewhat stiffly at us and managed a brusque 'Good evening.'

I tried in vain to determine who it was that he reminded me of. There was something forbidding about him. His dark, watchful eyes moved restlessly around the room, as though he could think of a dozen places he would rather be.

Cecile had realised, it seemed, that her brother did not intend to be sociable, for she led us away from him and towards a grouping of furniture before the fire.

'Won't you sit down? The others should be here shortly. At least . . . Beryl should be.' She smiled a bit humourlessly. 'My brother Michel may or may not join us.'

I found myself hoping that he would. I was curious about Michel Belanger. I thought there was a very good chance he might reveal something worthwhile about the family. Both Anton and Cecile were careful in all that they said and did.

I did not think Michel would have that same reserve.

A few moments later Beryl Belanger came into the room to greet us. She looked a bit better than the last few times I had seen her, not quite as pale and strained. She greeted Cecile with a hesitant smile. 'Good evening.'

'Good evening, Beryl,' Cecile said without any particular warmth. 'Monsieur and Madame Ames have come for dinner.'

'Yes, I knew they were coming. I encountered them in the park only this morning.'

'Did you?' Cecile said.

'Perhaps we English are drawn to one another,' Beryl said.

'What part of England do you hail from, Madame Belanger?' Milo asked.

'I come from Southsea,' she said.

'I have never been there, but I am sure it must be a charming place if it is your home.'

She smiled up at him, the dimples in her cheeks making an appearance.

'I have always found it a lovely place,' she said and, for just a moment, the cares that had shown in her eyes faded away. Milo had, with his unerring instinct, found just the way to put her at ease.

'Beryl has been planning a trip home to visit her relations. She will be leaving soon.' I looked up, surprised that Anton had deigned to join our conversation.

I glanced at Beryl to see what her reaction to Anton's announcement would be. She looked a bit uncomfortable, and I wondered if it had come as a surprise that her stepson meant to send her back to her home. Perhaps he meant her stay in England to be indefinite. I had no doubt it would be easier for Anton and Cecile if their stepmother was no longer living with them.

'Dinner will be ready soon,' Cecile said, breaking into the conversation. 'Madame Ames, would you like to come to the table in the corner for a moment? I have a few scents I would like you to smell.'

'Certainly.'

I followed her to a table in the corner where she had arranged three small wooden racks that held an assortment of glass vials. I saw that each row of vials was labelled according to scent type. Soliflores, bouquet, fougère, chypre, and several others. There were dozens of scents in each rack, a whole world of scents at our fingertips.

'What sort of scents do you enjoy?' she asked.

'I normally wear gardenia,' I said. She chose the vial from the soliflores and unstopped it, handing it to me.

'What is it about that scent that you enjoy?' She was waiting for my answer with a rather intent look on her face, and I realised that the question was a significant one.

I had to think about it for a moment. 'I like the sweetness of it, I suppose.' I remembered something else, a more personal reason for my preference, and I decided to tell her. 'It also reminds me of my courtship with my husband. The first time we were alone together, it was in a conservatory. I remember it smelt of gardenia.' I hadn't thought about that in years, hadn't realised that it was perhaps why I had selected the scent.

'Then you enjoy scents with a more personal connection.'

'Yes, I suppose I do.'

'Then perhaps we shall include it in your custom scent,'

she said. 'It is not at all scientific, but I have always felt that a scent is enhanced by the preferences of its wearer. It is as though their love for it interacts with the oils to make the scent something greater than itself.

'Now, if you'll smell these and let me know your impressions of them.' One by one, she selected and unstopped several vials and held them up for me to sample. Pausing occasionally to 'let my nose rest', as she called it, she asked me a series of questions about the scents, my preferences, even certain traits of my personality. I felt rather as though I were taking some sort of test for which I had not studied, but I could not help but enjoy the process as each new scent was unveiled to me and I was forced to consider what I felt about it. My selection of perfumes had always been in an offhanded manner based on superficial preference. I had not realised the depth of the art.

'I know it must seem as though I'm asking a great deal of personal questions,' she said, 'but it's necessary in order to determine which scent will suit you best.'

'I understand,' I said. 'I appreciate that you are willing to take the time to make the perfume such a personal reflection of me.'

'To me it is more than a business,' she said. 'And if we intend to attach the name of Belanger to what we create, I want to make sure that it is a quality scent.'

'I'm sure it will be lovely,' I said.

A movement at the door caught my eye just then, and Michel Belanger came into the room. His expression was one of boredom as his gaze scanned the room, but suddenly his eyes widened.

'Madame!' he said, coming directly to my side and

holding out his hand. I placed my hand in his, and he clutched it. 'I have been wondering if ever I would see you again, and here you are. It must be fate, don't you agree?'

'I'm not entirely sure,' I said, a bit surprised by this rather enthusiastic greeting.

'I searched for you at the party, but you had disappeared. Like the Cinderella of the story, only I had not even a shoe to know you by.'

'I see you have already met my brother,' Cecile said, her tone dry.

'Yes. How are you, Monsieur Belanger?' I asked, deciding I was more amused than startled by his rather forward manner. 'I hope that the friend you had mistaken me for was able to console you.'

'Alas, I could not find her either. We were like the ships that passed in the night.'

'How very tragic,' I said.

'Hello, Michel.' Milo appeared suddenly at my side, his arm sliding around my waist in a show of possessiveness that was uncharacteristic of him.

Michel's eyes moved from me to Milo and back again, his brows rising in mock dismay. 'Do not tell me that Milo Ames is your husband.'

'Yes, he is,' I said.

Michel turned to Milo. 'You break my heart, my friend. I had hoped to find her married to an old man and in need of more youthful company.'

'I'm not that old yet,' Milo said. 'Allow me to express my condolences upon the death of your father.'

Michel appeared completely unabashed by this not-so-subtle reminder of his recent bereavement. 'Thank you. It was sudden,

228

but my father would have preferred it to some lingering illness.'

His gaze returned to me. 'Husbands have never been an obstacle to me, but I very much feel that my old friend is more competition than I am used to.'

I smiled in the face of this rather forward remark. 'You should be warned, Monsieur Belanger: I take marriage very seriously.'

His smiled broadened. 'Charming. So very charming. You are a lucky man, Ames.'

'Yes, I know,' Milo replied.

Michel reached out to take my hand again. 'Should he ever neglect you, know that I am waiting in the wings.'

I laughed. 'I shall keep that in mind.'

'Michel, do stop annoying Madame Ames,' Cecile said. There was affection in her tone, and I could tell at once that her relationship with her younger brother was much less strained than with the elder.

'You did not tell me we were having such charming guests tonight, Cecile,' he said. 'I might have gone out and missed them entirely.'

'That would have been a pity,' Milo said with a complete lack of sincerity.

We were called into dinner then, and I found myself seated between Anton and Cecile. I decided to try my hand at making a friend of the impassive elder Belanger brother.

'It was so kind of you and your sister to invite us to dinner,' I said as the first course was serviced.

'Cecile enjoys having company,' he said, his eyes on his plate.

'Your brother and my husband are old friends, it seems,'

I said. 'Have you and my husband met before this?'

'No,' he said somewhat tersely. 'Michel and I do not keep the same sort of company.'

It seemed that he wasn't in the mood for pleasantries, but I was undaunted.

'I am so enjoying learning about perfume,' I tried again. 'One rather takes things for granted sometimes, not stopping to think where they come from. It is thrilling to see how the process works.'

'Yes,' he said. 'I suppose that it is.'

It was perfectly obvious that he didn't wish to have a conversation with me, and this made me more determined than ever to win him over. I would just have to take a note from Milo's book and try to charm him.

'I am so pleased that you and your sister agreed to create a custom perfume for me,' I said, deciding to try flattery first. 'I am simply thrilled to be able to wear my very own Belanger scent to events in London. My friends will all be terribly envious.'

'I am sure you will enjoy it,' he said blandly. I could tell at once that this was not the method to win his friendship. He cared very little for society women and their vanities. I wondered, then, what it was that moved him.

Despite what others had said about Anton's being primarily interested in business, I thought that there was more to him than that. I felt as though there were things to be learnt about him if only one had the opportunity to break beneath the hard exterior.

'Have you always been interested in the perfume industry, Monsieur Belanger?'

He looked as though he didn't want to answer the

question, but he did. 'I have not my father's flair for it, perhaps, but I do enjoy the idea of it, the way something lasting may be made from something fleeting.' This bit of insight surprised me. It was a good reminder that outward indifference did not always indicate lack of feeling.

'That's very true,' I said. 'When it's cold and grey one may long for roses, and with perfume you have them at your fingertips.'

He offered me a small smile, the first I had seen on his lips that evening, and I could not help but feel that I was making progress.

'It is exactly that,' he said. 'I like the essence of the thing. That is why I have always enjoyed the soliflores, the purity of a single scent. My father, Cecile, they revelled in making combinations, but for me the true nature of the thing is always preferable. Of course, one must give the people what they want. My father was renowned for the clever combinations of scents that he created. Parfumes Belanger will strive to live up to that reputation, even now that he is gone.'

'Your sister seems to have your father's knack for perfumery,' I said. I wondered if this might be the wrong way to go about earning his friendship, but I was also curious what his reaction would be. To my surprise, he did not seem much annoyed by my statement. Instead, he nodded.

'Cecile has always been much like our father in many ways. Sometimes too much like him.'

'Oh?' I asked, very curious as to what this might mean.

'Certain traits are not attractive, in men or in women.' To my disappointment, he did not elaborate. Instead he went back to the subject of perfume. 'I have long been considering launching a new line of soliflores, made of rare and expensive ingredients. For discerning clients, such as yourself.'

'That sounds like it has the makings of a successful venture,' I said encouragingly, hoping he would continue.

'My father did not think so,' he said flatly. 'However, it may be something that I will still consider pursuing. Of course, we will continue on in my father's legacy. We mustn't disappoint the masses.'

There was the faintest tinge of disdain in his manner, and I was surprised. Anton was, of all the Belangers, the one who I would have least expected to look down upon the customers who had made Parfumes Belanger a household name.

'I don't mind giving them what they want, of course,' he said, 'but it has always seemed to me that they are terribly easy to influence. Once a name has been established, they will accept almost anything.' His eyes met mine, curiously intent. 'Don't you find this to be true?'

I wondered if this little speech had anything to do with the missing formula. Was he trying to convince himself that he could fool consumers with an imitation perfume should he be unable to produce L'Ange de Mémoire?

'Well, I don't know,' I answered slowly. I was not certain I agreed with him on this score. There were many scents I was sure I would not enjoy, just as some of the more outlandish modern fashions would never be my taste. 'I suppose it is a matter of individual preference.'

'As you say.' He shrugged. '"To each his own," as the saying goes.'

'What of your brother?' I asked. 'Do you suppose he may ever be interested in the perfume business?'

His gaze moved to Michel, but he lifted his glass to his lips and took a drink before he answered. 'I don't suppose my brother will ever be interested in anything really worthwhile.'

'Oh, one never can tell about people,' I said.

He looked back at me. 'No,' he said. 'Perhaps not.'

It had meant to be an encouraging thought, but I found it rather disheartening at the moment. It seemed that the better I got to know the suspects, the more difficult it was to determine which of them might be guilty.

When dinner was over, I would have to set my plan into motion.

CHAPTER TWENTY

The rest of dinner was rather uneventful. After my conversation with Anton, Cecile had once again engaged me in conversation about perfume and it had lasted for the remainder of the meal. I found myself swept away by her enthusiasm and her vast knowledge of the subject.

Afterwards, we had returned to the drawing room for coffee. I was seated near the fire with Cecile, plotting a way to get into Monsieur Belanger's study, when Michel came up.

'Cecile, do let me steal her away for a few moments,' he said. 'You've monopolised her all evening.'

'You will behave yourself, Michel.'

'Of course.'

Cecile rose, turning to me. 'If he makes a nuisance of himself, you've only to shoo him away.'

I smiled. 'I don't think that will be necessary.'

Cecile went away to talk to Milo and Beryl, and Michel took a seat on the divan next to me. 'I'm sorry if I have been too intrusive, Madame Ames. It is only that I thought perhaps you needed rescuing from Cecile's lectures. She has a head for perfume and little else, my sister,' Michel said with a smile.

'Are you at all interested in perfumes, Monsieur Belanger?' I asked.

He smiled. 'Only in the way they smell on a woman's skin.' I wondered if he ever allowed himself to drop the guise of seducer. Surely there was more to him than that.

'Then you don't have much interest in Parfumes Belanger and the development of its perfumes?' While I didn't think he would let anything slip if he was responsible for stealing the perfume formula, I hoped I might be able to detect some hint of guilt in him.

'I'll admit that it has never much been my forte,' he said. 'I am not what you might call scientifically minded.'

Somehow this didn't surprise me.

'Oh, it isn't that I didn't attempt it. I knew from a young age that his perfumes meant more to my father than anything else. Cecile knew it, too. Even from the time she was a child, she did nothing but follow my father about. He shared all his secrets with her. It made me envious, so I tried to follow her lead.'

'And did you learn your father's secrets?' I asked with a smile.

'Some of them,' he said. 'But the love of perfume was not something that I inherited. I much prefer the love of women.'

So we were back to that again. I might as well use the subject to my advantage.

'I have heard a good many things about Angelique,' I said. 'I believe she was a special friend of yours?'

I had meant to throw him off guard, but I did not succeed. Instead, his smile widened. 'There are a great many things to tell about her,' he said. 'She is a fascinating woman.'

'But not fascinating enough to hold your interest?' I asked, brows raised. I wanted to know what it was that had really driven them apart. Somehow I didn't think that Helios Belanger's disapproval would have bothered Michel.

'We, both of us, found that our attention wandered.'

'I wondered if perhaps she had taken a fancy to Jens Muller,' I said.

Michel threw his head back and laughed boisterously. 'That sculptor? No, no. Angelique cared nothing for him. He was obsessed with her, but he would not have been the first man to feel that way.'

'Yourself included.'

He shrugged, his eyes alight with amusement, and his hand moved to my knee. 'I find that I fall in love quite easily.'

I picked it up and set it aside, smiling coolly. 'And you fall out of it just as easily, I imagine.'

Michel laughed. 'I like you very much, Madame Ames. May I call you Amory? It is a lovely name, very like our word for "love", is it not?'

'Michel.' It was Anton. He had come up and was frowning down at Michel. It seemed that he disapproved of his brother's frivolity.

'Yes, Anton?' he replied.

When Michel looked at his brother, his smile remained intact, but there was a difference in his eyes that might not have been noticeable if one wasn't paying attention. Suddenly

236

I understood something. There was a deceptive carelessness about him. No matter what he was feeling, he would always appear perfectly at ease and unmoved by emotion. It was a quality I recognised, for Milo was the same way.

I thought of the rumours I had heard of his violent temper, a trait that had not seemed to fit with his carefree personality. Now I wondered if I had underestimated him. I suspected there was much more to Michel Belanger than met the eye.

'I need to speak to you a moment.' Anton turned to me. 'You will excuse us, Madame Ames?'

'Of course. In fact, I think I shall just go and powder my nose.'

If I was going to try to get into Anton's office, now would be the ideal time. I was very much hoping that he didn't keep it locked.

I turned back to see if anyone would notice I had slipped away. Milo was still engaged in conversation with Beryl Belanger and Cecile. Anton was speaking earnestly about something to Michel, who only seemed to be half listening. Michel had that same vague expression on his face, but his gaze was watchful. He was paying close attention to everyone who was in the room. It was almost as though he, too, was waiting for the chance to escape.

I left before his eyes came back to mine.

I was alone in the hallway and walked quickly towards the door that I knew led to Anton's office. I tried it and, as I had feared, it was locked. That meant that I would need to try the door that led out onto the garden, the one where Anton and Cecile had spoken on the night of the party.

I tried the next door down the corridor and found it

unlocked. I stepped into the room, hoping it would have a door to the courtyard. There were heavy curtains drawn across the windows and the room was dark. I moved through it, feeling for furniture and hoping that I wouldn't knock anything over.

It was imperative that I hurry before I was missed.

I reached the curtains and pulled them aside, relieved to find that these, too, were doors leading out into the courtyard. I opened them and slipped out into the cool, fragrant night air.

The door to Anton Belanger's office was the next one over, and I tried it. I half expected it to be locked and was relieved to find that it was open.

With a furtive glance over my shoulder, as though some unseen presence might be lurking in the courtyard, I slipped inside and shut the door behind me.

The curtains were drawn here, too, and I didn't know how I was going to be able to find anything in the dark. Nevertheless, I thought it probably too risky to turn on the lamp. The light might shine beneath the door and into the hallway, calling attention to what I was doing.

I pulled back one of the drapes slightly to let in the moonlight. It wasn't much, but it might be enough for me to see what I was looking for.

There was a vast desk of dark wood not far from the window, and I moved to it. I tried the first drawer and found it unlocked. I pulled it open and discovered that it held a leather case full of paper. I opened it, squinting, and found that it was a thick stack of legal documents. It was rather difficult to tell, but I didn't think it was anything of importance.

It was then I realised what a daunting task this was. The desk might be full of papers, and my time was very limited.

I opened another drawer and found it full of empty perfume bottles of different designs. Prototypes, perhaps. They rattled slightly as I pulled the drawer open, and I held my breath, the sound terribly loud in this quiet room.

The next drawer contained only a piece of paper folded in half. I opened it and saw it had been written by hand, not a typewriter. I read the first line, which translated from French to something very like the opening lines of an English will. 'I, Helios Belanger, being of sound mind, declare this to be my last will and testament.'

Against all odds, I had found it. I was just about to read further, when I heard the unmistakable sound of the door knob turning. My heart froze in my chest, and then I realised that I had to move quickly. I closed the drawers as quietly as possible and turned back towards the window.

The door to the office opened just as I slid behind the curtain, and there was not time for me to go back out into the courtyard without being heard. I would have to wait it out. It was only then I realised that I still had the will in my hand.

I waited for a lamp to be lit, but there was only the scrape of a match. A pale orange light shone in the room, and I hazarded a glance around the edge of the curtain. I was surprised to see Michel Belanger.

He was standing before a painting on the wall. In the dim light cast by the match, I saw that it was a portrait of a woman. There was something a bit familiar about the shape of her face, and I realised that she resembled all of the Belanger siblings. No doubt it was their mother.

Surely, however, he had not sneaked into this room to gaze at the portrait of his dead mother. What was he doing here? How had he entered the room when the door was locked? He must have a key. I wondered if Anton knew his brother had access to this room. What was more, I wondered if Helios Belanger had known. Of course, with the door to the courtyard left unlocked, anyone might enter this room. I had proven that. Perhaps nothing of importance was left out in the open.

The match burnt down and he shook it out. A moment later, I heard the scrape of a second one being lit, and I peeked around the curtain again. He was reaching up to touch the portrait. I thought for a moment that he might be reaching up to caress the image of his mother's face, and I felt embarrassed that I was witnessing such an intimate moment of sentimentality.

Then I heard the faintest click as his fingers pressed a place on the frame and the portrait moved on hinges away from the wall. He was looking for the safe.

The second match died away, and he lit a third. He moved faster now, with more purpose. Holding the flame high, he reached into his pocket and removed a second key. I heard the safe's lock release and then he stepped behind the barrier made by the painting, and I could no longer see what he was doing.

How was it that he had a key to the safe? Madame Nanette had mentioned that only the solicitor and Monsieur Belanger had had keys. If that was the case, it seemed that Michel must be in possession of his father's missing key. That meant he might have taken the copy of the perfume formula from the safe before the solicitor arrived.

His mother seemed to look disapprovingly at me from her portrait, but I ignored her. I wanted to see what he was doing in the safe.

A moment later, he slipped something into his pocket. It wasn't a piece of paper, and so far as I knew, there had been only one other item of importance in the safe: the mysterious key that had been present when the solicitor had come to read the will.

He closed the safe and I moved back behind the curtain. I heard the click of the portrait as it swung back into place.

The room went dark again as his match went out, and I heard him move to the door, open it, and a moment later slip out into the hallway.

I stood in the quiet darkness for a moment to be sure he wouldn't come back, my mind racing. The evidence was piling up against Michel. After all, if he alone had access to the safe, it seemed certain that he had stolen the formula. But why steal the formula from the safe only to come back later to take the key? It didn't make sense. I had been confident that once we discovered who had access to the safe we would have our killer. Now I was less convinced. There was something else going on here, and I needed to discover what it was.

I moved quickly out the doors back into the courtyard. Only then did I remember I still held the will in my hand. I considered replacing it in the drawer, but I needed a better look at it. So I folded it into a small square and slipped it into my décolletage. I started towards the door from which I had entered the courtyard, greatly relieved that I had not been caught. Or so I thought.

I rounded a bush and walked directly into a dark figure.

I only barely kept from exclaiming aloud. 'Oh, excuse me,' I began. 'I . . .'

'What are you doing?' Milo asked in a low voice.

I was both relieved and somewhat irritated to realise it was him. It seemed he was always popping up when I had been doing something I oughtn't. 'I . . . I just needed some air.'

'Liar,' he said. 'You've been up to something.'

'I'll tell you about it later,' I said, starting to move past him. 'We'd better get back inside.'

He reached out an arm to stop me, pulling me against him. 'I think we have a moment to spare.'

I thought he might intend to press me further on what I had been doing, but it seemed that was not what was on his mind. 'I've been wanting to be alone with you all evening,' he said. 'I am very much looking forward to getting you back to the hotel.'

'Milo . . .'

'Someone's coming,' he said in a low voice. He lowered his head and kissed me then, and, despite being attuned for approaching footsteps, I allowed myself to be caught up in his embrace.

At last I pulled away, breathless. 'We've got to go back in,' I said. 'They'll wonder where we've gone.'

'I would not wonder,' Michel Belanger said, stepping around the path, a cigarette in his hand. 'Were I your husband, I should make use of every opportunity to be alone with you. Forgive my intrusion, but Cecile sent me out to see what had become of you.'

Milo smiled, his arms still around me. 'My wife wanted a bit of air.'

'And you wanted a bit of her. Perfectly understandable.'

I stepped back out of Milo's embrace. 'It was very ill-mannered of us. Let's go back at once.'

Before either of the gentlemen could say another word, I turned and hurried back to the doors leading to the drawing room. Under other circumstances, I might have been incredibly embarrassed to have been caught kissing my husband at a social engagement. As it was, I felt relieved that Michel Belanger had not caught me in a much more compromising position: behind the curtains in his father's office.

'I'm so sorry,' I said, as I entered the drawing room. 'I went to powder my nose and then I suddenly felt very warm and wandered out into the courtyard for some air. Please forgive my rudeness.'

I thought Anton was looking at me rather searchingly, but Cecile waved away my apology. 'There is something very enchanting about the garden at night.'

'Very enchanting, indeed,' Michel said with a knowing smile. 'Alas, my dear friends, I'm afraid I must be off. I have a pressing engagement later this evening.'

I heard a faint scoffing sound come from Anton's direction. 'Something very important, no doubt,' he said.

Michel smiled. 'I'm afraid so.'

'I'm afraid we must be going as well,' I said. Milo glanced at me as though wondering what had brought about this sudden decision, but I didn't meet his gaze. There would be time to tell him later.

'I want to thank you so much for having us. It was a lovely evening.'

'I am glad you could come,' Cecile said. 'We will meet again to discuss the next stage of the perfume?'

'Yes, that would be very nice.'

We went about collecting our things and making our goodbyes. I was worried that Michel would leave before we got the chance to follow him out, but it appeared that he meant to walk out with us. That was lucky, for I meant to follow him.

CHAPTER TWENTY-ONE

We left the house together, and Michel Belanger turned to me, taking my hand in his. 'I am so pleased to have met you again tonight, Madame Ames.'

'It was nice to see you, Monsieur Belanger.'

'We shall meet again soon, I trust.' It was not a question, so I did not answer it.

'Good to see you, too, Ames,' he said, turning to Milo.

'Good evening, Michel,' Milo replied.

With that, Michel Belanger took his leave and began walking down the street. I wondered if he meant to take a cab and why he had not made use of one of his own cars. Perhaps he did not want anyone to know where he was going.

We got into our cab and I leant forward. 'We need you to follow that man,' I said to the driver.

If the driver thought this request was unusual, he gave no sign of it. 'Yes, madame,' he said. 'If he means to get a cab, he will likely walk to the boulevard. I will drive past him so that he will not suspect us.'

It appeared it was not the first time our driver had engaged in such activity, and I didn't know whether to be pleased or slightly alarmed.

He pulled away from the curb, and we passed Michel, who was walking at a steady pace. He didn't look at us.

'Darling,' Milo said, leaning back in his seat and lighting a cigarette. 'I hesitate to ask, but why are we following Michel Belanger?'

'He took the key from the safe in Helios Belanger's study.'

'How do you know?' Milo pressed.

'I . . . saw him,' I said, trying my best to evade the question. For all his reckless behaviour, Milo was terribly conventional when it came to my doing reckless things myself. It was most annoying.

'What were you doing in Helios Belanger's study?' Milo asked.

'I wish you wouldn't ask so many questions,' I said impatiently.

'Yes, I'm quite sure you do,' Milo replied easily. 'Alas, my curiosity will not be suppressed. What were you doing there?'

'That's not important now.'

'Amory.'

I sighed. It appeared he expected an answer. 'I was looking for the draft of the will that Anton Belanger said his father had written before his death, the one that supposedly gave Anton complete control of Parfumes Belanger. After what you told me that Helios Belanger said when he crashed his plane, I was sure that it must hold some hint of who might be responsible for his death. While

I was in the room, however, Michel Belanger came in and took a key from the safe.'

'Ignoring, for a moment, your imprudent behaviour, how do you know that he intends to use the key tonight?'

'It's bound to be missed. He'll have to use it and put it back before Anton realises that it's gone.'

Talking of things that were bound to be missed, it was then I remembered that the will was still inside the bodice of my dress. I would have to remove it later so that we could get a better look at it. I hoped I could think of some way to get it back into Monsieur Belanger's desk. Perhaps Madame Nanette would be able to sneak it back for me later.

'He is hailing a cab, madame,' the driver said. 'I will follow it.'

'Thank you.'

'You do realise, darling, that in all likelihood, Michel is going out for nothing more than a night on the town,' Milo said.

'It's possible,' I admitted. 'But the timing seems rather suspect.'

'Everything about Michel is suspect.'

'He is rather . . . bold,' I said.

'That is, perhaps, the nicest word that might be used to describe him,' Milo replied.

'You don't like him,' I said.

'Not particularly.'

'I thought you were friends.'

'We ran in the same circles, but I never much cared for him.' I felt that there was more to the story than he was revealing, but I didn't press the issue.

'What do you suppose he means to do with that key?' I asked.

'I suppose we shall find out, if we're fortunate,' Milo replied.

We settled into silence as our cab followed the one Michel had taken. The streets were fairly busy, and I hoped that he would not realise he was being followed.

We had been driving for a good while, and I had just begun to fear that we might either lose him or be noticed, when we turned a corner and I suddenly recognised where we were, on the rue de Tolbiac.

'Milo,' I said. 'This is the flat where the woman lived. The one I told you about.'

'Is it?' he asked. 'I'll admit, it's an interesting coincidence.'

Our cab pulled to a stop down the street, and we watched as Michel got out of his and went into the building.

'Do you know which is her flat?' Milo asked.

'The one there,' I said, pointing. 'In the corner.'

We waited. A few moments later the light went on behind the lace curtains.

'He's inside,' I whispered.

The light stayed on for several minutes and occasionally Michel's figure could be seen in front of the window, as though he was moving about the room. Then it went out again. I didn't think he had been looking for the missing woman, for, if he had known where she lived, he might have gone there without the key. It seemed, then, that he must have known she had gone and had come to the flat looking for something. I wondered if he had found it or had merely given up the search.

A moment later he came back out of the building and got back into his cab.

'Follow him, madame?' the driver asked.

'Yes, please.'

We drove for a few moments, and then suddenly his cab came to a stop and he got out and began walking. I wondered if it was possible he knew that he was being followed, but he didn't appear uneasy at all.

'Continue, madame?' the driver asked.

'No,' I said. 'I think we shall get out here. Thank you.'

'Darling, don't you think we've played detective long enough tonight?' Milo protested as we got out of the cab.

'You're free to go back to the hotel if you wish,' I replied, starting down the street.

Milo muttered something beneath his breath, which he was probably fortunate I didn't hear, and paid the driver before catching up with me.

We rounded the corner, and I saw Michel stopping before a door. I grabbed Milo's arm and pulled him back with me into the shadows.

'What's that building that he's going into?' I asked. 'I don't see any sort of sign. Is it a private residence, do you suppose?'

'It's a nightclub, of sorts,' Milo said. 'A somewhat private one.'

'Do you think we should try to go in?' I asked.

'No.'

'I think we should,' I said, my eyes on the door. 'We might be able to . . .'

'No, Amory,' he repeated firmly. I looked at him, surprised. I had scarcely ever seen him so implacable.

'Why not?'

He sighed. 'Because it's a brothel.'

I looked sharply at him. 'How do you know?'

'I recognise the street name,' he said.

'Then you're familiar with it?'

'I've heard of it,' he admitted.

'You've heard of it, have you?' I asked. Michel Belanger forgotten for the moment, I was beginning to feel the first faint signs that we might be on the precipice of a very nasty row.

'Before you jump to unsavoury conclusions, let me say that there's no need for you to do so.'

'Oh?' I asked. 'And why not?'

He smiled. 'I've spent money on a lot of frivolous things, my love, but I can assure you that I've never paid for a woman.'

No, of course not. Why should he pay for women when they threw themselves at him with alarming regularity?

It appeared we had come to a dead end as far as the evening was concerned. It seemed that Michel Belanger had accomplished whatever he wished to at the mysterious woman's flat and had decided to spend the rest of the evening indulging his baser urges. I was disappointed. I had hoped, somehow, that he would lead us somewhere important. There was nothing for us to do but to return to our hotel.

'Well, darling, did you learn anything of use this evening?' Milo asked as we entered our room.

I sighed heavily. 'I'm not certain. I feel as though there are plenty of clues to be had, but there is a great deal of information to be sifted through in order to find them. One thing seems obvious: Michel Belanger is up to something.'

'I hate to disappoint you, darling, but Michel Belanger is always up to something. If I had to hazard a guess, I would say it had nothing whatsoever to do with his father's death.'

'But he had the missing key to the safe, which means he likely took the formula. And he knew about the woman Helios Belanger had been seen with,' I said.

'Neither of which proves that he killed his father.'

'It proves something,' I said stubbornly. 'We thought whoever stole the formula was the likely killer, and only Michel had access to the safe. He might have murdered his father so he could sell the formula to the highest bidder.'

'Or he might have come across the key to the safe and taken advantage of his father's death to take the formula. That's more in Michel's style.'

'That doesn't account for the incorrect formula that was substituted into Monsieur Belanger's attaché case.'

Milo shrugged. 'Perhaps that was merely some sort of mistake.'

He knew as well as I did how unlikely that was. With a sinking feeling, I recognised this offhand answer for what it was: the indifference that came when an amusement had begun to run its course. For whatever reason, Milo was losing interest in the case.

'There's more to him than meets the eye,' I pressed. 'I just have to determine what it is.'

'Whatever you say, my sweet,' Milo replied. 'I just hope you won't continue sneaking about in that careless manner. You're bound to be caught.'

That reminded me. I still had the will in my bodice. I reached into my gown and found that it had slid too far down for me to remove it. The dress was quite tight, and I could feel the paper lodged against my stomach.

'Come here, Milo,' I said. 'I've got to get out of this dress.'

He smiled. 'Certainly, darling. Had I known how eager you were, I might have started undoing it in the cab.'

I shot him a look and turned my back to him, and his fingers moved deftly, unbuttoning my dress with impressive speed.

The dress pooled to the floor and I stepped out of it. I shook my slip and the piece of paper fluttered to the floor. I reached to pick it up.

My eyes scanned it. There was no way Anton could have claimed this to be a legitimate will, as this was clearly a draft that had not been completed. It had been written hurriedly, and some of it was illegible.

What was clear, however, was that this will was very different than the official one. As Anton had claimed, it appeared that the company was left to him, with smaller legacies left to Cecile, Seraphine, and Beryl Belanger. Michel was not mentioned.

I looked closer. There appeared to be notes in the margins. One read: 'He cannot be trusted.' It was underlined with bold scratches that went nearly through the paper. Though it was not written near anyone's name in particular, my automatic assumption was that he meant Michel. It seemed Helios must have been very angry when he had written it. The rumour that he had meant to disinherit his younger son seemed to be true.

This meant that the motives we had considered before were still valid. If Anton had believed he was going to inherit, he might have killed his father. If Cecile or Michel had seen it, either of them might have had reason to kill their father before he could revise the will.

'I'm not sure this helps much,' I said. 'It seems as though it still leaves everyone in his family with a reason to kill him.'

'That's often the case when a rich man dies,' Milo said.

'It doesn't make much sense,' I said. 'It seems a very informal document.'

'I suppose he was making a draft for himself before he met with his solicitor.'

I looked again at the document. There was something at the bottom of the page. There, written in small letters, were the words 'She shall have the rest. My dear one.'

'My dear one,' I said aloud. 'Who do you suppose that is? Cecile, Beryl, Seraphine? Or perhaps even the mysterious woman who might have been his mistress?'

'I suppose now we shall never know,' Milo said. Again I had the distinct feeling that he was swiftly losing interest in the will and perhaps the entire matter.

I sighed. It seemed that I had placed myself at risk for very little reward. This will didn't prove anything, not really. Even Michel's access to the safe, though definitely suspect, was not satisfactorily conclusive. After all, we could not prove he had taken the formula since we didn't know exactly when it had gone missing.

The hunt for Helios Belanger's killer would have to continue, but there was little I could do about it tonight. Milo sat down to smoke, and I went to the bedroom to change into my nightclothes.

A moment later I heard the telephone ring, and by the time I had come back to the sitting room, Milo was setting it back on the receiver.

He looked up, and I knew at once that he was going to leave me again. 'Darling, I need you to be patient with me.'

My brow rose. 'I believe you've reached your patience quota.'

'Yes, I know, but something's come up and I need to go out for a bit.' He came to me and slid his arms around me, looking down into my eyes. 'You will forgive me, won't you?'

'Stop trying to look contrite, Milo,' I said resignedly. 'You don't know how to do it correctly.'

'I won't be gone long,' he said. He leant in to give me a brief kiss, began to pull away, and seemed to think better of it, instead pulling me more tightly against him and kissing me in earnest.

As ever, I found it maddeningly difficult to remain cross with him when he went out of his way to be charming. Knowing his tactics did not lessen my susceptibility to them.

He released me then with a sigh. 'You make it difficult to leave, darling. I'd much rather stay here with you.'

I didn't bother to point out that this was, indeed, an option. 'Yes, well, I hope your evening is a success,' I said. 'Have a nice time.'

I went to the bedroom then, and I heard him go out a moment later.

I was half tempted to dress quickly and follow him, but I didn't think I could manage it without being detected. He might even expect it.

There was nothing for me to do, I supposed, but go to bed. I went to lie down, but my mind would not let me rest. Instead, the details of the case kept flashing across my brain. Everything that I learnt seemed to point to multiple suspects. I went through the list of possible motives.

After tonight's events, the most obvious suspect was Michel. It seemed very likely that he had taken the formula, if the copy had indeed been present there at the time of Monsieur Belanger's death. But why had he taken it? Did he mean to sell it? To sabotage his brother and sister out of spite? He might have accomplished either of those things, of course, without having killed his father. Perhaps, as Milo had suggested, he had come across the key to the safe and merely taken advantage of the opportunity it presented to him.

But if the formula wasn't motive enough, the second draft of the will also provided Michel with a reason to want his father dead. If it was true that his father had meant to disinherit him, then it would have been to his advantage had his father died before the will went into effect. It all made for rather compelling conjecture, but it wasn't the only plausible theory.

I had to admit that Anton Belanger was also a likely culprit. He had wanted control of his father's empire for years. Perhaps he had finally been pushed to the edge of his patience. Anton had discovered the second draft of the will indicating that Parfumes Belanger would be left to him and might have believed it to be representative of the legally binding will. Perhaps he had decided to seize his chance at power.

Then again, Cecile had seemed to realise that she would inherit under the will that was in effect. Madame Nanette said she had not seemed at all surprised to learn that she and her brother were to have an equal role in Parfumes Belanger. Was it possible their father had given them different impressions of what his will entailed? That would explain the confusion.

If Anton had seen the second draft, however, it was just possible that Cecile had seen it, too. Perhaps she had realised that, despite her assumption that she would inherit, Monsieur Belanger might change his will to leave the company to Anton. She might have killed her father before he could remove her from power. I didn't like to think that she might have done it, not after the loving way she had spoken of her father. I knew, however, that appearances could be deceiving.

As far as appearances went, how much of Beryl Belanger's grief was genuine? She had been left quite a handsome sum. She was now a rich woman who could live independently. In addition, the child, Seraphine, had been left a good deal of money in trust. Beryl would never want for anything again. She and her child could go anywhere in the world and live quite comfortably for the rest of their lives. Had the temptation to do so been too great? I didn't like to think she would kill her child's father, but I could not rule it out.

There was also the disgruntled sculptor, Herr Muller. He and Helios Belanger had been on bad terms, and Herr Muller had benefitted financially from the timing of Helios Belanger's death. There were also my suspicions that he might be involved with Beryl Belanger. There was so much to consider.

And what of the two players we had yet to meet: the mysterious woman who lived in the flat and had disappeared shortly before his death; and Angelique, Michel's volatile former lover?

I couldn't do much about the woman who had left Paris, but there was always the chance that Angelique might tell me something. After all, Michel Belanger was at the top of my suspect list, and she might be willing to discuss some of his habits now that they had parted ways.

As far as that went, there was no time like the present. I threw back the covers and rose to get dressed. Milo was being evasive and secretive, and it was time that I took matters into my own hands.

CHAPTER TWENTY-TWO

I dressed and freshened up my make-up, warming to the idea of my mission. The more I thought about it, the more I was convinced that Angelique would be able to tell me something important.

I had picked up my handbag and was prepared to leave when Winnelda came into the room.

'Good evening, madam. I just thought I would stop in to see if you needed anything.'

'No, thank you, Winnelda. I'm about to go out.'

I went out into the hall and she came with me. There was a pretty dark-haired girl standing outside, apparently waiting for her.

'This is my friend, Trudy,' Winnelda said.

Trudy bobbed a little curtsey. 'Good evening, madam.'

'Good evening, Trudy. It's nice to meet you. Winnelda has told me you've been having a lovely time exploring Paris.'

'Yes, madam,' she said.

'We met two very handsome gentlemen who want to

take us to a jazz club. Isn't it thrilling?' Winnelda enthused.

'Yes,' I said, 'but do be careful.'

'Yes, madam.' Winnelda suddenly seemed to consider something. 'Are you going out alone, madam?'

'Yes, Mr Ames had some business to attend to.'

'You can come with us, if you like,' she said.

Trudy nodded agreement. 'It's a very nice club. The music is wonderful. And there will be many handsome gentlemen.'

'She's a married lady,' Winnelda said, affronted.

Trudy shrugged. 'It doesn't hurt to look.'

'That's very sweet of you to offer,' I said, breaking in before a disagreement could develop, 'but I'm going to La Reine Bleue.'

Trudy looked me over before saying hesitantly, 'I beg your pardon, madam. But are you going to wear that?'

I looked down at what I was wearing. It was a very modish gown of dark green silk, and I could think of no reason why Trudy should disapprove of it.

'Is there something wrong with this?' I asked.

'Oh no,' she said quickly. 'That is, it's a very nice gown, madam. But you're sure to stick out in something like that. It's a bit too proper, if you catch my meaning.'

I did indeed. For the space of a moment, I pondered the problem. If my gown was not what ladies wore to cabarets, I might make myself conspicuous. What was more, I might not be able to speak to Angelique if I appeared to be, as Trudy had phrased it, 'too proper'.

I looked at Trudy. She was just about my size. 'Do you happen to have anything suitable you could lend me?' I asked.

* * *

259

An hour later found me entering La Reine Bleue in a black-beaded gown with a scandalously plunging neckline and a low-cut back. Trudy had very much warmed to her role as my makeshift stylist, and she and Winnelda had done my make-up, applying a good deal more of it than I would usually wear. Sultriness was not something I had ever managed to achieve, but I felt I gave a fair imitation of it tonight.

The cabaret was in a building that looked somewhat the worse for wear, but it seemed the outward appearance did not discourage its customers in the least. There were a great many people coming and going beneath the glow of the lighted sign above the building, and the building seemed full to capacity.

I made my way through the dense crowd and requested a seat near the wall, hoping to remain inconspicuous. Not that there was much chance I would attract attention. There were a great many women here who were more eye-catching than I.

The waiter came to my table. 'Good evening, mademoiselle. What is it that you would like?'

'I'm looking for Angelique.'

He smiled. 'Yes, most people come here for Angelique. You are in luck. She is due to perform next.'

'Thank you.'

I ordered a cup of coffee, which seemed to amuse the waiter, and settled into my seat to wait. A moment later she walked out onto the floor and into the glow of a spotlight that cut through the smoky darkness.

When I saw her, I'm rather afraid I blushed. She wore only what appeared to be a long, strategically draped strand of diamonds. They glittered brightly in the light, and a cheer went up from the crowd.

She smiled, tossing her head, and began to sing in a low, pleasant voice.

Further description is beyond me, for I have never seen anything quite like Angelique's performance. The dance routine proved her to be quite flexible. Suffice it to say, angelic was not the word that came to mind.

She had finished her song and was met with a roar of applause when the waiter brought my coffee and nodded towards the stage. 'Did you enjoy the show, mademoiselle?'

'Yes, she was . . . very dramatic. I wonder, would it be possible for me to speak to her?'

He laughed. 'Everyone wants to speak to Angelique. She comes out onto the floor sometimes when she has finished her routine. Perhaps you may have a chance to speak to her then. She usually comes out there,' he said, nodding in the direction of a door that I assumed led to the dressing rooms. 'Though it may be some time before she comes out.'

It didn't matter how long it took. I would wait.

I skirted the dance floor, which had become particularly lively following Angelique's performance, and worked my way towards the door. I hoped I could stand outside and have a chance to approach her before anyone else did.

I had almost reached the door when I moved too quickly and bumped directly into a man.

'Pardon, monsieur . . .' I looked up just then into Milo's eyes. I felt a flicker of surprise followed by pure annoyance.

'*Enchanté*, madame,' he said dryly. If he was as surprised to see me as I was to see him, he didn't show it.

'What are you doing here?' I demanded.

'I might ask you the same question.'

I felt disinclined to answer him, but I supposed that now that he had seen me there was no reason to keep things quiet.

'I've come to speak to Angelique,' I said.

'So have I,' he replied.

'You didn't tell me.'

'You didn't tell me either,' he replied, his eyes moving over me. 'I must say, you look rather fetching in that ensemble. You haven't worn that dress before. I would have remembered.'

'Never mind that,' I said. 'I'm extremely annoyed with you.'

'I don't see why you should be. I told you something had come up.'

'You didn't tell me you had come to watch Angelique prance about practically in the nude. I suppose you enjoyed her performance immensely.'

'I did,' he replied. 'Do you suppose you could ask her to teach you how she did that last dance . . . ?'

Luckily for Milo, I was distracted by something behind him before he could finish his sentence.

'Milo,' I hissed, cutting him off. 'Did you see who else is here tonight?'

'Who?' he asked.

'Jens Muller.'

'Is he?' Milo said. 'It's not really surprising, I suppose, that he should come to see his muse.'

'Yes,' I said. 'But perhaps we can learn something from him about his relationship with Beryl Belanger.'

'Perhaps. You go and talk to him, and I'll talk to Angelique.'

My eyes narrowed.

'Divide and conquer, that was our plan,' he replied with a smile.

Somehow I didn't fancy the idea of my husband conquering Angelique. Nevertheless, I supposed the idea had merit. Though I hated to admit it, Milo probably had a better chance with Angelique than I did. When she came into this room, it certainly wasn't going to be me to whom she was drawn.

I walked towards where Herr Muller sat. He was alone at a table, though I had half expected him to be in the company of a model or two. He looked up when he saw me, though he didn't seem particularly surprised.

'Good evening, Madame Ames,' he said, rising from his seat. 'Are you here alone?'

'No,' I said. 'My husband is somewhere about, but he has so many friends that I sometimes lose track of him.'

I glanced in Milo's direction. Almost as though he had been trying to prove my point, he was no longer alone. There were two women seated at the table with him, neither of whom were Angelique, and they all appeared to be getting on famously.

I fought down my annoyance. Try as I might to pretend otherwise, Milo's effortless magnetism was sometimes a source of great vexation to me.

Herr Muller's gaze followed mine before coming back to search me speculatively, and I supposed he must think me a very obliging wife. 'Would you like to sit with me for a while?'

'Thank you, that would be very nice.'

He pulled out the chair for me and I sat. I saw his gaze drop from my face to my bodice, and for a moment I wished that I had not let Trudy talk me into wearing something quite so revealing.

'Can I offer you a drink?' he asked. 'A cigarette?'

'No, thank you,' I said.

He lit one for himself then and drew a deep breath before observing: 'You do not seem, if I may say so, to be much enjoying yourself. I don't think this type of place suits you.'

I smiled. 'I don't like to let my husband out alone.'

He chuckled. 'I would think he would not like to let you out alone either,' he replied, taking another thorough look at my décolletage.

I decided it was time to change the subject. 'You came to see Angelique.'

'Yes, she fascinates me.'

'She is very fascinating,' I agreed.

'Her body, I find it mesmerising.'

I supposed it had mesmerised a great many people this evening.

'It seems everyone was taken with her but Helios Belanger,' I said lightly.

This comment had the desired reaction. 'That man did not know good from bad,' he said heatedly.

'What was it that caused the rift in your friendship?' I asked. I did not think it likely that he would confide in me if he was having an affair with Beryl Belanger, but one never knew. People had confided strange things in me before.

'He had grown paranoid. He was convinced that someone was trying to sabotage him, to steal his secrets.'

I thought of the missing formula. It seemed that Helios Belanger might have been right.

'Do you think it was possible?' I asked.

He shrugged. 'I don't know. Nor do I care. I want to avoid all mention of him from this point on.'

'I thought I saw you yesterday, in the Jardin du Luxembourg,' I said, hoping to get to the matter of Beryl Belanger.

'Yes,' he admitted readily. 'I was walking there, but left because I saw Madame Belanger and did not wish to speak with her. I am through with the Belangers.'

So this was why he had avoided Beryl Belanger. It seemed, then, that he was not her lover. He might be lying, of course, but somehow I didn't think so. I had never quite been able to picture the two of them in a passionate affair.

'"I am being destroyed from the inside," he said to me one day,' he went on, apparently not quite through with the Belangers. 'I think he believed that someone was plotting against him, but did not know who to blame. So he blamed me. I tell you, from anyone else I would not have tolerated it. I only put up with it at first because I believed his illness had made him irritable.'

This was a conversational opening I had not expected, and I took advantage of it. 'Yes,' I said. 'I heard he was ill, that he had hired a nurse.'

'A fine woman she was, too,' he said. 'I noticed her at once. She had a wonderful figure.'

'What type of illness was it?' I asked, hoping at last to have the answer to this lingering question.

He shrugged. 'That I do not know. I do not concern myself with illness.'

It seemed that his observational powers had been otherwise engaged.

His next words, however, proved to be of great interest.

'I would have liked the nurse to model for me, but she was not interested in such things,' he went on. 'I do not know what became of her. Perhaps she went home. She was from Beauvais, I think.'

I stilled. Beauvais. That was where Milo had gone on the train. Had he gone to see the nurse? I could think of no other reason why he might have gone there.

I rose abruptly from my seat. 'I'm sorry, Herr Muller, but I must be getting back to my husband. It was very nice to see you again.'

'And you, madame,' he said. I hated to appear rude, but his gaze had already travelled to the woman who had taken the stage, a shapely redhead attired only in feathers, and I knew he would not miss my company.

I made my way back towards Milo's table, ready to confront him on the matter of the nurse. It was then that I saw that he was no longer seated with the two young women. I could tell by their annoyed glances, however, in which direction he had gone. My eyes followed their gaze, and I found him standing with Angelique. I was not really surprised at his quick success in capturing her attention. After all, he had never had to do much seeking where women were concerned; they were drawn to him naturally.

I might have left him alone to learn what he could, but then she leant into him, saying something into his ear, and I decided that it might be best if I made my presence known to her.

I walked to where they stood and Milo looked over at me.

'Ah, darling, there you are. This is Angelique.'

I turned to the woman at his side. She was tall and very thin, her graceful body draped in a red satin gown with a neckline that plunged nearly to her navel. Her hair was cut in a sleek, black bob, and dark make-up lined glittering green eyes. She was quite stunning, and I distrusted her instinctively.

'How do you do?' I said.

She was looking me over as I had done her, and she was in no rush about it. Finally, her eyes came back up to mine. The corner of her mouth tipped up in a languid smile.

'I think I know why you are here.'

'You do?'

'Yes,' she said, her eyes hard, despite the carelessness of her tone. 'And you have nothing to fear from me. I don't want him.'

'I . . . I beg your pardon?'

'You are one of Michel's lovers, are you not?' she asked. 'His newest, perhaps?'

I ought to have been surprised by the question, but, having met Michel Belanger, I could see how she might make that assumption. Perhaps she thought I was the diplomat's wife with whom Michel had recently been connected.

'No,' I said quickly and indicated Milo. 'I'm his wife.'

She laughed, a throaty sound. 'That has never stopped Michel.' Her gaze moved to Milo. 'But I suppose this one is man enough for any woman, eh? He looks as though he knows his way around a bedroom in the dark.'

She smiled at my husband and he smiled back.

I cleared my throat. 'I have come to you because I believe you know Michel better than anyone else.'

Reluctantly, her eyes came back to me. She hesitated. 'What do you want to know?'

I hadn't expected her to ask this question, and I was unprepared to answer it. Should I tell her the truth? What if she was still friendly with Michel Belanger and let him know that we had been asking questions?

I was trying to think of the best way in which to couch my questions about Michel Belanger when Milo decided to take matters into his own hands.

'The truth of the matter is that my wife has had a very brief affair with Michel Belanger,' Milo said.

My mouth nearly fell open, but I managed to keep my lips together. He had better have a good reason for this.

Angelique's eyes narrowed ever so slightly at this bit of information. It seemed that, despite what she had told me, she still felt something for Michel.

'I told her we would overlook the matter, but she has some concerns,' Milo went on.

'You are more forgiving than most husbands,' she told Milo.

'She has realised the error of Michel's ways,' Milo said.

Again, that cynical smiled flickered over her lips. 'Yes. Michel is a difficult man to resist.'

'That isn't the full story,' I said, unable to allow him to continue to malign my character. 'You haven't told her what you did to provoke me into that episode.'

Milo's brow rose ever so slightly in what I took to be a challenge. I accepted it.

I turned to her. 'He had been carrying on behind my

back, keeping secrets from me. And what is worse, he gave me a pet monkey, expecting that would make everything all right.'

She gave me what I think was supposed to be a sympathetic look. 'Men, they are all the same. They think that we will forgive them anything if they lay gifts at our feet.'

'Yes,' I agreed. 'I'm afraid it is true.'

'How little they know us,' she said.

'We have agreed to forgive each other,' Milo said, interrupting our newly developed camaraderie. 'However, my wife is uneasy about Michel's temper.'

'Yes,' I said, taking this cue. 'I have heard that he is very unpredictable, even violent. He did not take our parting well, I'm afraid. I would hate for him to harm my husband.'

'Michel can be violent,' she agreed. 'But in the heat of the moment. He is not one to plot and plan.'

'Are you sure about that? Michel once confided in my wife that he wanted to kill his father,' Milo lied smoothly. I was always a bit startled when I saw how easily untruths flowed from his lips. I sometimes worried about that particular skill.

'And now his father is dead,' she said. Her brows rose along with the corners of her lips. 'I do not think Michel would kill anyone. He has a temper, yes, but he knows how to control it. I should think that if anyone would have wanted Helios Belanger dead, it would be Anton.'

'Anton?' I repeated. I was curious to hear her thoughts on the elder Belanger brother.

'He wanted everything his father had. Now he can have it. He has won his prize.'

'He has to share the company with Cecile,' I said. 'That isn't everything.'

'Parfumes Belanger is not the prize I mean.'

'I'm afraid I don't understand,' I said.

She laughed suddenly. 'Oh. I see you mean what you say.' Her smiled broadened and her eyes glinted. 'Then you don't know. Anton Belanger is in love with his father's wife.'

CHAPTER TWENTY-THREE

'Anton is in love with Beryl?' I repeated. I was stunned. It was almost too incredible to be true. Yet the more I pictured sweet, pretty Beryl, the more I thought that she might be just the sort of person to win stoic Anton's heart.

'Are you sure?' I asked.

She laughed. 'Quite sure. Michel told me about it more than once, how his brother watched her with sad eyes but was not man enough to do something about it.' I realised then why Michel had taunted Beryl in the drawing room that morning I had been at the house. He knew that his brother and stepmother had feelings for each other, that they met in secret in the park.

Suddenly I wondered if the motive for murder might have been under our noses the entire time.

'You will excuse me now,' she said.

'Yes, of course,' I said. 'Thank you for your time.'

She gave me a half nod and then gave Milo one last smouldering look. 'If there is anything else I can do for you, you have only to ask.'

Then she turned and walked away.

'I can see how she and Michel would be well matched,' I said.

'Are you ready, darling?' Milo asked, glancing at his wristwatch.

'Yes, I think we've learnt all we're going to,' I said. I wanted very much to question Milo about what I had learnt about the nurse in Beauvais, but the crowded, noisy confines of this cabaret were not ideal for what I felt sure would develop into a heated conversation. I decided to hold my tongue for the time being.

Milo took my arm and we made our way through the crowd towards the door.

'It's a good thing I came here tonight,' I said, as we walked out together into the cool night air. 'I'm quite sure Angelique would have pounced upon you had you been alone.'

Milo steered me towards a cab. 'I think much of what Angelique says is a show.' He smiled. 'I did, however, receive a very interesting offer from the two young women I was speaking to at the table.'

My eyes narrowed. 'I don't care to hear the details, thank you,' I said.

Milo held the cab door open for me, and I slid inside. It was only then I realised that he didn't intend to join me.

'Wait,' I said, before he could close the door. 'Where are you going?'

'I have one more stop to make, darling. I'll be home before long.'

He closed the door before I could protest, and, though I was half tempted to get out of the cab and confront him, I decided against it.

Let him do as he pleased. I would find out the truth one way or another.

I slept deeply and awoke with Milo beside me, having no recollection of his having come in. I supposed he had wandered in extremely late again, and I fought the urge to search through the pockets of his evening clothes, which were, once again, strewn about the room.

At least he was still coming home to our bed, I reasoned. I did not care to repeat those several months of our marriage when we had not slept in the same room.

I tried to remind myself that this current break in communication that we were experiencing was not indicative of any great rift in our marriage. Milo was notoriously uncommunicative about some things. Whatever he was keeping from me would be brought to light eventually.

If I expected to spend the day discussing the merits of the case with him, however, I was to be disappointed. It seemed he had decided to make up for his late nights at last, for he slept very late, and when he awoke he hurried me out to lunch where he avoided every mention of the case, save for one comment.

'I've tried to convince Madame Nanette to forget all of this and leave Paris,' he said, 'but she won't leave the child.'

I was surprised by this sentiment. 'I wouldn't have thought you inclined to give up so easily,' I said.

'Sometimes the best solution is to walk away,' he replied.

It seemed that he was doing his best to forget the reason we had come to Paris, and I could not help but feel a bit frustrated by his attitude.

'Milo,' I said suddenly. 'Why didn't you tell me that you had gone to see the nurse in Beauvais?'

As always, he gave no indication of surprise at my sudden question. It was no wonder he was such a marvellous card player.

'Because I didn't learn anything of importance,' he said.

'Then why did you refuse to tell me when I asked you why you had gone there?'

'Because I was being very ill-tempered,' he replied. 'I was unable to find her and didn't learn anything. It wasn't worth mentioning.'

He was lying. He had lied to my face that night he had come back from Beauvais, and he was doing it again now. There would be no reason to hide the truth from me if it was insignificant. So what was it that he had learnt?

He changed the subject then, and I knew it would be useless to question him further at present. I was left feeling suspicious and dissatisfied.

My feelings were compounded as we reached the hotel and Milo was stopped by the concierge.

'A message for you, monsieur,' he said, handing Milo a slip of paper.

'Thank you.' Milo took the message and glanced at it.

'Anything important?' I asked.

'No,' he said, slipping the note nonchalantly into his pocket, and left it at that.

By the time we reached our room, I could no longer hold in my thoughts. 'Milo, I think there are some things we need to discuss.'

'Are there?' he asked, taking a seat on the sofa. 'I'm all ears.'

I looked down into his level gaze and almost lost my nerve. I had never been good when it came to confronting my husband, but I was learning that some things have to be said. 'I want to know what you've been doing,' I said.

'Doing?'

'All these late nights and secret messages.'

He smiled. 'I'm afraid you're reading a bit too much into things.'

'I think I have a right to know where my husband spends his nights,' I said mildly.

'I thought you'd agreed to trust me.'

'That doesn't mean I want to be kept in the dark.'

'That note was from an acquaintance. He mentioned a new gambling club to me,' he said. I didn't believe him for a moment. Something about this did not ring true. I suspected that it was something to do with Helios Belanger, and I wanted to know what it said.

'I thought you must know all the gambling clubs in Paris,' I said lightly.

'There may be one or two that have escaped my notice,' he said with an easy smile. 'I may go out and have a look at it later this evening.'

He must have seen my doubtful expression, for his smile broadened and he added, 'You needn't look so suspicious, darling. Not every note is a secret missive. Sometimes a man just wants to spend his evening out and win his wife a monkey.'

He had presented Emile as a peace offering, but my good graces extended only so far. He clearly intended to keep hiding things from me. Well, this time I was going to find out.

I decided on my tactic at once.

'Very well,' I said. 'I may go out tonight myself.'

I went into the bedroom. Trudy, in the course of making me up for my night at the cabaret, had lent me two gowns, and I put the second one on. It was silver lamé and much more risqué than the black one I had worn to meet Angelique, which was saying quite a lot. It was tightly fitted to the hip with thin straps and a neckline that plunged so low it was rendered practically superfluous. The skirt was long and clung to my legs as I moved back into the sitting room.

Milo was still sitting on the sofa, smoking a cigarette, and glancing over a newspaper.

'I think I shall wear this tonight,' I said.

His eyes came up and slowly ran the length of me, and I knew instantly that the gown had been a success. 'Where did you get that?'

'Do you like it?' I asked, turning so he could see it to its full advantage before walking towards him. 'I daresay I shall be able to find something to amuse myself this evening. Perhaps I'll go back to La Reine Bleue.'

A smile touched his lips. He knew what I was about, and yet the dress had had its desired effect. 'I find the gambling club less appealing by the moment,' he said.

I smiled softly. 'I'm glad to hear you say so.'

It was very hard to pretend I was feeling amorous when I was furious that he was hiding things from me, but I needed to do my best, and so I sat down on his lap. 'It seems as though we've barely spent any time together since we arrived in Paris.'

'I am at your disposal, madame,' he said in a low voice,

his eyes on mine even as his arms moved around me. 'Though I'd like very much to know what you're up to.'

I took his cigarette from between his fingers and leant to put it in the ashtray. Then I reached up to slide one of my hands into his hair.

'What makes you think I'm up to something?' I asked softly as the fingers of my free hand moved to his jacket pocket.

'I'm certainly not complaining,' he murmured, before he lowered his mouth to mine.

I kissed him as my fingers closed around the paper in his pocket. Slowly, slowly, I began to ease it out. It was imperative that I not be caught. If he realised what I was doing, it would ruin everything.

The paper came free, and I held it up over his shoulder as he kissed my neck, trying to read it. It was written in a bold hand and contained only an address and the words 'Tonight at ten o'clock'. The address seemed familiar, but I couldn't place it. It was possible that it was, as he had told me, an invitation to a gambling club, but somehow I didn't think so.

Just as I had folded the paper to slip it back into his pocket, he shifted me to push me back onto the sofa. Before I lost my balance and tumbled backward onto the cushions, I managed to slip the piece of paper into the crack of the sofa.

'You're going to wrinkle my gown,' I protested as he leant down to continue kissing me.

'The welfare of your gown is the very last thing on my mind at this moment,' he said.

I realised then that I had perhaps made an error in

judgement. I had divested Milo of the mysterious note, but I was going to have a difficult time divesting myself of Milo. In all honesty, I was beginning to wonder if I actually wanted to. I had not exactly considered the repercussions of this plan.

It was at that moment that Winnelda chose to walk blithely into the room.

'Oh!' she cried, when she saw us entangled on the sofa. I tried to sit up, but Milo was not moving very quickly, and the skirt of my gown was caught beneath his knee.

'I'm sorry. I'll just . . . shall I go? I'll go,' Winnelda said, turning back towards the door.

'No, no, you needn't go,' I said, managing to pull my skirt loose, roll inelegantly off the sofa, and rise to my feet. Milo unhurriedly took his seat on the sofa, completely unruffled.

I noticed that he was sitting on the side opposite of where I had stashed the note. I needed to get it back into his pocket before he noticed it was missing.

Winnelda turned back towards me, though she didn't look up. Her face was crimson. 'I'm sorry, madam,' she said, her gaze firmly planted on the floor. 'I . . . I didn't think about knocking. I suppose I ought to have . . .'

'It's quite all right, Winnelda,' I said, quite sure my face must be as flushed as hers. 'Mr Ames and I were just . . . ah . . .' I faltered.

'In conference,' Milo supplied, the only one of us not the least bit embarrassed. 'Is there something you need, Winnelda?'

'I . . . I . . . No. That is, I don't . . . I came to bring Emile a treat. I bought him a macaron.'

I had forgotten all about Emile. I turned to where his cage was resting in the corner of the room. He was looking through the bars at us. If possible, I felt even more mortified realising that we had had an audience the entire time.

'You may as well give it to him,' I said. I felt quite sure that Emile would not care for a macaron, but I was rather desperate to get us past our mutual discomfiture.

Winnelda went to the cage and opened the door. Before she could hand in Emile's treat, he hopped out of the cage and bounded over to the sofa.

Almost before I realised what he was doing, he had reached his tiny paw into the crack between the sofa and the cushion and pulled out the paper I had hidden there.

He then walked across the cushions to Milo and handed it to him, chattering happily.

Traitorous little beast.

'What's this?' Milo asked. He looked at it and his eyes came up to mine. I did my very best to feign surprise, but I knew how very difficult it was to fool Milo and I was not at all sure I succeeded.

'What is it?' I asked, hoping I sounded mildly curious and not guilty.

'My note,' he said, his eyes still on mine. 'It must have fallen out of my pocket.'

'How very sweet of Emile,' I said.

'How clever he is!' Winnelda said, walking to the sofa. 'Tell him I've bought him a treat, will you, Mr Ames?'

Milo translated obligingly, and Winnelda gave Emile the macaron. He took it from her and brought it back to his cage where he began to eat it daintily.

'I'll just be going now, shall I?' Winnelda asked. 'Unless there's anything you need?'

'She won't be needing you, Winnelda,' Milo said, rising from the sofa and walking towards the door to see her out. 'Rest assured, I shall tend to Mrs Ames.'

'Very well,' she said. 'If you're sure?'

'Quite sure. Thank you.' He ushered her out, locked the door behind her, and turned back to me.

'Poor girl. I'm terribly embarrassed,' I said.

'It was bound to happen one day, the way she charges into rooms.'

'I suppose we were lucky it wasn't Parks. He might have resigned on the spot.'

'Now. Where were we?' he asked, pulling me to him and kissing me.

Emile took the opportunity to screech loudly and clap his paws.

'Don't, Milo,' I said, pulling away. 'Emile is watching us.'

'I am not the least concerned with that monkey.'

I was glad of that. Perhaps he would forget that the monkey had discovered his purloined note. With any luck, Milo would believe it had fallen out of his pocket.

The telephone rang then, sparing poor Emile any more of our shocking behaviour, and I moved out of Milo's embrace as I went to answer it.

'Madame Ames?' said the voice on the other end of the line. 'This is Cecile Belanger.'

'Oh, hello,' I said.

'I worked for most of the night, and I think I am nearly finished composing your perfume. I realise this is

280

short notice, but I thought you might like to come and sample it.'

'I would like that very much,' I said, wondering what had spurred this sudden productivity. I had thought it would take much longer to finish developing the scent. I had certainly not expected it to be finished in a single night. 'What time is convenient for you?'

'Would three o'clock be all right with you?'

I glanced at the clock. That was a little over an hour from now. 'Yes, that would be fine.'

'Excellent. I shall see you then.'

I rang off and turned to Milo. 'Cecile has nearly finished with my perfume. She wants me to come back to the house this afternoon.'

'It seems you are becoming very popular with the Belangers.'

'It may be a chance to learn something. I don't know why, exactly, but I feel as though we are close. It's as though the answer is right in front of me, and I just haven't grasped it.'

'That may very well be,' he said without any particular enthusiasm.

'I may also be able to return that draft of the will,' I said. 'I can only hope that it hasn't been missed by now.'

'Well, in that case, I have an appointment of my own to keep. I daresay I'll be back before you are.'

He kissed me deeply and then went out, and I stood for a moment looking thoughtfully at the door.

I had an uneasy feeling about Milo. Despite my best attempts to draw it out of him, I had learnt nothing about his activities. I wondered what his appointment today might be, and I wondered even more where he was expected at ten o'clock tonight.

First things first, however. I went to the bedroom to change out of the silver gown into something more presentable. It was time to visit Cecile.

CHAPTER TWENTY-FOUR

'I'm so glad you could come,' Cecile said when we met in the drawing room. 'I'm sorry for the short notice, but I am leaving in the morning and I wanted to get your opinion before I go.'

'Leaving?' I asked.

'Yes, I have some business to attend to. It came up rather unexpectedly.'

'I see,' I said. I wondered if it could have anything to do with Michel's secret errand last night. Did she know anything about her brother's mysterious behaviour?

'I'm not sure how long I shall be gone. Once I have your opinion on the scent combination, I can go ahead with producing it. I'm very pleased with what I have developed. Will you come out to my laboratory?'

'Yes, I'd love to.'

We rose from our seats, but before we could make our way outside, the butler entered the drawing room. 'Monsieur Duveau is here to see you, madame.'

I was looking her way as he said these words, but I

could detect nothing on her features to indicate how she felt about the arrival of her former fiancé.

'Have him come in,' she said.

André came into the room a moment later and stopped when he saw me there. 'Oh, Amory. How delightful. I didn't know you were here.'

'Hello, André.'

'You'll forgive me for dropping in unannounced, Cecile,' he said, 'but I was wondering if you were able to find the book I had left here.'

'Yes, I think it may be in his room,' she said. 'I'll go up and see if I can find it.'

'Shall I come with you?' he asked.

'No. Things are quite out of order at the moment. I had the maids sorting through my father's things. They brought a good many documents and books to his office, but one of them took ill and left the job unfinished. It has been a nuisance. Madame Ames, will you excuse me for a moment?'

'Yes, of course.'

She went out of the room, and Monsieur Duveau and I took seats across from each other.

'As I told you, I had a book on perfumery that Monsieur Belanger was kind enough to annotate for me,' he said.

'Yes,' I said. 'I imagine you will be very glad to have his notes.'

'You'll also realise, perhaps, that I had ulterior motives for coming here.'

'Oh?' I asked. I had been a bit curious about his sudden appearance, but I hadn't liked to draw conclusions. After all, the two were on good terms. There was no reason why he should not visit her, so far as I knew.

'Yes, I came to see how things stand with Cecile. I have been thinking things over, and I wonder if we did the right thing in parting.'

'I see.' I wondered, a bit cynically, if his sudden change of heart had anything to do with the fact that Cecile had just inherited half of Parfumes Belanger.

'I know what you must think,' he said with a smile. 'But I truly care about her. I should hate to lose her.'

'Then it's good that you came to speak with her about it,' I said. 'I believe she means to leave Paris.'

I could tell this surprised him, though he tried to hide it. 'Does she? Then I'm glad I came when I did.'

She came back a moment later with a book in one hand and two small silver tins in the other. 'I think this is it,' she said, holding the book out to him.

He rose and went to take it from her. 'Yes, this is it.' He flipped through the pages. 'It looks as though he left me a great many notes.'

'Good,' she said. 'And I thought you might like this as well.'

She handed him one of the little silver tins.

He looked down at it and then back up at her. 'What is this?'

'My father's lavender pomade,' she said. 'His personal stock. He made the last batch not long ago, and I should hate for these tins to go to waste. Would you like one, Madame Ames?' she asked, handing one to me.

I took it. 'That would be lovely, thank you.'

Cecile had mentioned Helios Belanger's unique lavender pomade and I would be pleased to try it, but I couldn't help but feel there was some other reason Cecile had gifted this to me in front of André. Perhaps she had wanted him to have it, but, not wanting him to attach too much personal significance to the gesture, had decided to give one to me as well.

'I shall enjoy this,' André said. 'Each time I use it I shall think of your father.'

They looked at each other.

It seemed that she was waiting for him to leave, and I was aware that there was more André wanted to say to her that could not be said in my presence.

I wondered if I should find a way to excuse myself and was glad when he made his intentions plain. 'I wonder if I might speak to you for just a moment, in private.'

'I have a guest,' she said. From another woman, I might have thought the words held alarm, but Cecile seemed perfectly composed. Perhaps just disinterested.

'Oh, you needn't worry about me,' I said quickly. 'I'll just step out into the garden. I did want a chance to have a better look at it.'

It appeared that she was hesitant, but she nodded. 'Thank you. I won't be long.'

I turned to André. 'It was nice to see you, André.'

'And you. Perhaps you and your husband might have dinner with me soon?'

'That would be nice.'

'I'll ring you up.'

I went out into the garden and walked along the path a little way. I couldn't help but wonder what he would say and how she would respond to it. The timing of his renewed suit might be suspect, but I wanted to believe that it was made from true feeling rather than anything less noble.

286

Was there any chance of a reconciliation? Some part of me always hoped that the flame of true love could be rekindled. I supposed it was having been able to revive my own relationship that always made me hopeful for others.

I had walked along the little path that looped back around to skirt the house. I stopped when I realised that the doors to Monsieur Belanger's office were wide open. Cecile had mentioned the maids had been cleaning. Perhaps they had left the room open to air it.

I glanced inside. The door to the hallway was closed and the room was empty. I had intended to return the will. Now seemed like the perfect opportunity to do so.

I slipped into the room and opened the drawer where I had found it. I quickly slid the paper inside, closed the drawer, and was about to leave the room when something on the desk caught my notice.

There was a box filled with notebooks and assorted papers. These must have been the items Cecile had mentioned. There were a great many items in the box, but there was a stack of letters in yellowed envelopes on top, and something about the handwriting looked familiar. I picked one up and took the letter out.

My dearest one,
I cannot stop thinking of you. My heart aches and I
feel as though my world has come to an end. What
we have was meant to last for ever.

These were love letters. I didn't read further. Such things were private. I couldn't resist, however, turning the paper over to see why it was that the hand seemed familiar. The last words were written in darker ink than the rest, as though the pen had pressed hard into the paper.

> *The only thing that can stop my love is death.*
> *Yours for ever,*
> *Nanette*

They were the letters from Madame Nanette.

Judging from the date on the front, she must have written them when she and Helios Belanger had parted ways all those years ago. And he had kept them. I felt a little pang of sadness that her first love should have brought her such sadness.

I heard voices in the garden and hastily put the letter back into the envelope.

I hurried back outside and took the path away from the house, rounding it to find Cecile and André outside.

'Here it is,' she said, and he came around from another part of the path. She pointed out a plant to him. 'You see it grows quite well in our climate.'

'Yes,' he said. 'I shall have to add it to my own garden. Thank you.'

They both looked up as I approached. I tried to detect the atmosphere between them, but it was difficult. Cecile was always cool and reserved, and André seemed perpetually good-natured. Whatever they had discussed, it was not apparent on their countenances.

André made his farewells and, after he had gone, Cecile turned to me. 'I apologise for the delay, Madame Ames. Monsieur Duveau can be persistent.'

'He seems fond of you,' I said, hoping she would choose to confide in me.

However, it seemed that confidences were not in Cecile's nature. 'André is very genial,' she said mildly. 'We can go to the laboratory now, if you are ready.'

She led me through the courtyard towards the greenhouse. Once again, we made our way through the fairy garden of foliage to Cecile's laboratory at the back.

She had told me she had worked most of the night, and it was evident. There were bottles and beakers and a great many other pieces of equipment scattered about. The scent in the air was fresher than it had been the last time I was here. It smelt of living flowers now rather than dried ones.

'Please excuse the mess,' she said. 'I got rather carried away. Once I begin making a scent, it is as though I am almost unaware of my surroundings.'

'I greatly appreciate your taking the time to finish it,' I said. 'You needn't have rushed.'

'I was inspired,' she replied, picking up a bottle. 'I combined several scents, and I think you will find it to your liking.'

She unstopped the bottle of perfume that she had created and held it out to me. I breathed deeply of the scent. While I had known it would be a quality scent, I had not expected the reaction it would evoke, the uncanny sensation of happiness and longing and nostalgia it created within me. She had taken the information I had given her – my likes, feelings, and memories – and had somehow managed to put it into a bottle.

'It's wonderful,' I said sincerely. 'I love it.'

A small smile touched her lips. 'I thought it would please you. It is a very complex scent. Most notable are the sweet aromas of gardenia, jasmine, and tuberose, but there are also notes of patchouli, sandalwood, and myrrh, among other things. There's an earthiness behind the floral notes that grounds them. It has a poised and elegant exterior with a strength beneath the surface. Much like yourself, I believe.'

I could not argue with this assessment, and I found it touching somehow that she had detected it in me. 'It's perfect,' I said.

'I'm glad to hear you say so. Of course, this is only the prototype. The scent will be layered more subtly when we create it officially.'

'I can't believe it will smell any lovelier than this.'

'You may take that with you, if you like. I've written down the necessary formula.' She picked up one of her scent journals from the table, but in doing so, she knocked over a bottle that rested too near the edge. It wavered for a moment before it fell onto the flagstone flooring, shattering into several large pieces.

The base had fallen with a little liquid still in it, and, without thinking, I reached to pick it up. She quickly caught my hand. 'You must not touch that, Mrs Ames. It will absorb through the skin and harm you. There are a great many things in here that are harmful to the touch, I'm afraid. I'll clean it up later.'

We left the mess and walked back through the greenhouse and returned to the courtyard.

'This may be goodbye, Madame Ames,' she said. 'I have my doubts that I will return to Paris before you and your husband return to London.'

I couldn't help but wonder what had brought about this decision to leave Paris, but, as usual, she was not one to elaborate.

'You'll be in touch about the payment?' I asked.

'Yes, Anton will handle it,' she said. 'In fact, you will find him in the drawing room, should you want to leave him an address where he may reach you. We are going to put L'Ange de Mémoire into production, so I must devote the whole of my attention to its success. My father's good name rests upon it. The formula is a complicated one, and so I must oversee it myself.'

'The formula?' I repeated. They had the formula? This revelation was startling. How was it that it had been discovered?

'Yes, the formula for the perfume. We are a bit behind on its production. It was briefly misplaced among my father's things, you see,' she said, answering my unspoken question. 'He was constantly moving things from room to room when he worked on them. It was Michel who discovered it only last night, a great relief to all of us, I can assure you.'

So Michel had discovered the missing formula, had he? If he had taken it from the safe, why had he brought it back? Was that what he had retrieved from the woman's flat? Perhaps he had known that his father's mistress had vacated her lodgings and had hidden it there, as a means of insurance, until he could make sure his inheritance was secured.

'Yes,' I said absently. 'I imagine so. I know the world will be glad that L'Ange de Mémoire will soon be released.'

'Yes,' she said. 'Parfumes Belanger will continue on as it was. It is my hope that we can create a fitting legacy.'

'Of course,' I said thoughtfully. I was glad that Helios Belanger's perfume formula had been discovered, but I had lost what I had assumed to be a very likely motive for his murder.

I left Cecile and went back into the house and to the drawing room. Too late I heard the murmur of voices. I walked in to find Beryl Belanger in Anton's arms.

They practically sprang apart as I entered.

'Oh, Mrs Ames,' Beryl said, her pale skin flushing crimson. 'Anton and I were just . . . I was feeling very upset, and he . . .'

'I'm sorry,' I said. 'I came to leave you my address, Monsieur Belanger.'

Anton's expression was dark. He was, I supposed, angry both that they had been discovered and at the situation itself.

'There is paper on the desk,' he said.

I went to it and wrote down my London address. When I turned back to them, they were both watching me. Beryl was wringing her hands, though she didn't seem to realise it. 'I know how this must look, but I . . .'

I smiled, hoping to reassure her. 'You needn't explain.'

'But I must,' she said. 'It isn't . . . it isn't how it looks.'

The situation was growing very uncomfortable, and I wished I could think of some graceful way to make my exit. It was Anton, however, who decided to take his leave.

'If you will excuse me,' he said, walking from the room before either of us could say anything.

Beryl turned to me, tears glistening in her blue eyes. 'He doesn't know what to do about this,' she said. 'Neither of us have an answer.'

I was about to protest again that she needn't explain herself to me, but she went on before I could, the words spilling out as though they had been held at bay too long.

'Helios was kind to me, and I cared for him. I thought we could be happy, and we were for a time. But this past year, he became so distant. He was not at all like the man I married. I felt isolated, and Anton was kind to me. Almost before I realised what had happened, I began to fall in love with him. He feels the same way. But we have been circumspect. We haven't . . . I remained faithful to Helios.'

I wondered if this was true. Whatever the case, it was really none of my business.

'Nevertheless, I have felt so much guilt over it. You see, the night that Helios died, I was not with him. Anton and I spent the night in the Jardin du Luxembourg. We talked the night away. Only talked, I swear it. But the next morning, Helios was found dead, and I couldn't help but think that if I had been there I might have done something . . .'

'It isn't likely you could have done anything to help him,' I said. I certainly didn't know that, but I didn't think the killer would have been thwarted by her presence.

It crossed my mind that she and Anton might have poisoned him and then left the house to remove themselves from suspicion. Their whereabouts, in the park alone all night, could be more easily interpreted as a motive than an alibi, however, and I didn't think either of them so careless that they would have risked being seen together the night Helios Belanger died.

'We both have so much guilt,' she said. 'I just don't know what to do.'

'Perhaps it will all work out,' I said tactfully.

'No,' she said, the tears welling again. 'We can never be together.'

'Why not?' I asked.

'I am his stepmother,' she said in a horrified whisper.

It was a bit of an unusual situation, to be certain. A horrible scandal would no doubt ensue should they make their relationship public.

'I don't know what the answer is,' I said. 'But there are worse things than scandal.'

She looked at me with glistening eyes. 'Do you really think so?'

'I have lived through a good deal,' I said. 'People forget.'

She drew in a deep breath. 'Thank you, Mrs Ames. I don't know what will happen, but you have given me hope.'

'I wish you every happiness, Beryl,' I said sincerely.

I left the house, not entirely sure what to think of that particular situation. I certainly didn't envy them, and I hoped time could bring about some kind of resolution.

I returned to the hotel, my mind in a whirl with all I had learnt, especially that the formula had been discovered. If Helios Belanger had not been killed for the perfume formula, then what was the reason for his murder? I had been so sure that if we discovered who had taken the formula, we would be able to find his killer. Now it seemed that we were back at the beginning.

If it was a murder for profit, it still might have been any of Helios Belanger's family. My mind went back again to the draft of the will that I had secreted from his office, but the document I had seen had clearly not been intended to be legally binding. In all likelihood Anton's assertion that his father meant to leave the entirety of Parfumes Belanger to him had been nothing but bluster.

Who, then, was the likeliest to have wanted him dead?

Cecile had loved her father, and had been his right hand. I could see no reason why she might have chosen to kill him now. Even if she had wanted to take control of his business, after the release of L'Ange de Mémoire would have been a better time. His sudden death had only complicated matters, made the release unsure.

Michel had been threatened with disinheritance, but his father had threatened him for years and he had never appeared concerned before.

What of Beryl Belanger? She had, in all probability, married Helios Belanger in hopes of making a better life for herself rather than for any kind of abiding love. But she had loved Anton. And love could be the most powerful motive of all.

Love. A sudden awful, traitorous thought crossed my mind. *The only thing that can stop my love is death.* The note from Madame Nanette. She had written that line more than thirty years ago, but what if she had really meant it?

I tried to put it out of my mind, but the thought was persistent. And the more I thought about it, the more the pieces seemed to slide into place.

Helios Belanger had taken ill the first time shortly after Madame Nanette's arrival. Cecile had even told me that Madame Nanette had brewed a jasmine tea of which Helios Belanger was very fond. Was it possible that she had put something in it the night that he died?

Madame Nanette had taken a job with Helios Belanger, the man she had loved and lost. She might have thought that he meant to pursue her again, to make up for lost time. Instead, he had treated her as nothing more than another member of the household staff. He had moved on with his much younger wife and left Madame Nanette with nothing but the bitter memory of the love they had shared.

There was also the matter of the will. That second draft had read: 'She shall have the rest. My dear one.' My dearest one. That was what she had called him in her letter. Was it possible she had believed, after that one tender moment they had shared that night on the landing, that she might inherit a great deal from him? He had indeed left her a sizeable amount of money. Was it enough to kill for?

I tried to reconcile this story in my mind with the sweet, caring woman I had come to know. She didn't seem like a killer. Then again, so few of the killers I had encountered ever had. As much as I hated to admit it, it was possible.

Worse than the acknowledgement of this possibility was the realisation that I was going to have to tell Milo.

I suddenly began to think that Winnelda's friend Trudy might be right. It would be lovely to run away just now to a harem and not come back.

CHAPTER TWENTY-FIVE

Milo returned from his outing, but I didn't have the heart to bring the matter up. I didn't know what to say. Indeed, I had the strong inclination not to mention it to him at all. In my heart, however, I knew I needed to tell him. If Madame Nanette was the killer, we would need to decide how to proceed.

I couldn't help but feel that, if she should prove to be guilty, Milo would not want her turned in to the authorities. My husband's sense of morality was flexible, and I could think of no one who he was more likely to protect than the woman who had raised him.

I continued to fret about it as I dressed for dinner. Winnelda had come back, knocking hesitantly before entering, and I was glad for her chatty presence; it spared me having to make conversation with my husband, who would easily have been able to tell that something was amiss.

At last I finished dressing, choosing a red satin gown, and Winnelda departed for another night of adventuring with Trudy. Milo had finished dressing long ago and Parks had gone, so we were alone. It was time.

I briefly considered waiting until dinner, or perhaps even until we got back to the hotel tonight, but I knew that I would not be able to conceal my anxiety from Milo. Besides, he had his mysterious appointment at ten o'clock and might decide to leave at any moment. I needed to have this conversation and be done with it.

I came out of the bedroom. Milo sat smoking a cigarette and flipping through a newspaper.

He looked up as I moved into the room and rose. 'You look stunning, darling, as always, though I must say I miss the silver gown you were wearing this afternoon.'

'Milo, I need to talk to you about something.'

He looked at me, his attention caught, I supposed, by something in my tone.

'Whatever's the matter, darling?' he asked. 'You've gone all white.'

I couldn't remember a time when I had been so nervous. Normally, I was fairly adept at facing whatever needed facing. This time was different, however. I knew what Madame Nanette meant to Milo.

I took a seat on the edge of the sofa, my hands in my lap. 'This isn't easy to say.'

'Better just have out with it, then,' he said mildly, taking his seat again.

I drew in a breath and then let it out in a rush, the words with it. 'I think Madame Nanette may be the killer.'

He looked at me for a moment. Then the corner of his mouth tipped up and he leant to grind out his cigarette in the ashtray. 'It's not a very good joke, darling,' he said.

'You know I wouldn't joke about something like this,' I said. 'I . . . I learnt something today.'

'Oh?' The single syllable held something I couldn't interpret.

'I found a letter that Madame Nanette had written to Helios Belanger when they parted ways.' I briefly outlined what I had found, the way the evidence seemed to point towards this conclusion. 'If you think about it logically, all the pieces seem to fit.'

His eyes came up to mine. 'I don't need to think about it logically. It wasn't her who killed Helios Belanger.' There was something in his tone, or perhaps in his gaze, that should have been a warning. But I was so caught up in my own emotions that I failed to take notice of it.

'I never considered her for a moment,' I said. 'But think of it, Milo. She had a motive, she had the means, and the opportunity. She has loved Helios Belanger for years and he cast her aside. Even after he asked her to be his daughter's nanny, he treated her poorly. She had only to slip into Cecile's greenhouse and get the necessary ingredients. It would have been an easy thing to slip into his drink.'

'You forget that that scenario might fit any of the Belanger family,' he said.

'Except that Helios Belanger fell ill for the first time a month after Madame Nanette's arrival.'

He sighed. 'That might be a coincidence. Or someone might have done it purposefully to cast suspicion upon the new arrival.'

'But there is also the matter of the letter,' I said.

'A letter expressing a thirty-year-old sentiment is hardly proof of murder,' he said dismissively. 'Besides, even if

I believed any of this, which I do not, I think you have forgotten one important fact. Why would she call us here? Why would she ask us to look into a death that had already been determined to be of natural causes?'

This had been the one point I had hopefully fallen back on myself. But then I had realised the error of it. 'She couldn't have known that the matter would be brushed aside,' I said. 'She contacted you on the very day that Helios Belanger died. For all she knew, there would be a post-mortem done and she might have been accused. We were insurance against that.'

'That's a bit of a stretch,' Milo said.

'She knew we would stand by her, knew we would find another culprit to blame.'

'Amory, I know you mean well, but I really don't think you've thought this through.' His words were cool, measured, and I understood suddenly that he was trying very hard not to become angry. Milo seldom let his true feelings show, but I supposed the depth of what he was feeling now was too great to suppress.

'I know it's difficult to believe,' I said carefully. 'I don't like to believe it either. But the evidence . . .'

'Your so-called evidence can go to blazes,' he said steadily.

I realised that he meant it. He wasn't going to be swayed. I didn't know whether to feel relief that he was so sure or distress that he was willing to overlook everything I had just laid out before him.

'What you haven't taken into account is that you don't know Madame Nanette,' he said. 'Not like I do. She would never do something like this.'

'This is why I was afraid to tell you,' I said. 'I knew you wouldn't like it and wouldn't want to listen.'

'I have listened. I just happen to disagree.'

'Is it possible that your vision is clouded by your feelings for her?' I asked softly.

'No.'

'You're being unreasonable.'

'Am I?' His voice was still calm, but his eyes were darker than I had ever seen them. 'I seem to recall your reaction to a similar situation. When your former fiancé was accused of murder, you would have gone to the ends of the earth – fought to the death, if necessary – to prove his innocence. Nothing anyone said could sway you from your conviction that he hadn't done it.'

'I was right,' I said.

'And so am I.'

Our eyes met, and I realised that there was nothing more to say on the matter.

I didn't know where to go from here, but it seemed that Milo had no such qualms. He rose from his seat.

'If you'll excuse me,' he said. 'I'm afraid you'll have to go to dinner alone.'

'Milo . . .' I said pleadingly. I didn't want the conversation to end like this.

He didn't reply, didn't even look back, as he walked to the door and out of the hotel room.

He wouldn't be back tonight, of that I was sure.

I sighed miserably. I was plagued with doubts. Perhaps Milo was right. He knew Madame Nanette much better than I did.

But then another thought occurred to me. Perhaps in

knowing her as he did, he had known all along.

I thought of everything that pointed to this conclusion: his sudden disinterest, the way he had dismissed my clues and tried to dissuade me from pursuing the case. He had even tried to convince Madame Nanette to leave Paris. Was it possible that he had begun to suspect she was the killer and was trying to throw me off the track?

I felt a sick feeling in the pit of my stomach. I no longer knew what to think.

He had asked me to trust him. Could I? I just wasn't sure.

Not knowing what else to do, I sat down and picked up the book Madame Nanette had given me. Flipping through the pages, I looked at the photographs she had saved of Milo, the memories she had collected and kept. On every page the evidence looked back up at me. This was a woman who cherished love, not one who would have nurtured bitterness or hatred.

In my heart, I felt that Milo was right. She was a sweet, caring woman and, no matter what had passed between her and Helios Belanger, I did not want to believe that she had killed him. I had seen the sorrow in her eyes when she had talked of the loss of Milo's mother. I did not think she could deprive Seraphine Belanger of a father.

A thought occurred to me suddenly. Milo had steadfastly refused to believe that Madame Nanette was guilty, but what if it was more than his loyalty to her? What if he knew something I didn't? Not that Madame Nanette was guilty, but that someone else was.

It had been obvious to me that he was carrying on a series of activities in secret. I did not think it had been because of their illicit nature that he had been hiding them.

In fact, I rather suspected he had been pursuing a series of enquiries of his own.

That note he had received had been further proof of it. I had memorised the address in the brief time I had seen it. Perhaps I could meet him there and find out what he had been doing. It seemed, at least, that this was my only option.

I couldn't sit here doing nothing.

In a last moment's instinct, I went to the bedroom and took out my pearl-handled pistol, depositing it in my purse. I sincerely hoped there would be no cause to use it.

Then I put on my coat and went out to find my husband.

The note had said ten o'clock, and that was still more than an hour away as the cab pulled up before the address. I paid and got out, only then realising why it was that the address had seemed familiar to me. This was the location of the brothel to which we had followed Michel Belanger.

I was curious as to why my husband had received a note with this location. One thing was certain: I no longer harboured any illusions that he had gone out to a gambling club.

There was a cafe across the street but, just as I was thinking it might be an excellent vantage point for watching the brothel, I saw a familiar figure walking towards the building from the opposite direction. I was standing in the shadows and could therefore observe him without being noticed. Though it was fairly dark, I would have known him anywhere. It was Milo.

He walked directly to the door and tapped on it. While I felt a certain rush of indignation upon seeing my husband at such an establishment, I could only assume that he had a very good reason for being here. At least, he had better.

A moment later the door opened and Milo disappeared inside.

I stood there wondering what I should do. Though I had never set foot in a brothel, I didn't much like the idea of leaving my husband to his own devices in one. Though I was sure there was some ulterior motive, I was tired of his lies and excuses. I needed to find out what was going on once and for all.

After the briefest moment of hesitation, I hurried after him and knocked on the door.

I expected to be questioned by the doorman, but the gentleman let me in without so much as a second glance.

I stepped inside and looked around. I was not entirely sure what I had expected, but the interior of this establishment was much the same as the cabaret we had visited last evening. It was smoky and dimly lit inside, and tables and chairs were arranged around a dance floor, where, at the moment, a woman stood singing a mournful song. Most of the tables were occupied by gentlemen in evening dress, glasses of liquor before them and half-dressed women on their laps.

Milo was standing near the entrance to the room, and I went directly to him. He had left our hotel angry with me, but I felt that we were on even ground as far as indignation was concerned. He had some explaining to do.

His eyes scanned the room as though looking for someone and it took a moment before he saw me. Though the music was too loud for me to be sure, I was fairly certain that he swore beneath his breath.

'I was afraid you would show up here,' he said with a sigh. I was relieved to see that there was more exasperation than anger in his expression.

'How did you know I would know where to find you?' I asked.

'Because you took that note from my pocket,' he said.

'I need to talk to you,' I said, changing the subject. 'And, now that I've found you, I'm rather curious to know what this is all about.'

Before he could reply, raucous laughter sounded as a man and a woman fell to the floor in an embrace.

I looked at Milo, who appeared perfectly at ease in this rather unsavoury atmosphere. This was one of those moments where I realised how very little I knew about the life Milo had led before he met me, the life he quite possibly led when he was away from me.

'Darling, now isn't the time . . .'

A gentleman came up to us then, his eyes moving over me. 'Whatever he is offering, I will give you double.'

It took a moment for me to comprehend what he meant. My lips parted in surprise. He had mistaken me for a prostitute! I looked at my husband, waiting for him to refute the claim. Instead, his arm slipped around my waist, pulling me against him.

'I'm afraid this one is mine,' Milo said with genial finality.

I was rendered quite speechless by this reply and hadn't time to formulate a response before the gentleman turned to me, ignoring Milo. 'I am just a lonely man, looking for a woman to mend my broken heart.'

Milo's smile was no longer friendly. 'Look elsewhere.'

The man frowned and seemed prepared to protest, but then he thought better of it and moved away.

Milo released me. 'Amory, you've got to go back to the hotel.'

'I will not,' I replied. 'I want to know what you're doing here. What's going on?'

'I will explain it to you later. You'll have to trust me.'

I let out an irritated sigh. 'Trust you? After the way you've kept secrets and lied to me repeatedly?'

'I'm sorry, darling, but you'll understand why when I've explained things.'

I crossed my arms. 'Then explain.'

He let out a short breath. 'I haven't time for this now. If you don't go this moment, I will pick you up and carry you out.'

I felt a flood of indignation. 'You'll do no such thing.'

'I certainly shall.'

Our eyes met, neither one of us willing to relent.

'I'm going to go and sit in that chair there,' I said, pointing at a vacant table, 'until you decide to tell me the truth.' I started to turn away from him, but he caught my arm.

'Don't say I didn't warn you,' he said pleasantly.

Before I knew what he was going to do, he had picked me up and put me over his shoulder.

I struggled against him, kicking my legs, but his grip was quite secure.

'Milo!' I exclaimed. 'Let me down this instant.'

He paid me no heed, but began walking towards the door. Despite the fact that no one seemed at all surprised by this appalling behaviour, I was mortified.

I weighed my options. If I wanted to get down, there

were certainly ways I could accomplish it. Then again, we were already drawing a great deal of unwanted attention to ourselves. Several smiling faces had turned in our direction. Luckily for Milo, the only thing keeping me from kicking him very hard and screaming was the desire to keep from making an even bigger scene than the one we were already making.

'Let me go,' I said, struggling against him. 'Put me down, Milo. I mean it.'

Still, he didn't heed me. The two men standing by the door were of no help whatsoever. Not to me, at least. One of them held the door open for Milo, and I heard the second chuckle as we passed through. '*Bonne chance*, monsieur.'

CHAPTER TWENTY-SIX

Once outside, Milo set me down, and I turned on him, seething. 'If you *ever* dare to manhandle me again in such a fashion, they will be investigating *your* murder,' I ground out.

He looked very much as though he was trying to hide his amusement, and it was all I could do to keep my anger in check.

'Amory, I really do need you to go back to the hotel,' he said, in what I assumed was meant to be a soothing tone. It only made me angrier.

'I won't,' I said. 'I want to know what you're doing.'

He glanced around as though weighing his options. At last he seemed to realise that I was not about to be thwarted. 'All right,' he said with a sigh. 'But we'll be seen here. Let's go to that cafe, and I'll explain.'

We crossed the street and went in. The cafe was warm and the air smelt of coffee and fresh bread. It was nearly empty, and we had our choice of seats.

There was an empty table near the corner. It was a bit secluded but also close enough to the window that we had a clear view of the building across the street.

We settled into our seats and Milo ordered coffee.

Though there were flickering candles in little glass holders on the tables, the light was dim. There was a distinctly romantic air to the place, and I could not help but feel the tug of nostalgia. There had been many nights like these on our honeymoon, cups of coffee in shadowy cafes as we held hands across the table.

It seemed a very long time ago, almost as though I had been another person then. Our marriage had not been, as I imagined it would be then, a constant state of bliss. We had had more than our share of difficult times. In fact, I was not altogether sure we were not in the midst of one now.

I looked across the table at my husband. He had a great deal of explaining to do, but I supposed that I could begin.

'Before you begin what will no doubt be an enthralling tale, I want to say something, Milo,' I said. 'I think you're right. I don't think Madame Nanette killed Helios Belanger.'

'I'm glad to hear you say so, but must you have followed me to a brothel to do it?' he asked lightly. It seemed that his anger of earlier in the evening had all but evaporated. It should not have been surprising given that Milo was extremely even-tempered, but I had expected another terse exchange over the subject, not this easy reconciliation.

'In my head it all made sense, but in my heart I knew as you did that she hadn't done it.'

'That's very sweet, darling,' he said as he flicked his silver lighter, 'but it was rather more than my heart that made me sure.'

'What do you mean?'

'I asked her,' he said, lighting his cigarette.

I looked up. 'You asked her?' I repeated.

'Yes. That night after she told us about her inheritance. When I saw her down to her cab, I asked her to tell me if she had anything to do with his death.'

'What did she say?'

'She tut-tutted me for the suggestion and assured me that she had no reason to kill him.'

'What made you so sure she was telling the truth?' I asked.

His eyes met mine. 'Because she knew I would have protected her if she had done it.'

I knew that he meant it. There were very few things that were important to Milo, but the things that truly mattered trumped all else.

'You could have told me,' I said. 'We might have avoided a row.'

'Yes, you're right. I shouldn't have lost my temper. You caught me off guard with your accusation. I am a bit defensive when it comes to Madame Nanette.'

'You care for her a great deal,' I said, ready to forget the argument once and for all.

'Yes. She has always been very kind to me.'

'Why do you never talk about your childhood?' I asked him. I had so many things I wanted to know about what had transpired here in Paris, but they suddenly seemed less important than learning about his past.

If this line of questioning surprised him, he didn't show it. Instead, he shrugged. 'There isn't much to tell. I'm afraid it was very much like any other English boy's childhood.'

'You didn't have a mother,' I said.

'Many people grow up without mothers,' he replied.

'Yes, I suppose.'

The corner of his mouth tipped up in amusement. 'Why all the questions, darling?'

I wasn't even sure I knew myself. It was difficult, somehow, to put into words what I was feeling at the moment. I felt as though I was so close to discovering some elusive part of him that had always been just beyond my reach.

At last I answered him. 'I sometimes feel as though I don't know you very well at all.'

'You know me better than anyone else,' he said, his eyes on mine.

Did I? Sometimes I felt very far away. Sometimes I longed for those early days, when I had been so blindly in love that the world seemed like paradise.

'Why are you looking at me like that?' he asked.

'I don't know,' I said. 'I suppose I'm feeling a bit nostalgic. I was thinking about our honeymoon. This place reminds me of it.'

He smiled, his eyes warm. 'When I think about our honeymoon, I do not think of nights spent in cafes.'

'But we did spend evenings in places like these. I remember how very happy I was.'

'I remember thinking how lucky I was to have convinced you to marry me.'

I smiled. 'I think about it often,' I said. 'That night you asked me to marry you, quite out of the blue.'

I still recalled it as though it was yesterday. I had been engaged to another man, but Milo and I had met often at social occasions. He had pursued me with that relentless charm for which he was infamous, and I had been fighting a losing battle with my attraction to him.

Then one night we had been at a party and Milo had

swept me away into an abandoned conservatory, redolent of gardenias, so we could be alone. He had kissed me then for the first time, and I had let him. When at last my conscience could no longer be ignored, I had pulled away. 'I'm engaged to be married, you know,' I had told him breathlessly.

'Marry me instead,' he had said, and for a moment I had been unable to speak.

I sighed at the memory. 'I thought it was quite the most romantic thing I had ever heard of,' I said.

'I rather thought I bungled it. I didn't propose to you on one knee, did I?' he said.

'No,' I replied, 'but I didn't mind.'

'Would it surprise you to learn I was afraid you would laugh in my face?'

I looked up at him, surprised indeed. 'Surely you knew that I was mad about you.'

'I knew that you liked me. That's not at all the same thing as wanting to spend the rest of your life with someone.'

I felt the prick of tears behind my eyes at the sentiment. Milo so seldom revealed his feelings to me that I was almost at a loss as to how to respond. 'Did you want to spend the rest of your life with me?' I asked softly.

'I'd had no intention of ever getting married until I met you,' he said. 'And if you'd refused me, I'd be a bachelor still.'

'Do you think so?' I whispered.

I had always been under the impression that Milo had married me because I was engaged to another man and he knew he couldn't have me any other way. I had occasionally felt like the prize he had meant to win at all costs. It was touching to realise that there had been more to it than that.

He leant towards me across the table, lowering his voice.

'You are the best thing that has ever happened to me.'

Tears filled my eyes, and I was just about to respond when a movement across the street caught my attention. I looked closely, and soon I was convinced I was right. It was Michel Belanger.

'Milo, you haven't told me what's going on,' I said, the spell of the moment broken. I had been so caught up in romance that I had forgotten the matter at hand. 'Who was that note from? Who were you going to meet?'

'Michel.'

'He asked you to meet him at a brothel?' I asked, growing more confused by the second.

'I asked to meet with him. I chose this place because it was where we came last night. I wanted to see if it would happen again.'

'If what would happen again?'

'If someone would follow him.'

'Milo, you're not making sense.'

'Darling, while you were busy following Michel Belanger last night, you didn't realise that we weren't the only ones to do so.'

'Why didn't you say something?'

He didn't answer this question, but rose from his seat. 'And there is the person I meant.'

I looked outside. For a moment, I couldn't see anyone other than Michel, who was walking unhurriedly down the street. Then the person who was standing in shadow moved. I could not make out if it was a man or a woman. Milo, however, might have got a better look, for a strange expression crossed his face.

He rose, throwing some money on the table, and moved

towards the door. I followed him and caught his arm before he could step outside. 'Milo, maybe we should ring the police. It's not safe.'

He turned to me. 'Amory, I need you to go back to the hotel. Telephone Madame Nanette and tell her not to let the child out of her sight. Stay in our room and don't let anyone in until I get there.'

'But, Milo, I don't . . .'

He grasped my arm. 'Please, darling. Trust me.'

I looked into his eyes, and knew that I must.

'All right,' I said. 'But be careful.'

I didn't want to leave him there, but there had been something in his tone that had convinced me to do as he said. I hoped I had made the right decision.

I hurried to a cab at the corner and got inside.

As I rode back to the hotel, my mind was in a whirl. There was so much about this I didn't understand. Who was following Michel Belanger? I supposed it was possible that he was being followed for some other reason than Helios Belanger's death. After all, he had a reputation for seducing other men's wives. It might simply have been a jealous husband who was following him. Somehow, however, I didn't think so.

If it had something to do with the formula that had been in his possession, however, who might be following him? His siblings or Beryl might have confronted him at home at any time. Why trail him to a brothel? It didn't make sense.

I thought that Milo had recognised the person who was following Michel, and it appeared that it had not been who he'd expected.

I went into the hotel, my nerves very much on edge.

Milo had asked me to trust him, but I needed to do something. But what?

I was about to walk past the front desk when the clerk stopped me.

'Madame Ames?'

'Yes?'

'You have a visitor.'

I cast a glance around the lobby, half expecting someone to have been waiting there.

The man shook his head and glanced upward at the ceiling, pointing. 'No, madame. In your rooms.'

I was a bit surprised, as I could think of no one who would be visiting here. Not many people even knew that Milo and I were in Paris . . . unless perhaps my cousin Laurel had made an unexpected appearance, as she was sometimes wont to do.

'My cousin, perhaps?' I asked.

He shook his head. 'No, madame. Your brother.'

'My brother?' I repeated.

'Yes,' he said. 'He was most anxious to see you and asked if I could let him into your rooms. It was just a few moments ago. But perhaps I should not have told you. Perhaps it was meant to be a surprise.'

It was indeed a surprise, especially considering I had no brother.

CHAPTER TWENTY-SEVEN

Who was in my suite? I contemplated asking the clerk to go up with me or, more drastically, telephoning the police, but then I decided that perhaps the only way to learn the truth was to face whoever was there. I had the beginning of an idea, and I needed to see if I was right. After all, my visitor had been seen coming here. Surely he wouldn't try anything drastic.

But first I went to the telephone booth in the corner and rang up the Belanger residence, asking for Madame Nanette. It was a few moments before she came on the line and when she did, I could hear the concern in her voice.

'Hello?'

'Hello, Madame Nanette. It's Amory,' I said. 'Milo told me to ring you up.'

'What is it?' she asked. 'Is there something wrong?'

'I . . . I'm not sure,' I said. 'He told me to tell you not to let Seraphine out of your sight.' Somehow, given the gentleman in my room, I didn't think she had to worry. If there was danger, it was here and not there.

Madame Nanette, with the uncanny ability that only nannies had, seemed to have read my thoughts.

'Amory, are you in danger?'

'I don't think so,' I said slowly. 'I'm at my hotel. Milo will be here shortly. We'll ring you up again then.'

'You will be careful,' she said, her tone unconvinced.

'Yes,' I said. 'I'll be careful.'

We rang off, and I walked slowly across the lobby to the lift, my thoughts moving rapidly, the little pieces of the puzzle beginning to come together in my mind.

As I took the lift to my room, I opened my handbag and made sure the revolver was still there.

I reached my room and inserted my key into the lock and pushed the door open to find André Duveau standing before me. 'Good evening, Amory,' he said.

'Good evening, André,' I said a bit cautiously, closing the door behind me. Somehow I had known it would be him.

He smiled, a bit sheepishly. 'I suppose you're wondering why I'm here.'

'As a matter of fact, I am rather curious. Won't you sit down?' I asked, leading the way towards the sitting area. 'Can I offer you coffee or tea? It will only take a minute to have something sent up.'

'No, thank you. I apologise for dropping by and slipping into your suite, but I have very good reason. There was a matter of some urgency I wished to discuss and I realised that a gentleman arriving at this time of evening might be cause for speculation.'

'It wouldn't have been so very odd for Milo to have a late visitor,' I said in a casual tone.

'But he isn't here, is he?'

'No, but he shall be back soon,' I said, hoping that it was true.

'Well, it's you I've come looking for,' he said.

'Oh?' I asked. We were playing a little game of politeness, but we both knew that this was no ordinary social call.

'Yes. It's about your visit with Cecile yesterday.' His tone was friendly, his handsome features as pleasant as ever, but I could detect that there was something less cordial that lay just beneath the surface.

'Oh?' I asked. 'What about it?'

Emile, in his cage, suddenly started jumping and shrieking excitedly. It was just the opportunity I needed, a few moments to gather my thoughts and to determine how to proceed in the face of this newest development.

'If you'll excuse me for just a moment, I need to feed the monkey.'

'Very well.'

I picked up a knife and an apple from a bowl on the table and went to Emile's cage.

I cut the fruit into slices, while Emile watched, still chattering away excitedly, but the slices were too large to fit through the bars of the cage. I opened the door to hand them in to him. I should have expected he had just been biding his time.

Emile darted from the cage, rushing past me.

There was a surprised murmur from André as Emile attached himself to the man's lapel and gibbered noisily.

'Emile, you naughty thing,' I said. 'Come here at once.'

I had expected him to ignore me, but instead he looked over his shoulder at me and responded excitedly. I was quite sure he was trying to tell me something, but I had no notion of what it was. In fact, I was beginning to suspect I was half mad for trying to communicate with the creature.

Then, suddenly, he hopped to the floor and ran over to me, leaping up into my arms. 'What a naughty boy you've been, Emile,' I scolded him. 'I'm very sorry, André.'

He laughed, though I could tell that he was not exactly amused. I could not blame him, for it had to be most disconcerting to be unexpectedly pounded upon by a primate. 'It's no matter.'

'All that fuss, Emile,' I said, carrying him back to his cage. 'You must learn to be polite.'

It was then that I felt his furry little hand press something into mine, something he had taken from André's pocket. I looked down at the little tin of lavender pomade. Why had he stolen André's tin? Then I looked at the table where I had taken my tin out of my handbag earlier in the day in order to put the gun inside. My tin was gone. So it had been the one in André's pocket, and Emile had wanted to return it to me.

And suddenly the last piece clicked into place. Even as I considered it, it all began to make sense. From the beginning, the answer had been obvious. I had just not been able to see it because I had been looking at it in the wrong way.

It had been André all along. André who had infiltrated the Belanger family with his good-natured interest in the industry, André who had charmed Cecile Belanger, who wanted Helios Belanger's perfume formula. He had been the most obvious suspect from the start, but he had not been in Paris when Helios Belanger was killed. Now I knew how he had done it.

Emile clicked his tongue and tilted his head, as though

waiting for me to compliment him. 'Very good, Emile,' I whispered. 'You've done very well indeed.'

I turned away from Emile's cage to find that André was pointing a gun in my direction.

'Where is it?' he asked pleasantly.

'Where is what?' I asked.

'You know what I mean,' he said. 'I saw you go into Helios Belanger's office and take something from his desk only this afternoon.'

I was confused at first, but then I realised he must mean Madame Nanette's letter. 'I didn't take anything,' I said. 'It was a letter, and I only looked at it.'

'You'll forgive me if I don't believe you.'

'Do you mean the formula?' I asked. 'Cecile has it. She told me.'

'I haven't time to play games with you,' he said. 'Please tell me, Amory. I like you very much, and I should hate for things to get unpleasant.'

'I don't have it, André,' I said, trying to decide what I should do. The pistol was still in my purse, but I didn't think that I could reach it before he had a chance to pull the trigger on his.

'I want that document,' he said. 'Give it to me now, or I will wait until your husband comes in the door and I will shoot him.'

It seemed inconceivable to me that the formula for a perfume might have been worth a man's life. Looking at André's face, however, I could tell that he was completely in earnest. He had killed before, and there was no doubt in my mind that he would kill again. I had to get him away from here before Milo returned.

320

An idea began to take shape in my head. I wasn't at all sure it would work, but right now it seemed to be my only option.

'I don't have it,' I said. 'But I know where it is.'

'Where?'

'I'm very nervous, André. Might I have a cigarette?' I asked, glancing at the box on the table near the paper and pen I had left out earlier in the day.

'Very well, but you'd better not be stalling.'

'I wouldn't do that,' I said. 'I'll take you there, and you shall have the answers you need. Everything will end well.'

I very much hoped that this would prove true.

A few minutes, we went down the lift and into the lobby, André's gun in the pocket of his jacket. I considered the possibility of attempting an escape or raising the alarm, but there were several people milling about the lobby and outside the hotel. If André began shooting recklessly, many people might be hurt.

And even if I got away, there was still the chance that he might wait for Milo to return and harm him. No, the best thing I could do was lead him away and try to bide my time. I only hoped that Milo would receive and understand the subtle message I had managed to leave for him.

We went out of the hotel and into the cool night air. André had a tight grip on my arm, though there was no need. I didn't intend to run. There was a car parked along the curb and he steered me towards it, opening the passenger-side door.

'Get in,' he said, grasping my arm even tighter and pushing me into the car.

Threats have always induced in me a strong feeling of non-compliance, but in this instance I felt that I should do as he said.

I got into the car, and he went around the driver's side and got in, starting the engine. As we pulled onto the street I couldn't help but wonder if I would make it through the end of the night alive.

I gave him the address and we drove along in silence. I wanted to talk to him, to try to make sense of what was happening, but I felt that I would be better served to do so once we had reached our destination. The more time I could buy, the better.

After what seemed like a very long time, the car came to a stop at the curb before the empty flat of the mysterious woman, the flat Michel Belanger had entered when we had followed him. I didn't know what he had been doing here, but it was just possible that whatever André was looking for would be here.

The little cafe across the street where I had spoken to Lucille seemed almost empty, and I felt a bit disheartened knowing there was little chance of being spotted or assisted by a passer-by. If Milo did receive my message and came after me, I was afraid that André would then dispose of us both.

'What are we doing here?' André asked.

'Michel came here last night,' I said. 'I believe he brought the document here.'

'Michel?' he scoffed. 'Why would he have it? Michel has never cared anything for his father's enterprises.'

I was suddenly confused. 'You must have known he had it,' I said. 'You were following him.'

'No,' he said. 'I was following you.'

Milo must have known that it had been André. That was why he had been surprised at whoever it was that followed Michel tonight. He had suspected André would try something, which was why he had wanted me to warn Madame Nanette.

I realised something else. 'You followed me today, to the Belanger's house, as well.'

'Yes. I wanted to know what you were doing. Luckily, I had unfinished business with Cecile that gave me a plausible excuse for following you inside. I made my conversation with Cecile brief and we went out into the garden. I saw that you had gone into Helios Belanger's office, and I know that you took the document. I meant to get into your hotel tonight and take it before you returned.'

'Along with the tin of lavender pomade Cecile gave me today,' I said.

'Yes, Cecile made a mess of things when she gave that to you. I was very much afraid you would use it.'

'And poison myself,' I said.

He smiled.

'You killed him using the technique of enfleurage.' I thought of what Cecile Belanger had told me about the process. The essence of certain flowers was slowly absorbed into the fat. He had used a similar method to kill Helios Belanger, a poison that absorbed through the skin and was slowly released into his system.

He smiled. 'You're very clever, Amory. Yes, I had access to Cecile's laboratory, and I added an ingredient of my own into his pomade. The idea was that he would use it and slowly absorb the poison. He would be dead when I was away and no one would be the wiser.'

'But how did his death benefit you?' I said.

'Because he had something I wanted, and no one was aware of it until you came along. Get out of the car.'

I got out and he came around to take my arm. We went inside and got into the lift. The lift operator who had been there the day I came to enquire about the mysterious woman was nowhere to be seen, and another chance at a rescue disappeared.

I knew the location of the flat, though I didn't have any idea how we were going to get in. When we reached the door, however, André proved he had no such qualms. A quick kick to the door and it flew open. He pushed me inside.

It was a comfortable flat, neat and somewhat sparsely furnished. Nothing about it spoke of anything sinister or extraordinary.

'Now,' he said. 'Where is it?'

'I . . . I'm not entirely sure. I only know that I saw Michel take it from the safe last night. He brought it here.'

He sighed.

'Sit down.' I took a seat on the white sofa, while André walked around the room. There was a small writing desk along one wall, and he went to it and began opening the drawers.

Something about this did not make the least bit of sense. In fact, I couldn't believe that it was the perfume formula that he was after. Even if he believed I was lying about Michel having discovered it among his father's things, how could André possibly hope to use the formula to create a new perfume without it being connected to Helios Belanger?

'It's not here,' he said, closing the drawer and turning to face me.

'It must be,' I said.

'I do hope you're not trying to lie to me, Amory,' he said. 'I don't know who you work for, but I don't suppose it matters. In the end, I will get what I want.'

Who I worked for? Did he believe that I was part of some rival perfume company?

'I'll admit, I didn't have any idea when I first met you in Como,' he went on. 'Your husband's reputation had preceded him. A rather clever disguise, I suppose. But when you came to Paris, asking questions, I knew at once that you were not what you seem. A custom perfume was rather a poor excuse.'

He turned to a shelf lined with books and began pulling them off, one at a time, flipping through them and then tossing them aside.

'What is this really about?' I asked suddenly.

He looked up at me but said nothing.

'What is that formula, really?' I asked. 'It's something more than perfume, isn't it?'

'It won't do any good to pretend as though you don't know,' he said. 'It is a shame that things have come to this. I wish that you and your husband would have stayed in Como. It would have been much better for all of us.'

I said nothing. I was quickly beginning to realise that there was more happening here than I had first believed.

He turned to me, then, the darkness in his eyes belying his pleasant tone. 'I'm afraid I don't have any more time for this, Amory. I need you to tell me. Now.'

I tried desperately to think of something to say that

325

might put him off. Now that I was here, I realised the error of bringing him to this remote location. There would be no one to help me.

I still had the gun in my handbag, which I was clutching on my lap. If I slipped my hand inside of it, perhaps I might have a chance to defend myself. I would have to move quickly, and I was not at all sure that I had the time to act. I carefully undid the clasp and slid my fingers into the opening. As if in response to this small movement, I saw André's finger began to tighten on the trigger.

Before I could react, a shot sounded, the noise deafening.

For a split second, I wondered if André had shot at me. And then I saw the perfectly round hole appear in his forehead before he slumped to the ground.

I whirled around to the door to see Cecile Belanger standing there, gun in hand.

'Cecile. You . . . you've shot him,' I said stupidly.

'Yes, well, he was about to shoot you, so something had to be done.'

She came farther into the room, and I stared at her, unable to believe that this sangfroid could be genuine. She had just killed a man.

I couldn't bring myself to look back at André's body on the floor. Despite everything, I had not wanted to see him dead. It had all happened so fast. I was glad that I was still sitting down, for my legs had gone completely numb. I was not at all sure they would have held me up.

I looked at Cecile, trying to determine if she might be in shock. It took me a moment to realise that she was doing the same to me.

'Are you all right, Madame Ames?'

'Yes,' I said, clenching my hands to stop their shaking. 'Yes, I'm fine, but what . . . ? How did you . . . ?'

'Why don't you tell me what's happening,' she said calmly.

I tried to collect my thoughts, to make sense of everything that had transpired. I supposed I needed to start at the beginning. I drew in a deep breath and then began. 'It has to do with the death of your father,' I said.

'Oh?' she asked. She did not seem at all surprised. 'Go on.'

The words spilt out in a torrent. I told her about Madame Nanette's connection with Milo and the letter she had sent us. I told her about our suspicions about Helios Belanger's death, how we had been trying to determine who might have had the motive to kill him.

'It was André,' I said. 'I thought from the beginning that he had the best motive, but he had been at Lake Como with us at the time and I didn't see how he might have done it. Then tonight I figured it out. He poisoned your father with the lavender pomade. That must have been what made him crash his aeroplane that night. You said your father was never without it. It made him ill, but he recovered. He must have used it again the night he died. When you gave me some of it today, André decided that he needed to stop me from using it, so he came to my hotel room.'

She said nothing and I continued. 'He kept demanding the documents – the perfume formula, I assumed – but he didn't seem to believe me when I told him you had discovered it. He wasn't making sense.'

She studied me, as though trying to determine if my confusion was genuine.

'We need to ring for the police,' I said. 'We need to tell

them what André has done. Once they understand, I'm sure that they will see . . .'

'No,' said gently. 'We're not going to call the police.'

I frowned. 'Why not?'

She seemed to consider something for a long moment and at last appeared to have made up her mind. 'Madame Ames, I am going to take you into my confidence. I trust that you will be discreet with what I am about to tell you.'

She hesitated, and when she spoke, her words shocked me. 'André Duveau didn't kill my father,' she said. 'I did.'

CHAPTER TWENTY-EIGHT

I stared at her, wondering if she had really said what I thought she said.

'You killed him?' I repeated. I was suddenly very aware that she still held the gun in her hand. Though she had it at her side, I couldn't help but wonder what she meant to do with it.

Her eyes must have followed mine, for she gave a wry smile. 'You need not worry, Madame Ames,' she said. 'You had it right. André was the villain of this story.'

'I'm not sure I understand,' I said, marvelling at how calm I sounded. I wondered now if I was in more danger than I had been with André.

'André wormed his way into my father's affections and made love to me. He wanted to steal from him the secrets my father had long worked to keep.'

Did she mean, then, that she had killed André tonight out of revenge? But why had she killed her father? None of this was making sense. I felt as though it ought to, as though the answer was staring me in the face, but I was still shaking and I couldn't seem to clear my thoughts.

'Did you love him?' I asked. It was, perhaps, the least significant question I could have asked, but somehow I wanted to know.

Again, she smiled, and it was a hard smile. 'I could not love a man such as he.'

Somehow I felt that I had realised this all along. Cecile Belanger was a brilliant woman; she was focused, dedicated. Her interest in someone like André could only have been fleeting.

'It was not only who he was, but what he was,' she went on. 'He did indeed try to kill my father with the poisoned pomade, but it was clumsily done. André was not a very good parfumier. I disposed of the poisoned batch. It didn't have time to harm my father. I gave you the tin today to draw him out, to let him know that I was onto his game.'

I had so many questions, but I didn't know where to begin.

'So, in the end, André had nothing to do with my father's death,' she said. 'I wish he had lived long enough to know that he had failed.'

'But why did you . . . ?' I began and then faltered.

'Why did I kill my father?' she asked. 'Because he was already a dead man.'

And suddenly I understood. The private nurse who had been hired then dispatched, the change in his temperament, the mood in the house.

'He was ill,' I said. 'More ill than anyone realised.'

She nodded. 'And it was worse because of how it affected him. His mind was deteriorating, a little at a time. It started first with his sense of smell. Horribly ironic. The thing he valued most was the thing that began to fail him. He thought at first that it was perhaps a cold, an infection of some sort. But it soon became clear to us that it was something more than that.'

I felt, amid the myriad emotions assaulting me, the pang of pity. I could not imagine how dreadful it must have been for a man who valued scent above all else to lose the ability to smell.

'He might have gone on making perfumes, even after that,' she said. 'Scent was a part of him. Nothing could take that away. As Beethoven continued to play when he'd lost his hearing, my father might have gone on making perfumes from his memories of the smell. Alas, his memory soon began to fade.

'He could not remember where he left things, confused ingredients when in the laboratory. It was when he began to forget the names of the flowers that I knew that we were truly losing him.'

'I'm sorry,' I said softly.

'He became obsessed with his past. He began to call Beryl by my mother's name. He remembered Madame Nanette and insisted that I contact her. I resisted that for as long as I could, but there came a time when he would no longer heed me. I helped him write to her, and, for the sake of Beryl, I did not mention their past connection.'

So that was it. I had wondered why he had contacted the woman he had loved so many years ago. Perhaps it was because his mind had become lost in the past and he'd desired to bring resolution to things left undone.

'As the wretched disease progressed, he began to become increasingly accusatory, paranoid. He didn't know who to trust . . . or who not to. And that was when it became dangerous.'

I thought of Madame Nanette's description of his change in temperament. Had that been a part of it? Had Cecile felt she had no choice but to kill her father to protect the others?

'He became violent?' I asked.

She shook her head. 'No, Madame Ames. He became a danger, not because of what he didn't know but because of what he did. You see, my father was a man of deep passion. Perfume appeared to be chief among them, but it was followed closely by a love for his country. He was trained in the art of secrets, as he was trained in perfumery, by the apothecary who mentored him.'

'The art of secrets?' I repeated.

'Yes. He collected information as he collected scents. Vital information to be used by our government.'

'Your father was a spy?' I said. The dizzying realisations were coming so quickly that I didn't have time to process them. I felt I was being pulled along in a swiftly moving tide and could do nothing but ride it out.

She nodded. 'Long before the war, my father was travelling the world, gathering intelligence to bring back to France. Those early days were dangerous for him. Many times he was very near death. It was, I think, why he must have broken off his connection with the nanny. He would have wanted to protect her.'

It was nice to think so, that he had put his need to protect her ahead of his desire to be with her.

'So you see,' she went on, 'that was why he became dangerous. In his paranoia, he began to believe that someone in the house was turning against him. It started first with Herr Muller, a German, and then he moved on to the members of his family. He suspected us all, in turn. When Michel and I wouldn't give in to his whims, he even went so far as to attempt to write us out of his will.'

That, then, had been the cause of the confused draft we had seen, the one in which Anton had been left everything.

'I believe he must have told Anton as much,' she said with a wry smile, 'for my brother was quite sure he would inherit control of Parfumes Belanger.'

'He didn't know about your father's illness?' I asked.

'Not the true extent of it,' I said. 'My father wanted it that way. Besides his doctor, I was the only one who knew, though I eventually confided in Michel. We did our best to conceal his increasingly frequent memory lapses. I told Anton that our father was developing a new and highly secretive process to account for his increasing distraction and paranoia. As time went by, however, it became nearly impossible to hide his condition. One night he was very confused and Michel tried to keep him from leaving the house. My father went to bed but slipped out the next morning. We did not know where he had gone. It turned out that he went to Grasse and returned unscathed, but things were very bad after that. He did not know who he could trust, so he could no longer be trusted with the information he was receiving from his contacts. We could no longer operate effectively, not with his condition.'

'We,' I repeated. 'Then your father made you aware of his work.'

She nodded. 'I was my father's protégée in all things.'

'But surely there was someone you could tell, some

superior?' There must have been some other way than resorting to such an extreme solution.

She shook her head. 'I'm afraid not. In the state he was in, he would not have understood. He might have let something slip, something of vital importance. It was not just a matter of his own life. There were others to be protected. Not just Michel and myself, but the many who rely on us.'

'Michel?' I repeated. Somehow I found I was not entirely surprised to learn that Michel was a member of this secret cause. It made sense to me now, the watchfulness I had noticed that did not match his careless reputation, his wide travels, the wives of government officials he had romanced.

'Yes, my brother is also a part of our work.' She smiled. 'He cannot abide perfumery, but this other work he likes very much.'

At the mention of perfumery, I thought of L'Ange de Mémoire. 'What of the perfume?' I asked.

'It was during the early stages of his illness that he conceived of creating L'Ange de Mémoire, the Angel of Memory. It would be his final bow, he said. His legacy. He made plans for the design of the bottle and for the ingredients he would use, many of them very rare. By the time he received many of the ingredients, he was too ill to create it.'

'But he created the formula for you to follow?'

She shook her head. 'There wasn't a viable perfume formula. My father tried to write it, but by then his mind was too far gone. It was senseless, unusable.'

So the illegible copy he had brought in his attaché case to Grasse had not been one that had been substituted for the real thing, but one that Helios Belanger had believed, in his confusion, to be correct. But what of the missing copy?

Cecile answered this question as though she had been following my train of thought. 'I had the key to my father's safe and took the duplicate copy. We didn't want Anton to know, and I needed time to create a new one. When it was finished, Michel pretended to discover it. We had to continue as though my father had created it, for the sake of Parfumes Belanger. It will still be his legacy. I shall see to that.'

'But what about André? Was he . . . ?' My voice trailed off as the implications hit me.

'Yes.' She met my gaze coolly. 'André Duveau was a German spy.'

I felt at a loss. Despite everything that I had learnt, all the pieces that had seemed to connect, nothing was as I had expected. It was as though I had pieced together a puzzle, but the picture was the wrong one.

'Are you . . . are you sure?' I asked.

'Yes,' she said. 'We knew from the beginning. Last year my father had acquired a very sensitive document, the details of which I am not at liberty to share. He was to keep it until such time as the information should be made useful. It might have been a month, a year, or longer. We had been warned that an operative would be attempting to make contact to retrieve the information. When André arrived, we knew it was he. He thought he was very clever with his charm and good looks, but we were not fooled.'

'But he was shot down, decorated, in the war.'

'Yes. He claimed to have been shot down, but that was a ruse. He was really making contact with the Germans. Oh, he came home to a hero's welcome and was hailed for his exploits. He was very clever at hiding what he truly was. But not clever enough.'

'And so the past year was a long attempt to retrieve that document?'

'Yes,' she said. 'He tried at first to romance me. I thought he could perhaps prove useful to me. He thought that I would introduce him to the family, that he would have time in the house to retrieve the document. He even went so far as to express interest in perfumery to win my father's trust and approval. When that didn't work and I eventually broke off our relationship, he decided that his only recourse was to kill my father so that the information would never be made public.'

'Then he didn't realise that you knew your father's secrets?'

'No,' she said scathingly. 'It did not seem to occur to him that I might be interested in anything other than perfume. I think he meant to kill my father and hoped the document would remain hidden away or be lost among his other papers until they were no longer of use. Then you and your husband arrived.'

I thought of what André had told me tonight, about not knowing for whom Milo and I worked. I realised now that he had thought us spies. 'He thought my husband and I were somehow involved in all of this.'

'I thought the same at first,' she said. 'But I soon began to realise that it was a different game you were playing. I just did not know what it was. It was when I saw Madame Nanette come to your hotel that I realised your connection and began to think you must be after something else. At least,

I thought you were. Your husband was another matter.'

'My husband?' I repeated.

'Yes, he was very close to the truth, I think. He and Michel gambled together frequently, and my brother told me that he asked some pressing questions.'

I wondered suddenly just how much Milo had known.

'I was hoping that if I created your perfume and left town that you would return to London. When André came to my house today, however, I knew that something was amiss. I gave him the pomade as a warning, one which he clearly did not heed. I thought he might attempt something tonight, so when your husband asked Michel to meet him, I knew that he must know something. So I followed my brother.'

Then it had been Cecile whom Milo had recognised as the figure across the street. No wonder he had been surprised. He had been expecting André.

'When I saw you leave, I decided to follow you and was outside when André forced you into his car.'

'But what is this place?' I asked. 'Why did Michel come here last night?'

'This flat belongs to the woman who was my father's nurse at one time. My father had begun to think of her as a confidante. So much so that we were forced to dispense with her services. He sought her out after that, however, and even came here to see her. One night he wandered here quite late and refused to leave. I sent a car to get him the following morning.'

So that was what Lucille the waitress had seen. The alleged mistress and the missing nurse had been one and the same.

'I began to wonder if, perhaps, he had entrusted her with anything she should not have,' she said. 'Then recently there was a death in her family, so she returned home for a time. It was the perfect opportunity to search. Luckily, Michel found nothing. The nurse is not the sentimental type, it seems,' she said, glancing around the sparsely decorated room.

'Milo told me to go back to the hotel and to phone Madame Nanette to watch over the child.'

She nodded. 'I was afraid, too, that André might get desperate enough to use Seraphine as leverage. Instead, however, he gambled on your having the documents he was seeking.'

'I can't believe he spent a year trying to obtain that document.'

'There is a great deal of unrest in Europe, Madame Ames,' she said. 'Peace is an illusion.'

'He even taught your father to fly,' I said, marvelling at the way he had inserted himself into their lives.

'Yes. I think he thought that he might find it a useful way to dispose of my father when he was finished with him. There are ways to cause a plane to crash. I'm sure he thought it was his poison that had done the trick that night, but it was my father's own confusion that caused it.'

I knew Helios Belanger had been a strong-willed man. No doubt they had been unable to keep him from doing as he desired. 'He wanted to continue flying,' I said.

'Yes. We tried to stop him, but he was a man of great determination. And there were still moments of great clarity. He was fine when he left, very much his old self. I had hoped he would make the journey without incident, but when he crash-landed I knew the time had come.'

The time had come. And she had killed her father.

'He was afraid from the beginning that this would happen, that he was going to say things, to reveal things that no one else could know. He told me a year ago, when he realised what was happening to him. He said, "I am relying on you to do what is necessary when the time comes." I agreed that I would, and I kept my word.'

I said nothing. I could think of nothing to say.

'You think me cruel, perhaps. Only a wicked woman could kill her own father.' She shrugged. 'Perhaps you are right. Perhaps I am wicked, in a way. But it had to be done. The cruel thing would have been to let him suffer, to let him live in a cloud of confusion, at a risk to himself and others. He did not want to live that way. To allow him to carry that burden, that would have been the malicious thing.'

There was movement at the door then, and I turned, startled, hoping that it was not some associate of André's here to finish what he had started. Not that I need worry; Cecile seemed more than capable of dealing with whatever problems might arise. I had seen that streak of steel in her when we had first met, but I had not imagined how deep it ran.

However, the figure at the door was Michel and, behind him, Milo.

My husband came at once to my side. 'Are you all right, darling?'

'Yes,' I said with a weak smile. 'Thanks to Cecile.'

Michel walked to André's body, looking down at him. 'You took your time about it,' he said, turning back to his sister. 'If it had been up to me, we would have ended him long ago.'

'I had meant to make use of him,' she said, 'but he got unmanageable. I'll need you to clean things up for me.'

'Of course,' he replied.

I turned to Milo, trying to put away the horrible casualness of their conversation. 'How did you know I was here?'

'When I saw that it was Cecile who had followed Michel to the brothel and not André, I realised that André might mean to do something desperate, perhaps even kidnap the child. I spoke with Michel and we hurried back to the hotel to meet you, but the concierge told me you had gone out with a man and I knew what had happened. I might not have thought to come here, but Emile told me.'

'So he managed it,' I said.

'Yes. When I arrived back at the hotel, he gave me this.' From inside his shirt pocket, he removed a cigarette. I could see where I had scrawled on it "flat" before dropping it into the couch cushion. I had hoped Emile, having frequently seen Milo smoking, would give it to him when he returned. It had been a ridiculous plan and quite unnerving to have one's fate resting in the paws of a monkey, but it seemed that it had worked.

'I was very worried, Milo . . .'

'There, there, darling,' he said, draping an arm around me and pulling me close. 'There will be time to talk about that later. Right now, I think we had better leave Michel and Cecile to take care of all of this.'

I glanced over my shoulder at the body on the floor. I still could not believe that she had done it, and with such very accurate aim. I shivered.

'We will not meet again soon,' Cecile said. 'I will be

gone before the night is out. Your perfume, however, will be sent to you when it is finished. Anton will see to that.'

'Does Anton know . . . ?' I asked.

'No,' she replied. 'Anton is weak. He has always been weak. My father knew it. He will do his best with Parfumes Belanger, but the . . . other matters are best left to Michel and me.'

Michel turned to us. 'It has been very nice to meet you, Madame Ames. My only regret was that I could not pry you from your husband's arms.' He shrugged. 'Alas, one cannot have everything.'

'Goodbye, Monsieur Belanger,' I said.

He winked at me, and Milo took my arm and we walked to the door.

Cecile's voice stopped me before I reached it. 'Madame Ames.'

I turned.

'Your perfume. I have decided to call it La Perception.'

Perception. 'I like that very much,' I said.

She smiled. 'I thought you might.'

She turned then, to help her brother with the body on the floor, and I allowed Milo to lead me out into the night.

CHAPTER TWENTY-NINE

We arrived back at our hotel, and I tried to shake the feeling that this entire evening had been some very strange dream. I could not believe that the truth had been so unlikely.

'I never would have imagined,' I told Milo. 'I never suspected even for a moment that they might be spies. It's too incredible.'

I noticed he had said nothing, and I thought of what Cecile had said about his being close to the truth. It all made sense: the secrecy, the trips into the night. He had known it was something like this, and he had been trying to work from that angle while discouraging me from continuing to pursue it.

'You knew,' I said suddenly.

'Yes,' he admitted.

'For how long?'

'Almost from the start,' he said. 'I had heard rumours about André Duveau, things that made me suspect there was more to him than met the eye. When I learnt that he was involved with the Belanger family, that confirmed it.'

'You knew about the Belangers?'

'I became acquainted with Michel Belanger shortly after the war. He had a wild, reckless reputation and was known for his temper, which got him into trouble more than once. He and his father were constantly at odds, as you know. As time went by, however, I began to realise that he was possessed of a second, more careful nature. Then one night, something went wrong, and we were very nearly ambushed.'

'Ambushed?' I repeated.

'Thanks to his quick thinking, we averted injury,' he said, brushing aside the encounter. 'Michel, however, was forced to reveal at least a little of the truth to me.'

'Then he is not what he seems?' I asked.

'Oh, he is most definitely what he seems,' Milo replied with a smile. 'Perhaps time has tamed his temper a bit, but he has a reputation to maintain and he greatly enjoys maintaining it.'

'So, knowing what you did about the Belangers, you came to Paris knowing that there was some secret information involved.'

'I didn't know anything,' he said. 'I suspected. After all, Duveau had been in Como with us at the time of Belanger's death. I encouraged our involvement initially because I thought it was just possible that his death was simply a family matter. However, I began to conduct enquiries on my own. When it began to be clear that this went beyond murder for profit, I tried to convince Madame Nanette to leave Paris and to convince you that it hadn't been a murder at all.'

'Why didn't you just tell me the truth?' I asked softly.

I wanted to be angry, but I was suddenly weary and my words lacked the bite I had intended.

'I was trying to protect you,' he said, his expression rueful. 'Fine job I did of it.'

'What about the nurse in Beauvais?'

'That wasn't quite the dead end I made it out to be,' he said. 'After a good deal of trouble, I was able to locate her and, though she didn't tell me anything specific, I began to get the idea that Helios Belanger's sickness had affected his mind.'

'And you drew the conclusion that his information might be in danger.'

He nodded. 'That's why I didn't want to tell you. I knew you would only want to pursue it further. When you mentioned the nurse that night I came back from Beauvais, I was certain you had found me out. When it became apparent that you hadn't, I knew I couldn't let you learn what I had discovered. Even when you confronted me, I could give you no good answers.'

'Your lies only strengthened my resolve to discover the truth,' I said.

'Yes, I might have known it's no good to lie to you,' he replied.

'It would do you well to remember that,' I said. 'Did you know it was her flat that night when we followed Michel?'

'Yes. That made things much more complicated. You were getting too close. I had hoped to get the matter settled tonight. I lost my temper with you this evening in part for your relentlessness. You're very difficult to keep out of trouble, you know.'

'And what about the other person who followed Michel last night?'